STARTING OVER AT THE VINEYARD IN ALSACE

BOOK 2, DOMAINE DES MONTAGNES

JULIE STOCK

CLUED UP PUBLISHING

Cover Design: Oliphant Publishing Services
Editing: Helena Fairfax
Proofreading: Perfect Prose Services

GET BEFORE YOU FOR FREE!

The prequel to my début novel, *From Here to Nashville*, is available **FREE** when you sign up to my newsletter. Find out what happened between Rachel and Sam before Jackson arrived on the scene in *Before You*, at **www.julie-stock.co.uk**.

To my friends, Tanya, Julia and Mandie.
Thank you for keeping me sane all these years.

CHAPTER ONE

Lottie

Lottie Schell gazed out of her bedroom window at the dormant vineyard estate of Domaine des Montagnes on the hillside in the distance. At last winter was coming to an end and soon the vines would be coming to life again as the new season got underway. The vineyard had been in the Le Roy family for generations and was now run by Didier, together with Lottie's sister, Fran. Lottie smiled as she thought how close she and her sister had become since she'd found out she was unexpectedly pregnant. When she'd had to return home to Alsace from her travels, Fran had taken her in.

Lottie glanced down at her stomach in the mirror, still unable to believe it had grown quite this big, even though she'd had eight months to get used to it. She turned from side to side, amazed at how taut and shiny her skin was. Her baby was due in about four weeks' time, according to the dates her doctor and midwife had given her, and she was impatient to meet him or her after all these months. At the same time, the thought of moving the baby from the relative safety of her body to face the dangers of the outside world scared her half to death.

As if to confirm agreement with her on that thought, the baby kicked, and Lottie touched her hand gently to the spot.

'I know you're ready to come out, little one. You're in the driving seat on that, I'm afraid.'

She slipped her clothes on before negotiating the twisty staircase of Sylvie's old cottage and emerging into the living room. Sylvie Le Roy was tucking away the knitting she'd been busy with for the past few months since Lottie had moved in with her. Lottie kept up the pretence of not knowing what she was up to so it would be a surprise when Sylvie finally gave her the gift she'd been making. This was sure to be at the upcoming baby shower, which the whole village seemed to have been invited to, despite Lottie's request not to make a fuss.

'*Bonjour*, Lottie. *Ça va ce matin?*'

'Yes, I'm fine, thanks. How are you today?'

Didier's mum was only just fully straightening up after pushing herself gently out of her chair, and Lottie caught the grimace that passed across her face as she did so. Not for the first time, she worried about the added pressure she was bringing to Sylvie's life by staying with her.

'I'm absolutely fine. Now, what can I get you for breakfast, before you go to the doctor for your check-up? You need to keep your strength up.'

Lottie willed herself not to roll her eyes at the older woman's mantra. Sylvie was always quick to deflect the conversation away from her aches and pains in favour of fussing over Lottie's wellbeing and, by association, that of the baby.

'Fran will be here to take me in a minute, Sylvie, and we're going to get breakfast on the way, I promise.' She didn't want to impose on Sylvie any more than she already felt she was doing by staying in her house.

Sylvie looked sceptical, but she didn't say anything else, and luckily Fran chose that moment to appear through the back door from the garden.

'*Salut, tout le monde*,' she said with a smile as she kissed them both. 'The garden's looking beautiful, Sylvie. It's ready for spring.' She touched Sylvie affectionately on the arm and was rewarded with a pat on the cheek.

'It's my favourite time of the year, but it's always hard work keeping the garden looking so lovely during spring. Thank goodness Frédéric is helping me now, which is making a huge difference. I don't think I could manage it on my own any more.'

Sylvie missed the glance that Lottie exchanged with her sister at the mention of the man who was now openly sharing Sylvie's life, having been kept a secret for quite a long while. Lottie was glad Sylvie had a companion in her older age, especially since she'd been without her husband for several years.

'Anyway, how's my Didier and little Chlöe?' Sylvie asked Fran. 'Will I be able to come over and see my granddaughter again soon for a sleepover?'

'Yes, of course, she'd love that. We'll sort something out later today, shall we?'

Lottie envied Fran for the easy way she had with Didier's mum, and she was glad they got on so well. She only hoped that things would work out as well for her one day, but whereas Fran was about to get married to the love of her life, Lottie was on her own and facing an uncertain future. With a great effort, she hauled herself back from her negative thoughts. Right now, all she needed was to give birth safely to her baby and to make a success of her new life as a single mum, and she was determined to do it.

Once she was safely in the car with Fran and they were on their way to the doctor's in Strasbourg, Lottie blew out a sigh of relief.

'Is everything okay?' Fran asked as she drove.

'Yes, I'm nervous about this check-up, that's all. I want to be sure everything's all right with the baby, with the due date being so close. Thanks for taking me, Fran.' Lottie didn't admit she was nervous about the impending birth, too. There was no way out of it now.

'You don't need to thank me. That's what sisters are for. I'm sure everything will be fine. How did it go with Thierry when you told him I was taking you today?'

'He wasn't very pleased about it.' Lottie shrugged. Although she'd been seeing Thierry for several months, it was still early days for them. 'He's so protective of me, which is great when it's not even his baby, but sometimes he can be so bossy.' She laughed despite her frustration.

'It shows he cares for you, even if he overdoes it a bit at times.'

Lottie chose to change the subject. 'How are things with you and Didier? Any more news about your wedding plans?' Since leaving her job in London and returning home to Alsace to work at the vineyard, everything in Fran's life had finally fallen into place.

Fran's face fell. 'No. We're too busy with the vineyard at the moment. It's not only all the work that needs doing in the vineyard itself, it's all the building work in the new Visitors' Centre and the restoration of the château. There's hardly time for me and Didier, with all that going on. And then, of course, we want to spend time with Chlöe.'

Fran bit her lip, and Lottie waited for her older sister to reveal what the real source of her worry was.

'The thing is, Lottie, Didier and I have been trying for a baby of our own for a good few months now, but I'm still not pregnant.'

'Oh, Fran, I'm sorry. There's me, having fallen pregnant with no trouble at all. It hardly seems fair for you to be struggling, when you and Didier are so in love and settled together.'

'That's the way it is, I suppose, but it's hard to keep on hoping month after month. I can't even think about a wedding when this is so much on my mind.'

'What does Didier think about it all?'

'Didier definitely wants more children, but as he already has Chlöe, he's not too worried about it. But I want us to have a child of our own, even though I love Chlöe as if she were my own daughter. Right now, it feels like it might never happen for me.'

Lottie's heart ached for her sister. Just when she'd got back together with Didier and everything seemed perfect, something else was stopping her from being happy.

Thierry

As he strode up the slope from his house on the other side of the estate, Thierry Bernard cast his critical winemaker's eye over the vineyard. Spring was his favourite time of the year, and he was looking forward to seeing the vines coming out of their resting phase after the harsh winter months. Buds would soon be appearing and the vines would start spreading along their canes, looking for the sunlight to help them grow. There was even some sunshine today, at the beginning of March, and although it was feeble by summer standards, he appreciated the warmth on his face.

He pushed his mop of dark hair out of his eyes and squinted against the sun. When he reached the top of the hill, he glanced across to the cottage to see if Fran's car was there. He wanted to catch up with Lottie after her appointment at the doctor's to see how things had gone for her. She'd not told him in so many words – when did she ever tell him what was on her mind? – but now that her due date was so near, her anxiety about the baby's health was increasing.

Fran's car wasn't there, so he continued towards the courtyard where the estate office was, planning to go and ask Didier when he expected them to be back. As he emerged through the archway that led to the courtyard, Fran was pulling in, and he was glad to see Lottie smiling in the front seat.

'*Bonjour*, Fran, Lottie. How did it go?'

'Everything's fine, thank goodness.' Lottie beamed at him and he sensed her relief.

'Are you walking back to Sylvie's now?' he asked. 'I can come with you if you like. I have some things I need to get in the village.'

'Okay. Thanks again for taking me, Fran. See you soon. Take

care, won't you?' They kissed each other goodbye, and Lottie turned to Thierry to follow the path back to the village.

'How are you feeling in yourself?' he asked, taking her hand as they walked at Lottie's waddling pace along the path.

'I'm relieved after speaking to the doctor, but he said it could be even more than four weeks before the baby actually comes. I'm not sure I can wait that much longer.' She rolled her eyes and Thierry chuckled. 'It's all right for you,' she said. 'You're not the one having to carry all this extra weight around.'

'I know it must be hard for you, but it's not so long to go now, and then you will have your baby with you.' He paused for a moment and then continued, 'Have you thought any more about my suggestion?'

'I have, but I'm happy at Sylvie's for the time being. And as I've said before, I can look after myself, and the baby, when it comes. I wish you could accept this and not keep asking me to move in with you.'

Lottie blushed as she finished speaking, which confirmed Thierry's thoughts. It was his turn to roll his eyes before cutting straight to the point she was trying to hide. 'I want to help, and I have plenty of room in my house for you and the baby, whereas at Sylvie's cottage it must be a squash, even with only the two of you living there. And I'm sure it's awkward for you knowing that, because you're there, Chlöe and Frédéric can't stay over.' He paused to let his words sink in. 'I don't understand why you keep fighting me on this when it makes perfect sense to me. It's as if you don't trust me.'

Lottie stopped on the path and turned to face him. 'Look, Thierry, we've discussed this. It's nothing to do with me not trusting you. After I had to move out of Fran's last year, I went to live at Sylvie's rather than moving in with you because I don't think it's fair for you to take on the responsibility for someone else's child, especially when you and I have only been seeing each other for a few months. It is a squash, that's true, but we've managed so far.'

Lottie started walking again, rubbing her lower back with one hand as they continued on their way into the village.

'But in that time, six months nearly, we've... we've developed feelings for each other, so there's no reason for us not to be together. We'll get to know each other more over time, and especially if you move in with me.' He wanted so much to tell her he loved her, but he was afraid he'd scare her off if he did, so he kept quiet.

'We don't need to rush this, Thierry. I want us to take our time getting to know each other before we take this next big step. I still know very little about you or your past, or about Nicole's death, for example. All that makes me feel you're still holding on to so many emotions you're not ready to share yet.'

Thierry turned the wrought-iron handle to open the back-garden gate and stood back to let Lottie go through first. She sat down on one of the wooden benches in Sylvie's beautifully tended garden, and Thierry took his place next to her. He rubbed his temple, his dark brows drawing into a frown as he wrestled with what he was trying to say.

'Why would you want me to talk to you about my wife? You didn't know her, so it would feel weird for me to talk about what happened between us with you.'

'I think the fact you don't understand why says everything. You still have a lot of pent-up emotion and grief to deal with,' she said softly. She reached out and stroked his stubbled cheek with the palm of her hand, and his body lit up at her touch.

'I still don't understand why any of this would stop you from moving in with me,' he retorted, turning reluctantly away from her and folding his arms as he stretched out his long legs on the still dewy grass.

Lottie laughed at his exasperation. 'I'm independent, I know that, but I have a right to do what I want to do, for me and the baby. After everything that's happened to me, and finding myself on my own now, I need to feel sure before making any more decisions.' She paused and he glanced at her to show her he was listening.

'Please will you think about it?' He took her hands in his. 'I want to be with you, and this arrangement with you living here doesn't make our relationship any easier. I can only see that getting worse when the baby comes, and there'll be even less room for you all at Sylvie's.'

Lottie opened her mouth to reply.

'No, don't say anything now,' Thierry interrupted. 'Just promise me you'll give it some thought.' He leaned forward and kissed her gently on the lips. 'I'll leave you to get on.' With that, he slipped back through the gate, shutting it firmly behind him, and disappeared away down the street.

———

Lottie

Lottie touched her fingers to her lips, still tingling from Thierry's kiss. He'd made her heart beat faster too, like he did every time he touched her. But those feelings were always swiftly followed by doubt, and the fear she had of ever giving her heart away to a man again.

She struggled to her feet to make her way indoors and out of the cold. Sylvie was watching from the kitchen window as she approached the cottage. She would have seen them talking and would want to know what it was all about. Lottie sighed as she crossed the weathered paving on the patio, anticipating her questions.

'Is everything okay between you and Thierry? I saw him leave in a hurry just now.' Sylvie's first question came as soon as Lottie opened the stable door at the back of the house.

'He still wants me to move in with him,' she replied honestly. 'And he doesn't like it when I say no to him.'

Sylvie nodded knowingly but, to Lottie's surprise, didn't say anything more about it. 'Most importantly, how did it go at the doctor's this morning?'

'He said everything was fine. It's a matter of time now. I just hope it isn't too much longer.'

Sylvie smiled. 'Babies come when they're ready, and not a

moment sooner. I know it feels like forever, but you have all the time in the world to enjoy together. Don't wish it all away.'

'I'm trying not to. I want to meet my baby, that's all. I'm ready to move on to the next phase in my life with my son or daughter, and I can't wait to get started.'

'It's an exciting time in your life, and I count myself lucky to have been able to share it with you.' She patted Lottie's hand.

Lottie smiled at the woman she'd become so fond of in these past few months. 'I know, and I appreciate your offering to let me stay here with you, but I feel terrible about imposing on you for this long, Sylvie. It was only ever meant to be for a short while until I got myself sorted out. I know you've missed being able to have Chlöe over to stay while I've been in the spare room, and it must have been awkward always having to go and stay at Frédéric's rather than inviting him to spend the night with you here.'

Sylvie sat down at the table, lowering herself gingerly onto the hard wooden chair. 'Frédéric loves having me to stay at his place, so that's not been a problem. I do miss having my little granddaughter to stay, but it's as easy for me to go and babysit her at Fran and Didier's. I don't mind.'

'Once my baby needs its own room, though, it will become more difficult. I'll have to look for somewhere else before too long. I have some savings to keep me going for a while, and you've been so lovely not letting me pay you any rent. But I do need to stand on my own two feet, Sylvie, now I'm going to be a mother.'

'I understand your need for independence, I really do. More than you realise, perhaps. But how will you manage when you're not even entitled to maternity pay from the nursery? You won't be able to go back to work for a while yet. I don't see how you can afford to rent somewhere else – it would make things even harder for you. Maybe you should reconsider Thierry's offer, after all.'

'Shall I make us a drink?' she asked instead of replying. At Sylvie's nod, Lottie took off her jacket and went to hang it up in the hallway under the stairs, before putting the kettle on to boil. While she thought about what Sylvie had said, she stared at the decorative plates hanging above the range. She'd become familiar with them after spending so much time in the cottage kitchen. Her favourite scene of Alsace was the one of La Petite Venise in Colmar, reminding her of home. She loved the quirky little boat trips along the canals, the little backstreets with their typical timbered houses and the unusual shops designed to draw the tourists inside.

Finally, she replied to Sylvie's point. 'It would be an easy solution for me to move in with Thierry, but there are lots of reasons why I don't think it would be the best idea right now.' She didn't elaborate, knowing how fond Sylvie was of Thierry, and not wanting to criticise him in front of her.

Sylvie fiddled with her rings. 'To tell you the truth, Frédéric has asked me to move in with him, and I've been weighing up all the pros and cons, just as you have. I like my independence too, you see.'

Lottie grinned. She and Sylvie had a lot in common.

'I can only see pros, Sylvie. You're finding it difficult to manage the garden on your own now – you said that yourself – and if you move in with Frédéric, you can tend the garden together, and you'll enjoy having his company. Not only that, but there would be plenty of room for Chlöe to come and stay. So what's stopping you from saying yes?'

'Well, first of all, I promised your family I'd look after you, and the baby, when it comes, and I don't want to let them or you down by going back on that promise.'

Lottie threw her hands up in the air. 'This is why I haven't ever learned to support myself, because my whole family treats me like I'm a child. You're not responsible for my welfare, Sylvie. You must put yourself first.'

'They're only looking out for you, Lottie. And I'd feel a lot happier about accepting Frédéric's proposal if you were settled somewhere else, with a support network around you, especially if you do want to go back to work eventually. There's no shame in accepting help, you know, and Thierry really wants to help you.'

Lottie placed their coffees on the table. She sat down again, trying not to take out her frustration with her family on Sylvie when she'd been so good to her.

'Thierry's not ready for me to move in, despite what he says. He's still not over the death of his wife, and I think he needs more time.'

Sylvie took a sip of her coffee. 'Yes, I agree. He's never got over what happened to Nicole. He used to be such a carefree young man before life intervened and changed his outlook forever. Such a tragedy, when they loved each other so much. But perhaps if you moved in, you could help him to come to terms with everything.'

Although Lottie was interested to hear Sylvie's take on Thierry's situation, she couldn't help feeling that there were too many secrets surrounding him. She wanted to hear about his past from him rather than from everyone else, but he showed no sign of relenting.

'If you want to move in with Frédéric, I will completely under-stand. It would make a lot of sense, and if I'm going to move out anyway in the near future, there's no point you hanging on here any longer than you need. Someone will be able to take me in. You mustn't worry about it.'

As much as she believed what she was saying, Lottie had no idea where she would go if Sylvie did decide to move in with Frédéric. Right now, Thierry seemed to be offering the only option.

───────

Thierry

By the time he'd returned to the vineyard, Thierry was feeling calmer. Just the sight of the rows and rows of vines in front of him, and the order they depicted, allowed his breathing to return to normal and his frustration to abate. Lottie had never been afraid to speak her mind to him – that was one of the things he liked best about her – but he wished she wasn't so perceptive sometimes. He was still grieving for Nicole – Lottie was right about that – and he had no idea how to start moving on.

He'd been angry ever since Nicole had died, but what husband wouldn't be, after losing his wife in such a senseless way? There wasn't a limit to how long it should take him to get over her loss, was there? But then an inner voice of doubt spoke up. *Shouldn't you be feeling less angry about it all by now? Is it time to start moving on?*

He couldn't answer any of these questions for himself, that was for sure. He found it hard to talk about his feelings at the best of times, so there was no way he was going to talk to his friends about it. He certainly couldn't talk to Nicole's parents, who were still struggling to come to terms with their own feelings after losing their only daughter.

He stopped in front of the pinot noir vines and stared out across the estate. He owed it to Lottie to tell her what had happened if they were going to be together, but right now, he wouldn't even know where to start with explaining how he felt. He'd been wondering for a while now whether counselling might help him, but he was afraid to take that step. He rubbed his eyes, trying to clear his mind. What was the right thing to do?

He took one last look at the estate, before turning away from the vines to head back to the office in search of Didier. He walked through the bare vines to the path that led up to the courtyard where the estate office was and made his way steadily up the slope.

Didier was alone and Thierry sighed with relief. He didn't want to talk in front of Henri, Didier's assistant, even though they were all good friends and had worked together for years. It would be hard enough having to reveal his weakness to Didier, his best friend, let alone anyone else.

'*Salut, ça va?*' he asked as he came in, closing the door behind him.

'Not bad, you? Do you want a coffee?'

Thierry nodded and sank gratefully into Henri's padded desk chair.

'I think I may need counselling.' He winced, embarrassed at saying it out loud.

'That's a great conversation starter,' Didier replied setting a cup of coffee in front of him. 'How did all this come up?'

'I asked Lottie to move in with me again, and she told me I still need to deal with my grief.' Thierry stared absently at his coffee. 'And the thing is, she only said what I've been telling myself for a while now.'

Didier blew out a long breath. 'And you think counselling might be the answer?'

Thierry nodded, looking up. 'But the trouble is, even the thought of needing therapy makes me feel weak and inadequate. Then after our conversation, as I thought about it, I wondered if she was right. If I want to be with her, I need to sort this out.'

'I agree counselling might be good for you. There's no shame in it, Thierry, and I think it could help you sort through the nightmare you've been living with. Do you know anyone you could go to?'

'No idea, no. I suppose I could check with my doctor about a referral.'

'Yes, that's a good idea. And you know you can always talk to me, don't you? Without judgment.'

'I know, and I appreciate it. I just feel guilty because you're always listening to my woes, but you never tell me any of yours.' After all they'd been through over the years, it meant a lot to him to have Didier's friendship.

'That's not strictly true, and you know it.' Didier sighed and took off his glasses.

Thierry waited for him to summon up the courage to say what he had on his mind. 'Without judgment, remember?' he prompted him gently.

'Fran's desperate for us to have a child together, but we're not having any luck with her getting pregnant. We've been trying for about five months now, but it's stressing her out that it's not happening more quickly for us.'

'How do you feel about it all?' Thierry asked.

'Well, if I only ever have Chlöe, that will be fine with me. But for Fran it's different. She loves Chlöe, but she wants a child of her own.'

'Have you been to the doctor about it?'

'Fran has, but they keep sending her away, saying it will happen in due course, that she shouldn't worry.'

'What about tests? Have you had any?'

'Well, I suppose everything's okay with me, as I've already had a child, but we don't know about Fran. She hasn't had any tests yet because it's still too soon. I'm not sure she could take it if she found out she was somehow "flawed", as she would see it, and that was the reason for her not getting pregnant. I don't want to put her through that, but I'm sure she will eventually suggest it if she doesn't fall pregnant soon.' Didier rubbed his hands over his face. It seemed like it was already too much pressure for him.

'I suppose you have to keep trying for as long as you want to, and then you'll need to decide whether to pursue treatment. I don't envy you, though, having to wait and see every month whether the news is good or bad.'

Thierry thought then about his relationship with Nicole and of his lasting regrets following her death. It was time for him to get some help in overcoming his guilt.

CHAPTER TWO

Lottie

Lottie was dreading the day ahead. She'd told Fran and her mum time and again she didn't want a baby shower, but they'd refused to listen and ploughed on with it anyway. Although she'd be grateful for the gifts people would bring, she didn't feel like making small talk with loads of people she hardly knew, or being forced to say the same thing over and over.

Sylvie had disappeared early that morning in a cloud of secrecy that only left Lottie more frustrated. They were all so excited about the event and looking forward to it – and she didn't want to spoil their fun – but at the same time it would have been nice if they'd asked her what she wanted. She would have preferred a small get-together with her family and friends, rather than this full-blown do with so many people.

Her phone rang as she sat down with her breakfast, and she sighed when her mum's name appeared on the screen.

'*Salut, Maman, ça va?*'

'Ah, Lottie, I'm so looking forward to the baby shower. And I can't wait to see you and Fran. How did it go at the doctor's yesterday?'

Lottie repeated the story again for her mum, giving her the reassurance she needed. 'What time will you be arriving today?'

'I'll be leaving shortly so I can help Fran and Sylvie get everything sorted in plenty of time.' Her mum sounded so excited, Lottie half expected her to squeal out loud.

'I'll see you soon, then.'

'Yes, and it will be great to talk about everything baby-related with you face to face, won't it? And what we're going to do once the baby's born, too. We've got plenty of room for you both here, you know.'

'Hmm,' was all Lottie could muster by way of a response. She said goodbye and resisted the urge to scream.

She'd known her mum would be pushing for her to come home to live with her and her dad after the baby was born. And that wasn't what she wanted at all. But now that she'd talked with Sylvie about her tentative plans to move in with Frédéric, she was going to have to make a decision about where she was going to live. Otherwise her mum would be moving her back home without a moment's hesitation.

She'd left home to travel in the first place because she was stifled by life in Colmar, and it was even worse when Fran moved to London after university. So the last thing she wanted to do was to go back home again now, but trying to get her parents to understand this was proving impossible.

She set off for the *Salle des Fêtes* a little before midday, wrapping her padded coat around her as best she could against the chilly spring day. On her way, she nodded at a couple of the mums she recognised from her time working at the nursery, and wondered what it would feel like to join their ranks as a new mum soon. Although she was frightened at the prospect of giving birth, and still hadn't confessed this to anyone else, she was looking forward to life with her new baby on the other side. It wasn't quite how she'd expected her life to turn out as she approached her twenty-sixth birthday, but she was ready for life as a single mum, all the same.

As she turned the corner, the *Salle des Fêtes* came into view in the distance, with a cluster of pink and blue balloons tethered on either side of the arched entrance. She had to smile at the lengths they'd gone to for her, and she resolved to be patient with them all and to try to enjoy herself. She waited for an oncoming car to pass before crossing the road, but the car slowed down and then pulled up next to her.

'Lottie, *ma chérie*, I'm glad I've caught you.' Her dad parked and got out. On reaching her, he threw his arms around her and gave her an awkward hug, due to the size of her bump. She'd missed his hugs.

'Hello, Dad, how are you?'

'I'm fine. I've just dropped your mum off for the big party.' He winked, as if Lottie didn't know that they'd been planning it for ages, and she laughed.

'What are you going to do while we're in there?' she asked, wishing she could go with him instead, wherever it was.

'I'm going to taste some of Didier's wines, of course.'

'Well, think of me while you're having fun, won't you?'

'Don't be like that, your mum is looking forward to seeing you, and I'm sure everyone else is, too. They've gone to a lot of trouble to make it a special event for you.'

'I know they have, but I didn't want a big do. I would have been happy with the family and one or two friends.'

'Well, it's nice to know you have so many friends looking out for you and the baby, isn't it? Your mum said everything went okay at the doctor's the other day, and you're looking well.'

'Thanks, Dad. I don't mean to be grumpy. I wish the baby would come, that's all.'

'You might be wishing the opposite soon. Try to enjoy this last bit of freedom while you have it.'

'Not that I can do much with it at the moment, apart from waddling everywhere.'

Her dad laughed and gave her another hug. 'Enjoy the party. I'll see you later when I come to pick your mum up. *Je t'aime, ma chère.*'

'Love you too, Dad. Bye.'

He climbed back into the car and was gone in a flash, leaving her loitering on the pavement opposite the *Salle*, summoning up the strength to go in and face everyone. Just as she was thinking about changing her mind, Fran popped her head out the front door, looking for her, no doubt, and ran across the road to join her.

'Everything okay? You're not going to change your mind, are you?' Fran tilted her head with a knowing smile.

'I did wonder about it, but only for a minute.' She grinned at her older sister, then tucked her hand inside Fran's arm and set off across the road to see what the baby shower had in store for her.

Thierry

Thierry was up early, as always. After checking on the vines, he changed back into his normal shoes and set off on the drive to Strasbourg. His doctor had recommended a bereavement counsellor to him and he'd made an appointment straight away, before he could change his mind. Didier had helped him get over his last mental hurdle, and he was glad to be doing something about it all at last. On the way into the city, he wondered what sort of questions the counsellor would ask him and how intrusive it would all be. He would have to be open if he was going to get anything out of this, but that wasn't going to be easy.

The counsellor's office was in a quiet backstreet, not far from the university. At least it wasn't near the hospital, a place he hoped he would never have to return to for many years to come. He parked the car right outside, fed some coins into the meter and went in, announcing his arrival to the receptionist before taking a seat.

'*Monsieur* Bernard?' An elegant blonde woman, who he assumed was the counsellor, called his name a few moments later.

He stood up and went to shake her hand. She turned to lead the way to her modern office down the corridor.

'Please, take a seat. I'm Dr Bartin. May I call you Thierry?'

'Of course.' He unzipped his jacket and sat down in one of the contemporary-looking armchairs. His hands were suddenly clammy and he took several deep breaths to calm himself.

Dr Bartin took the chair opposite. 'Now, I understand from your doctor that you're looking for bereavement counselling following the death of your wife. I'm sorry for your loss. Why don't you start by telling me how you're feeling now?'

Thierry cleared his throat. 'Well, even though Nicole has been gone for nearly two years, I still haven't come to terms with what happened to her. I'm often angry and I don't know how to control it. And I... I've started a new relationship with someone, and she's made me see that I need to get some professional help.' Thierry released a long breath, glad to have got that first bit over with.

'Well, the first thing you have to accept about grief is that everyone reacts differently to the death of a loved one, and there's no right or wrong about how long it takes to move on from that grief. Sometimes, you will feel you have moved on, and then a tiny thing will spark a strong memory that will suddenly fill you with sadness all over again. There are stages of grief, though, and denial and anger are common at first. It sounds to me like you're stuck at that stage, but that now maybe you're trying to move forward because you have a new partner.'

'I don't feel like I'm in denial. I do accept Nicole is dead, but I'm still so angry because it shouldn't have happened.'

'Why do you say that?'

Thierry shrugged. He couldn't bring himself to tell her the full story yet. It was only their first meeting, after all. 'It was a needless accident, and she shouldn't have died like that.'

'Sometimes, people do die in stupid accidents, and it's as hard to come to terms with deaths of that kind as with any other, when you're the one left behind.'

Thierry absorbed that information silently, understanding the counsellor's point. 'She was so young, though, and we'd only been married a few years. We had our whole lives ahead of us, but it was all cut short on that day.' He ran his hands over his face, swiping at the tears that threatened. He hardly ever cried, and yet here he was, embarrassing himself in front of a virtual stranger.

'Did you have any children, Thierry?'

'No. Why do you ask?' The question came out more sharply than he meant it to, and he regretted his tone at once. But the counsellor didn't seem to take any offence. She looked like it would take a lot to ruffle her feathers.

'You were newly married, so you might have been thinking of starting a family soon, or you might have already had a child, which would only have made things harder for you when Nicole died.'

'We'd been, er... thinking about it, but Nicole wanted children more than I did. It was something we argued about a lot.' He tipped his head back and closed his eyes, mortified at having to reveal this.

'That must have been difficult for you both. Have you told your new partner any of this?'

'No, we're not at that stage yet, and she has a lot on her mind at the moment. She's pregnant by an ex-partner who's no longer on the scene, and she's due to give birth soon.'

The hour session with Dr Bartin passed quickly, and Thierry almost couldn't believe how much he'd told her in that time. She'd drawn him out in a way he wouldn't have believed possible beforehand. It had felt good to get everything – well, almost everything – off his chest. He felt strangely relieved as he drove back to the vineyard, as well as hopeful the doctor could help him come to terms with all that had happened.

He and Lottie had a good thing going, and if he could conquer his grief and his anger, they might be able to build on what they'd started. He wanted nothing more than to be a good partner to her and to help her with her baby, and at last he could see a way forward. For the first time in a long time, he was looking to the future and making plans.

Lottie

'Lottie!' her mum cried, as Lottie pushed open the heavy wooden door to the *Salle*. 'How lovely to see you, sweetheart.'

Her mum flew across the room and enveloped her in a massive hug, as if she hadn't seen her in years, when in fact it had only been a few weeks. Sylvie and Chlöe came up to join them, and Lottie hugged and kissed them all in turn.

'Thank you all for doing this for me. I appreciate it so much.' She smiled her thanks despite her reservations, and they looked pleased she was happy.

'Let's get you a drink, Lottie,' Fran said, gently guiding her away from the older women to give her some space. Lottie took Chlöe's hand and followed her to the kitchen hatch, where Fran poured them both out a cup of juice.

'Thanks again, Fran. I know you organised most of it, and I am grateful, honestly.'

'I did try to keep it low-key, as you wanted, but Sylvie and Mum had other ideas, as you can see.'

Lottie turned round and did a quick count. There were at least forty people attending. She recognised some faces, but not many, guessing Sylvie must have invited a lot of her own village friends to join in the celebration. She tried not to let it annoy her, but to focus instead on the kindness they'd all shown by arranging the event.

'What's the plan, then?' she asked, eyes widening at the thought of having to open all the gifts one by one.

'I think we'll have lunch first of all – Sylvie and her friends did all the cooking – and you can mingle while you eat, or people can come to you. Then we'll have a moment for some brief speeches, and you could open some of your gifts then, if you want to. Sylvie really wants you to open hers.'

Lottie chuckled at that.

'I made up some little thank you gifts for people to take home with them, which include a card, so you don't have to worry about doing that afterwards.'

'That was so kind of you, thank you.' Lottie gave her sister a grateful hug, thanking heaven for her support, before looking down at Didier's daughter. 'Chlöe, I think I'm going to need your help with opening all these presents. Will you help me?'

The little girl nodded and laughed, before dancing off to count the presents once again.

Lottie managed to talk to a lot of people over lunch, and to thank them for the gifts they'd brought, which were all piling up on a side table. She opened Sylvie's gift at her insistence, and was delighted to see she'd knitted her a beautiful white shawl for the baby, with an intricate scalloped edging. She also opened a present from Chlöe, which turned out to be a fluffy rabbit.

'I've got one like this and I still love it,' the little girl told Lottie.

'Well, I'm sure my baby will love this one, too.' She pulled Chlöe gently to her for a hug and a kiss, delighted by her enthusiasm.

As the baby shower wore on, most of the guests wanted to know how Lottie was going to manage as a single mum with no job once the baby was born. After deflecting what felt like the hundredth person to ask her this, she wandered off to sit quietly on her own for a moment.

'Don't let them get to you,' a voice said from behind her. She turned to see Fran's English friend, Ellie, tucked away in a corner. Ellie stood up and came to sit next to Lottie. She'd been living in Alsace for about the same length of time as Lottie had since her return from her travels, but they hadn't spent much time with each other up till then.

'Why are you hiding away from everyone over there?' Lottie asked.

'All this talk of babies is making me twitchy. I'm not ready for any of that yet, to be honest.' Ellie shrugged in apology.

'Neither was I, but fate had other ideas. And now I've had some time to get used to it, I'm looking forward to it.' Lottie rubbed her bump and smiled.

'I'm glad for you, honestly I am. But the whole idea of settling down right now makes me feel queasy. There's so much I want to do before that.'

'Like what? I thought you and Henri were an item and getting ready to tie the knot.'

Ellie winced. 'I do like Henri, very much, but it's far too soon to be talking of marriage and babies. After I was made redundant last year, I began to think about travelling for a bit, but I got distracted when I came here and started work on the château. Now I'm wondering whether this might be the best time for me to do that before everything gets too serious between us.'

'Well, I definitely understand your need to travel, that's how I felt. I enjoyed it too, and you might as well do it while you're young. Have you spoken to Fran and Didier about it? They'd really miss you two.'

'I haven't even spoken to Henri about it. I don't think he'll understand where I'm coming from about wanting to travel. He loves it here so much.'

'Well, you need to start by talking to him then, I think.' Lottie gave Ellie a weak smile, not envying her that conversation at all.

'How about you? Have you enjoyed the party?'

'Sort of. It's just that everyone keeps telling me they know best for me and the baby, and no-one seems to understand that it's possible to raise a baby on your own.'

'It won't be easy, that's for sure, but you can do it. You'll need to be organised, I suppose. At least you can return to your job at the nursery in the longer term, and I'm sure Fran will help out with babysitting.'

'Thanks for being so honest with me. That's what I think, too.'

'What are you two doing all the way over here?' Lottie's mum appeared in front of them, wagging her finger dramatically.

'We're catching up and I needed a sit-down,' said Lottie.

Her mum pulled up a chair and looked from one to the other. 'How's everything with you and Henri?' she asked Ellie.

'Fine, thanks, *Madame* Schell.'

'Oh, do call me Christine, no need to be so formal. It's been a wonderful party, Lottie, hasn't it?' She went straight on, without waiting for Lottie's reply. 'You've had so many presents. People have been so kind, and all those things will come in very handy once the baby's born and you can't get out as much. Your dad and I would be so happy to have you at home again, you know, and I could help you, make life easier for you.'

'I know, Mum, but I've told you I want to stay here. My life is here now, what with my job at the nursery, and with Thierry living here, too.'

Her mum leaned towards Lottie, a worried look on her face. 'I wish you'd reconsider. I don't think you'll be able to manage everything on your own, especially when the baby is first born. And have you thought about money? You won't be able to go back to work straight away, and babies are expensive.'

Lottie was saved from having to answer when a cry rang out from the other side of the *Salle*. All three women turned and her mum rushed away to see what had happened. Lottie struggled to her feet and slowly made her way over to the gathering crowd.

'Should we call an ambulance?'

At the sound of her mum's panicked voice, Lottie nudged her way through the guests to find her with Fran on either side of a distinctly pale-looking Sylvie, who was sitting on a chair with her eyes closed. Lottie's heart sank at the thought that something terrible might be wrong with Sylvie, who'd been so good to her. She looked around for Chlöe, knowing she would be frightened to see her grandma like this, and spotted her hiding under a table.

'It's okay, Chlöe. Your dad will be here soon and he'll take your grandma to the hospital for a check-up, and then everything will be fine.'

Chlöe crawled out and Lottie put her arm round her, trying to soothe away the child's fears as much as her own.

'Didier's on his way, Sylvie,' Fran said. She put her mobile away and took hold of the older woman's hand. 'Everything's going to be all right.' She glanced up at Lottie, with fear in her eyes, and the only thing Lottie was sure of was that everything in her life was about to change.

Thierry

Thierry pulled up in the courtyard of the vineyard, after an uneventful journey back from Strasbourg, and made his way on foot to Sylvie's cottage in the village. He knocked on the front door, admiring the familiar brass knocker while he waited to be let in. When there was no reply, he wondered about going round the back. Most people tended to use the garden entrance, but he'd never done so before and didn't want to seem rude. He knocked more loudly, then glanced at his watch. He'd expected Lottie to be at home at lunchtime and couldn't think where she might be. Then he remembered it was the baby shower today.

Disappointed, he started walking back to the vineyard. Just before he reached the track that led back to the estate, he spotted Lottie in the distance. He was surprised to see her on her own.

'Lottie, is everything okay?' he called out. She was wiping her face with her sleeve. 'What's the matter?' he asked as they came face to face, frowning at her tears.

She threw herself into his arms and he pulled her close, relishing her need for his comfort.

'Oh, Thierry. Sylvie's not well. She almost fainted at the baby shower, so she'll have to go to hospital. Didier's there now. Fran's looking after Chlöe, and I'm going to get some things for Sylvie to take with her.' She pulled back, her face wracked with worry.

'I'll go with you. How did she seem when you left?' He took her hand as they turned to make their way back to the cottage.

'She looked so fragile. Her aches and pains seem to have been getting worse recently, but she never complains. I don't think she's been quite right since she was involved in that car accident last year. Even though the whiplash passed, I think it took it out of her.'

'She's always been so strong, but perhaps she needs to slow down and take things a bit easier.'

'I can't see her accepting that for a minute, but something's going to have to change. What were you doing out in the village, anyway?' she asked, letting go of his hand to tuck her arm through his as they walked.

'I was looking for you. I wanted to find out how the baby shower had gone.' He'd wondered about telling her about his counselling, but now didn't seem to be the right time. He wasn't sure he was ready to talk about it yet, either.

Lottie grimaced by way of an answer and he laughed.

'It was okay, and people were kind. It just wasn't what I wanted to do by way of a celebration. It doesn't matter now, with all that's happened.'

They reached the cottage a minute later and she led him round the back and inside to the little kitchen. Thierry waited downstairs while Lottie went and gathered a few things together for Sylvie, in case she needed to stay at the hospital. Soon, she was making her way down the stairs again, a small bag on her arm, and then they were on their way back to the *Salle*.

'Sylvie told me yesterday that Frédéric has asked her to move in with him.' Lottie glanced up at him as she finished speaking to gauge his reaction.

'And has she made any decision yet?' He hardly dared hope what this might mean for him and Lottie.

'Not yet, no. She likes her independence, but she also knows there could be some real advantages to taking him up on his offer.

Maybe what's happened today will encourage her to make a final decision.'

'And where would that leave you if she does decide to move in with Frédéric? I assume she'd sell her cottage.'

'Well, I could either move back home or... I could take you up on your offer, if it still stands.'

Thierry stopped in the street to face her. 'Of course it does. I hope you know how much I care for you, and how much I want us to build on what we've already started together.' He caressed her cheek with his hand, and she closed her eyes at his touch.

Lottie didn't say anything in reply, and he didn't know what to make of her silence. She turned and carried on walking and he followed, trying to be patient while she sorted things through in her mind.

'I'd like to build on what we've started too, Thierry. But even though I'd love to be with you every day, I do have my reservations, as I told you before. You still have to come to terms with Nicole's death, and I'm about to experience the biggest change of my life so far. If I'm honest, if I did move in with you, it would be against my better judgment.'

'You're right. We both have a lot to deal with, and more than anything, I don't want to let you and the baby down. But I can offer you a good life, and I think we could all be happy together.'

He didn't tell her he wanted to make amends for letting Nicole down in the terrible way he had – that would be a step too far – but he did mean everything he'd said.

Lottie was frowning by the time he'd finished speaking, making him more nervous about what she was about to say. 'I've given this a lot of thought since speaking to you about it last week, and now that Sylvie's situation has changed, I've had to review it all again. In an ideal world, I'd want us to keep things between us as they are so we can take things slowly, but that's not an option any longer. I really don't want to go back to my parents' house, so I'll accept your offer.'

'You'll move in with me?' He could hardly breathe while he waited for her confirmation.

She nodded, but followed it up with a warning. 'But don't go thinking this is going to be easy, Thierry. We both have a lot of baggage to sort out.'

He still swooped in for a hug. 'You won't regret it, I promise. It'll all be fine.'

CHAPTER THREE

Lottie

Lottie spent a few sleepless nights alone at the cottage after Sylvie was taken ill. Didier and Fran had taken her to the *urgences* at the hospital in Strasbourg. The doctors had found nothing wrong, but had decided to keep her in as a precaution. Since then, Lottie had been slowly packing up her things and preparing herself to move to Thierry's. She still wasn't sure she was doing the right thing, but she couldn't burden Sylvie any longer, and she definitely didn't want to go home.

She lay in her single bed, snuggling for a few minutes longer under the duvet, and thought about the baby's father for the first time in ages. She'd met Yiannis when she was visiting Crete. She'd found a summer job in a restaurant by the beach so she could top up her funds, and he'd been the resident musician. She'd fallen for him almost at once: his dark, wavy hair, his passion, his easy smile. Before she knew it, she'd found herself pregnant as well, and when he'd told her he wasn't ready to be a dad, she was faced with the prospect of being a single mum.

She hauled herself out of bed with a sigh. There was no point wasting time with what-ifs. Yiannis had made himself clear and Lottie was perfectly capable of managing without him. Without anyone, if she had to. Still, she regretted placing so much trust in him only for him to let her down when it really mattered.

An hour later, she called Thierry to let him know she was ready. She cast her eye round Sylvie's neat cottage one final time to make sure she'd not left anything behind. She'd loved living with Sylvie for these past few months. She was so grateful to her for taking her in after Didier had moved in with Fran, and for finding her the job at the nursery. Her kindness had allowed her to stay near Thierry while they were finding their feet with their fledgling relationship, and she would always remember it.

Thierry arrived to pick her up a short while later. 'C'est tout?' he asked, at the sight of her small collection of bags.

'Yes, I don't have much stuff. Just as well when I think of all the things I'll need to buy for the baby.' She frowned. There was a lot of expense ahead, and she wasn't even working at the moment.

'Don't worry. That's one of the things I want to talk to you about once you're settled.'

'What do you mean?' she asked, as she climbed into his Peugeot estate.

'Well, I can help pay for anything you need to get for the baby.'

She suppressed a smile as he pulled himself up straight, reinforcing the idea that he'd be the one doing the looking after, regardless of what she wanted. But she was ready with her answer.

'You don't need to do that, Thierry. You're already helping me by not letting me pay any rent. I still have some savings put by, and I'll be going back to work eventually, so I'll have enough money to get what I need.'

Thierry tutted softly but didn't say any more. He just drove slowly away from Sylvie's cottage towards the lane leading up to Didier's vineyard estate. He parked the car in the courtyard car park a minute or two later and came round to help her get out. She took his hand as she turned herself carefully and slid down onto the gravel. It was getting harder and harder to extricate her growing body from cars, and she was grateful to him for helping her to do it reasonably gracefully. He went to gather her few belongings from the boot and returned to take her hand for the walk down to his house.

'How long have you worked here as winemaker, Thierry?' she asked, as they went through the archway that led on to the vineyards.

'I came here straight after college, about ten years ago. I met Nicole at a wine tasting in Riquewihr run by the company she worked for. We were married a year later.'

It was the most he'd ever told her about Nicole without prompting and she was surprised. Maybe he had listened to her, after all.

Lottie stopped to inspect a row of vines, noticing the tiny green buds beginning to appear along the canes.

'I could see the vines from my bedroom window at Sylvie's, but I couldn't see these little buds growing. They looked so bare and forlorn. It's good to see the first signs of spring.'

'It is good, but it also means there will be lots of work to do soon to get the vineyard in shape before the summer.'

They carried on walking slowly down the slope alongside the vines. Lottie had been to Thierry's house a few times before when they'd been on some of their early dates, but she'd not been back for a while and things felt different now. Thierry opened the front door to the old stone house and showed her into the cool, tiled hallway. She pulled her coat closer around her. It didn't feel much warmer indoors than it was outside.

Thierry put down the bags and went into the spacious front room. 'I'll light the wood burner again. It does get cold very quickly when the fire's not on.'

Lottie followed him in and glanced around the room while Thierry sorted out the fire. It was furnished minimally: a couple of worn but comfortable-looking sofas were sideways on to the fire, and there was a single armchair by the window that looked out on the veranda and the vineyards beyond. There was an open book resting on the chair. It must be Thierry's favourite place to sit.

She turned to look at the mantelpiece above the fireplace, expecting to see some photos or knick-knacks, but there were no clues as to Thierry's background or his life with Nicole. It was as if she'd never been there at all. Lottie sighed. Not for the first time, she wondered how dangerous this whole arrangement might be for her heart.

Thierry

'I didn't know whether you'd want to share my room or be in a room on your own, but I've cleared some space for you in my wardrobe.' Now that Lottie was actually here, Thierry was nervous all of a sudden. Everything had seemed much easier before it became a reality.

'I'm happy to be in your room for now. When the baby comes, we both might feel differently.' She smiled, and he relaxed a little.

He picked up her bags and led her to the stairs back out in the hallway. At the top of the stairs, he turned right, following the bannister all the way along to the end of the corridor where his room was located. He put her bags down on the floor next to his king-size bed and walked over to the wardrobe.

'I emptied out this side of the wardrobe for you. Will that be enough space?'

'Of course. I don't have much. Thank you for doing that for me. It must have been hard to clear out Nicole's things.' She reached out and took his hand.

Thierry swallowed. 'I've moved them to the wardrobe in the spare room for now. To be honest, I still don't feel strong enough to get rid of them.'

'There's no rush. You'll know when you're ready.'

He showed her the chest of drawers and the little bedside table, before showing her where he kept the towels. He wondered if it all appeared very functional to Lottie. He'd not had the energy to decorate or add any more furnishings since Nicole had died – there didn't seem to be any point – but maybe now Lottie was here, he'd find more of a sense of purpose.

'This is a lovely house, Thierry. I didn't take it all in when I visited you before.' She blushed, and he remembered bringing her back here the first time they'd slept together. That was when he'd put all his pictures and mementoes of his life with Nicole away, not wanting to frighten Lottie off. And he'd not remembered to bring them out again since. His guilt resurfaced with a bang and he turned abruptly.

'I'll make us a drink,' he said, and shot off downstairs without waiting for her to catch up. Having Lottie here on a permanent basis was going to be more difficult than he'd realised, and he didn't have the first clue how to tackle it.

Lottie joined him in the kitchen a few minutes later. 'Everything okay?'

'Yes, fine,' he said, more gruffly than he intended.

'Did you put all your pictures of Nicole away before I visited here the first time?'

Her intuition was uncanny. Thierry stared at the coffee cups wondering what to say. 'Yes, I did,' he finally admitted.

'You can get them out again. I won't be upset. I know you had a life together before me and that you want to be able to remember her. You need to be able to do that if you're going to move on.'

'I know, but...'

She waited for him to continue, but he couldn't tell her what a reminder they were of his guilt.

'I don't have any pictures of my baby's father,' she said instead. 'I deleted them all from my phone right after he left me. I didn't regret that at first – I was still so angry with him then for abandoning me – but now I wish I had at least one picture to show the baby when they're older. They'll want to know about their father and I won't have much to tell them.'

Thierry had never asked about the father of her baby. It was too personal when they were first getting to know each other, and this was the first time she'd volunteered information about him since then. 'What was his name?' he asked tentatively.

She bit her lip while she decided whether to say more and he waited patiently. 'Yiannis.'

'And you loved him?'

She nodded but didn't say more. Tears sprang to her eyes and Thierry moved closer to take her in his arms. He held her tight while she cried for her lost love, and her regret. He knew exactly how hard that was to deal with. Eventually, she pulled away and gave him a wobbly smile.

'Sorry to burden you with all that,' she said, after wiping her eyes and blowing her nose.

'I'm glad you felt able to share with me. It's hard for both of us, but we need to do it if we're going to be living with each other, don't we?'

He passed her a cup of coffee and led the way back to the front room. Lottie took a seat on one of the sofas while he went to the cupboard next to the fireplace to retrieve one of his photos.

'This was always my favourite photo of Nicole.' He passed her a heavy silver frame containing a picture of his wife on her own.

Lottie studied it silently for a few minutes and he wondered what she was thinking. Had he done the right thing in showing it to her?

'She was beautiful. She looked very happy that day. Where did you take it?'

'At the lake. We'd taken a picnic one day and it was one of the happiest days we spent together.'

She passed it back and he went to put it back in the cupboard.

'Don't put it away again, Thierry. Put it somewhere you can see it and remember those good times.'

He hesitated and then took her advice, resting the photo frame on the mantelpiece.

'I'm sorry you don't have any photos of Yiannis to show the baby, but you should try not to feel guilty about it. It's understandable that you were upset with him for not wanting to support you.'

'It wasn't that so much – I can manage on my own, like millions of other women have managed before me – but I thought he loved me too, and it hurt to know he didn't feel the same way. I felt so stupid for trusting him.'

Thierry read between the lines; Lottie was wary of depending on anyone else after what had happened to her. He would have to work hard to gain her trust. He had no intention of abandoning her, but proving that to her was going to take time.

Lottie

By the time Lottie woke up the next day, Thierry had already left. He'd warned her that he got up early every day to do his vine-yard inspection, but she was still surprised when she found herself alone in the house on her first day. That was one of the things she'd loved about being at Sylvie's – that she was hardly ever on her own – and she missed the companionship of Didier's mum straight away. She wanted to find out how Sylvie was getting on today if she could. She hoped she'd left the hospital by now and was planning her house move.

She reached out to touch Thierry's side of the bed to see if it was still warm, but it was as if he'd never been there. She'd hoped they would make love on her first night, but he was treating her with kid gloves, as if she might break, and so nothing had happened between them. And now she wished she'd been able to wake up next to him, to see what that felt like, but she accepted he had reasons for getting up so early.

She rolled over onto her side and then sat up slowly, before pushing herself up and making her way to the en-suite bathroom. Thierry had cleared some space for her on the glass shelf above the sink, but she'd only got round to putting out the basics last night. She'd need more space than he'd made for all her lotions. She bent down to see if there was any room in the cupboard under the sink and found it stuffed full of Nicole's old toiletries. She closed the door quickly, feeling like she was snooping. She'd have to ask Thierry if he could clear the cupboard out as well, but she might try to manage for a while before doing that.

She was about to go downstairs when the front door opened. She immediately felt guilty for not having got dressed while Thierry had been out. Then she berated herself – she didn't have anywhere to be, did she?

'Lottie, what are you doing up? You should be resting,' Thierry chided her, as he took off his coat and boots in the hallway.

'Why? I'm pregnant, not ill. I was just coming down to make a cup of tea. Do you want one?'

She sensed his irritation, even though he didn't say anything at first, but busied himself hanging up his coat.

'Why don't you let me make it? I can bring it up to you in bed.'

'That's lovely of you, but I want to go and find out what's happening with Sylvie.'

'I spoke to Didier this morning while we were checking the vineyard. Sylvie came home yesterday. Apparently, she's fine. She was overdoing it a bit too much. Frédéric's going to stay at the cottage with her to help her pack everything up and then she'll be moving in with him.'

'Oh.' Now she didn't need to go and find out what had happened. She carried on making the tea, determined to show Thierry she was quite capable of looking after herself.

'I would like a cup of tea, if you're still offering. It's pretty cold out there first thing. You'll need to wrap up when you go out.'

She tutted, unable to hold it in, before plonking a cup down in front of him, and then taking hers back towards the stairs.

'Where are you going?' he asked.

'To get ready.'

When she came back down half an hour later, Thierry had disappeared again. She would have liked to have sat and chatted with him, but his mollycoddling was annoying, and she didn't want to give him any more opportunities to tell her what to do.

She was going to go and see Sylvie anyway, she decided, and she'd catch up with Thierry later. She pulled on her coat and scarf, shaking her head at Thierry's overprotective comments, and set off on the short walk into the village.

She took the slope up alongside the vines slowly, so she didn't wear herself out, and soon she was walking through the courtyard towards the path leading to Sylvie's cottage. The path was dotted with pastel-coloured houses with half-timbered frames, as per the Alsatian tradition, and Lottie delighted in the array of colours as she walked past: golden yellow, sky blue, raspberry pink. She looked forward to the time when all the window boxes would once more be filled with red geraniums, bright as lipstick, guaranteed to make passers-by smile.

She went round to the back garden of Sylvie's cottage rather than knocking on the front door, and it felt strange not to have her own key. She found Frédéric in the garden pulling out some of the weeds that had sprung up since he'd last visited.

'*Salut*,' she called, wanting to alert him to her presence.

He straightened and looked her way, shielding his eyes with his hand from the midday sun and trying to make out who it was. 'Ah, Lottie. *Ça va?*'

'Yes, I'm fine, thanks. How's Sylvie doing?'

'She's grumpy because she's having to rest and she doesn't like it. She misses you, too. Why don't you go in and say hello?' He smiled openly and she nodded.

'See you in a minute.'

She approached the stable door at the back of the house, knocked briefly and stepped inside. She walked through the small kitchen and into the lounge, where Sylvie was stretched out on the sofa.

'Lottie! How lovely to see you,' she cried, getting ready to sit up.

'Don't get up, it's all right. I can still just about bend down.' Lottie kissed her on both cheeks and then took a seat in the armchair next to her.

'How have you been? I've missed you so much. I wish you hadn't moved out so quickly.' Sylvie's face was etched with concern and Lottie was sorry for upsetting her.

'We thought it made sense with you not being well. You didn't need me to look after, as well. And you're going to be moving soon yourself, anyway.'

'Yes, and it all feels so sudden. I shall miss my cottage very much when it's sold.'

'I know, but it will be better if you're with Frédéric and not having to do everything on your own, won't it?'

'I suppose so.' She frowned, not looking for one minute like she agreed.

'You'll get used to it in time. Just like I'll have to, I guess.' Lottie pulled a face, remembering all the comments Thierry had made to her that morning.

'Is Thierry being overprotective, too?' Sylvie chuckled.

'Yes, he is, and don't laugh. Otherwise I won't be sympathetic towards you when Frédéric does the same.'

'I've missed your company, Lottie. I do hope we'll stay in touch.'

'Of course we will. You won't be far away. I can bring the baby to visit you when it's born.'

'I'd like that very much. Now, tell me, how are you feeling?'

'I'm absolutely fine, just keen to get on with it all now.'

'It's good you'll have Thierry by your side when it comes to giving birth.'

'Oh no, that's Fran's job. She's been my birth partner throughout, so she'll be with me when that day arrives.'

'But Thierry will want to come with you at least, won't he?' Sylvie frowned, looking worried.

'I suppose so. I hadn't given it much thought. It's not his baby, so I wouldn't expect him to want to come along as well.'

'That may be, but knowing Thierry, I think he'll have a view on what he wants to do.'

Lottie didn't want to depend on Thierry on that day of all days, but listening to Sylvie, she realised perhaps she'd already been planning subconsciously to exclude him from the birth. She had no idea how he would feel if she said she didn't want him to come, but she wasn't entirely sure she wanted him to be there, either.

Thierry

Thierry went out early again a couple of days later, but this time, he was planning to do something else after his inspection. Lottie had already shown him since she'd moved in that she could get on and do her own thing in his absence. He was gradually starting to accept that she didn't need him to manage her day or fuss over her. However, he did have something he wanted to do for her, and so he was making an early morning trip into Strasbourg.

When he got back, it was only ten o'clock. He was hoping that Lottie was still at home so he could put his idea to her. He collected his purchases from the boot and made his way inside.

'Hello!' he called, putting down his things. He hung up his coat and left his boots neatly on the doormat. Spotting Lottie's coat on the end of the bannister, he hung that up as well, trying not to be annoyed she'd left it there again.

'In here,' she replied.

He found her sitting at the kitchen table, eating a croissant.

'That looks good. How are you feeling today?'

'I'm fine. I had a walk to the *boulangerie* first thing, and it was good to get out and about. How about you?'

'Well, I've been into Strasbourg this morning.'

'Really? Why?'

He went back out to the hallway to collect what he'd bought. 'To get these.' He held up two large tins of lemon-coloured paint.

'Got some decorating plans, have you?'

'Well, yes.' He raised his eyebrows, expecting her to know what he was talking about.

'What?' she asked, putting down her croissant.

'The nursery,' he declared. 'The baby's going to need their own room and I thought I could make a start on decorating the spare room now your due date's getting closer.' He'd decided this was just the right project to revive his enthusiasm for sprucing up the house.

'I see.' Lottie pushed her chair back and stood up. Then she put her hands on her hips, and suddenly, all Thierry's confidence evaporated.

'I thought it was a good idea.' He shrugged, anticipating her irritation before she'd even said anything.

'Couldn't you have just talked it over with me first? You have no idea what colour scheme I would like, for example.'

'I bought lemon because that's what all the advice says to do when you don't know the sex of the baby.' He gave a little smile of apology.

'Who gave you that advice?' She rubbed her forehead, making him feel worse.

'I... I wanted it to be a surprise, so I looked it up online. I'm sorry for not talking it over with you.'

All the fight went out of her then. 'It's kind of you to do this, honestly it is, but I'd prefer you to discuss things with me first. So don't go out and buy anything else, please. I want to make up my own mind. And anyway, it's far too generous of you to dedicate one of your bedrooms to my baby.'

'But you're both going to be living here, and the baby will have their bedroom and we'll have ours.'

'As I told you before, it'll be best if I move into the other room when the baby comes. I'll want my own space while the baby and I get used to each other and find our feet. And I don't want to disturb you, either, when the baby's little because you'll have to get up every day to go to work.'

'Okay, that makes sense. But we can still redecorate, can't we?'

'The room's nice enough as it is. I don't want you to feel you have to go to lots of trouble for us.'

Thierry hung his head in defeat. He'd tried to do something to please her, but he'd got it all wrong. He turned away without another word and went to put the paint in the utility room off the kitchen. When he returned, Lottie was still standing in the same place, fidgeting with her hair.

'Don't worry. I'll take the paint back and we won't say any more about it.'

'Look, I'm sorry. I know you were trying to do something kind for me, and I do appreciate it. It's not that I'm against the idea of redecorating the room, although that was a bit of a surprise, but I'm used to making my own decisions about things.'

'Well, I should have spoken to you before getting the paint, I understand that now. And I understand you're used to making your own decisions, but if we're going to have a future together, maybe we should be making decisions together?'

Lottie swiped her hand through her dark blonde hair, gathering it into a ponytail over her shoulder. 'I agree, except that this baby isn't yours, and you're not responsible for it.'

'Damn it, Lottie. If we're together, then I *am* responsible for the baby and for you.' Why did she always push him away?

Her eyes widened. 'I don't know why you think that. I'm the only person who's responsible for the baby and I want to be able to provide for my own child, which is why I'll be going back to work as soon as I can. I know that's not going to be easy, but it's not impossible, either.' She stuck her chin out.

'When I invited you to move in with me, it wasn't meant to be a temporary solution. It was meant to be for good. I want to be with you because I... I care for you, and I'll care for the baby too, whether it's mine or not. That means I want to help you raise your child. I understand you want to go back to work at the nursery at some point, and I hope you'll let me help you care for the baby if you feel you have to do that. I don't want you to be dependent on me. I want you to know you can depend on me. There is a difference.'

He had no idea whether he would feel so loving towards this baby once it was born, but for now, this was his plan and he was sticking to it. He didn't want her to go back to work, either, but he wasn't going to tell her that. What he wanted to tell her was that he loved her, but his fear of rejection was too great and so once again, he left it unsaid.

CHAPTER FOUR

Lottie

Lottie was finding it harder and harder to get comfortable at night now she was only two weeks away from her due date. Her bump was so big she was having to use pillows to support it, and she worried about disturbing Thierry's sleep. At least the bed was big enough for them each to have their space. After rolling about for what felt like forever, she sat up to look at the clock and groaned softly. Three o'clock. She lay back down against the pillows, turned over gently towards Thierry and tried her best not to fret.

As her eyes adjusted to the darkness, it became clear Thierry wasn't in bed. She got up to get herself a drink of water and to go and check whether everything was all right.

She padded softly down the stairs and into the kitchen. There was no sign of Thierry, so she poured herself a glass of water and went back upstairs with it. As she reached the top of the stairs, she saw the light was on in the second bedroom. She hesitated for a moment wondering whether to go in. As far as she knew, only Nicole's old clothes were in there and she didn't want to intrude on his privacy. But then she heard him, and her heart broke at the sound of him crying.

'Thierry?' She pushed the door open slowly, giving him time to compose himself if he needed to. 'Are you okay?' she asked as he came into view.

Thierry looked up at her with tears running down his face, which he tried to swipe away as she came into the room. He was surrounded by Nicole's clothes, shoes and other bits and pieces that painted a picture of his former wife. 'She was so young, Lottie. So vital. Why did she have to die?' He sniffed and wiped his eyes again.

Lottie took a seat on the sofa bed and tried to compose herself before speaking. It was hard to see Thierry like this, even though she'd known for ages he was suffering, and that he was bottling it all up.

'It was an accident, Thierry. She wasn't meant to die. She was so very unlucky.'

'It's such a waste of a young life. She – *we* had everything to live for and it was all taken away in an instant.'

'I'm so sorry. I know you loved her so much.'

He scoffed. 'Not enough. It was my fault she died, you know.'

Lottie's heart filled with dread. 'What do you mean? That can't be right.'

'We argued that evening and she stormed out. I didn't go after her because I thought we could both do with calming down, and the next thing I knew, she was dead. If only I'd gone after her, I could have stopped her.'

'Oh, Thierry. You don't know that. You can't blame yourself for Nicole's death.'

'Yes I can, and I do.' He gave her a fierce look, as if daring her to contradict him but she wasn't afraid of him.

'Come and sit with me.' She reached out to him, then patted the sofa next to her.

After a moment, he stood up and came to join her. He rested his head on her shoulder and let out an enormous sigh. 'I'm so tired,

Lottie. I feel so guilty and I don't know how to get over it. I know deep down it wasn't my fault Nicole died, but I still feel so responsible. I let her down when she needed me most and I can never put that right.'

'Why did you argue?' She wasn't sure she wanted to know this much about Thierry's relationship with Nicole, when she was so concerned about whether his heart still belonged to her, but the question was out before she could help herself.

Thierry sat up at once. 'It doesn't matter any more.'

Lottie sighed. 'I won't push you, Thierry, but I think you need to confront that question before you can tackle your guilt.'

She stood up and bent to kiss his cheek before making her way back to bed. She waited for Thierry to come and join her but fell asleep before he did.

In the morning, Thierry's side of the bed was still empty. Lottie had no idea whether he'd come back to bed or not. She listened for sounds of him downstairs, but there was only the sound of the birds tweeting outside.

Seeing Thierry grieving like that had been hard, and it had only reinforced her belief that he still had a long way to go before he'd be able to move on from Nicole's tragic death. It was obvious he still loved Nicole, and that meant Lottie would always take second place in his heart. She couldn't resent him for that – Nicole had clearly been the love of his life – but she didn't know if they could build a relationship together when his love for his wife was still so present.

She sighed and threw back the bedclothes. She needed to get out and get some fresh air. Half an hour later, she was making her way over to the château, where Ellie had been put in charge of restoration work. Ellie had been Fran's best friend while she'd been working in London, but since Lottie had come to live on the vineyard, and especially since the baby shower, they were getting to know each other more and becoming good friends themselves.

'Hello?' she called, pushing open the heavy wooden door of the ancient building.

'I'll be right down,' Ellie called from somewhere upstairs.

Lottie had a look around while she waited. Didier had been living in the château when Fran first came back to Alsace to work for him. But since they'd been together, he'd moved into the cottage with her, leaving Ellie free to restore the château to its former glory. Sylvie had told Lottie that she and her husband had lived together in the château during their married life, but that her husband had never wanted to spend money on it, so it had fallen into a sad state by the time Didier had moved in. And Didier had never had the money to spend on it either, until now.

Ellie had already managed to achieve quite a lot on the ground floor, which Lottie hadn't seen for several months. The last time she'd been in the château was for the party they gave for Ellie's arrival, back when Didier and Chlöe had still been living there, and Fran had been living in the cottage on her own. All the rooms had now been replastered and repainted, and it looked as if all the woodwork had been spruced up, too. None of the rooms had doors on yet, though, and there was still some work to be done in the hallway.

'Hey Lottie, how are you? This is a lovely surprise.'

Lottie hugged and kissed Ellie, before gesturing at the progress she'd made. 'This looks amazing. You've done so much work since I was last here.'

'Yes, I had no idea what I would be getting myself into when Fran asked me to take on this job!' She laughed. 'I'm pleased with what we've done so far, but it's been so much more expensive than any of us first imagined.'

'I'm sure. Have you got time for a break? We could maybe go and get a coffee in the village.'

'Sure. You look like you need it more than me. Are you going stir crazy waiting for this baby?'

'A bit, yes. And then there's Thierry...'

'Let me grab my coat and you can tell me all about it.'

Thierry

'So, how have things been since the last time we met?' Dr Bartin smiled warmly, and Thierry relaxed into his chair a little, resting his hands on his thighs.

'A bit up and down, to be honest.' He told her about Lottie moving in with him and how hard they were both finding it to adjust to living with each other. Things still weren't much better on that front and he was also finding it hard to get back to the intimacy he'd previously shared with Lottie, despite them sharing the same bed every night.

'Still, it's good that Lottie took you up on your offer. You must have been pleased about that?'

'At first I was, but now I keep putting my foot in it by doing too much for her, and she doesn't like it.'

'You'll adjust to that in time, I'm sure. Tell me some of the good things that have happened since Lottie moved in.'

He told her how they'd talked about Nicole and also about Yiannis. 'Telling each other about our partners has definitely brought us closer, and I feel more comfortable talking to her about Nicole now. Then the other night, she found me crying, which was mortifying.'

Dr Bartin smiled kindly. 'It's okay for you to cry, Thierry. In fact, it's much better for you to let these feelings out than to keep them all in. Why were you crying?'

'About the fact that I feel responsible for Nicole's death. We'd been arguing again about having children. Nicole stormed out and I never saw her alive again. I should have gone after her, and then maybe none of this would have happened.' He rubbed his hand over his face, hating having to go over it all again.

'What did Lottie say about that?'

'I didn't tell her why we argued, but she's worked out that's the big issue for me to get past.'

'Why didn't you tell her?'

'I'm worried if I tell her I didn't want to have children with Nicole, she won't want me in her life any more. She's got a baby on the way and she's in a relationship with someone who doesn't even want to have children. How's that going to look?' Thierry threw his hands up and stood. He paced back and forth in front of the bay window that looked out onto the street.

'Why didn't you want children with Nicole?'

Even though he'd known this question was coming, his stomach tightened. 'I didn't want to share Nicole with anyone else. I'm ashamed to say it now. We'd not been married long and I wanted us to enjoy some time together as a couple first, maybe save up some money before children came along. I thought once we had children, they'd stop us from doing all the things we might be able to do without them. I hoped Nicole would eventually leave it alone. But she kept on bringing it up. There was nothing new to say, but she kept trying to make me change my mind because it was all she really wanted.'

'Thierry, please come and sit down.' The counsellor spoke so softly, he hardly heard her, but he went and sat down as she'd asked.

'I'm sorry I'm finding it so hard to talk about all this even though you're impartial. Although you do seem to have a skill for bringing me out of myself.'

Dr Bartin smiled again. 'That's my job, Thierry, and I only want to help you.' The counsellor read her notes and then changed tack. 'How do you feel about having children now you've met someone who's already pregnant?'

'I know I want to be with Lottie, and I want to look after her and her baby. I'm not against having children sometime in the future; I just didn't want to have them then. Now Nicole's gone, I regret not having agreed to have children with her.' He was so ashamed of what he'd admitted, he couldn't look the counsellor in the eye.

'We'd all like to be able to go back and change things in our past, Thierry, that's only natural. But just because you argued with Nicole about this, doesn't make you to blame for her death. You had a good reason for not going after her, and you had no idea she would be involved in an accident. You have to learn to forgive yourself for this if you're to come to terms with it and to begin to move on with your life.'

'Dr Bartin, I don't know if I can keep doing this. It's all so personal for me, and I'm not sure I'm strong enough to keep revealing this level of detail to you.'

'Okay, Thierry, let's call it a day for today to give you some time to think about what you want to do next.'

Thierry sat in his car for several long minutes before setting off for the vineyard. His head was spinning. On that final day, he'd said some awful things to Nicole, and she to him, but neither of them had had any idea what fate had in store for them, of course. He would always regret it. For her to have died with those bitter words ringing in her ears still filled him with shame, whenever he thought about it.

He parked in the courtyard, changed into his boots, and walked right across the vineyard estate to the furthest point, which took him about twenty minutes at the pace he set himself. As he strode along between the vines, the frustration and misery began to seep out of him, and his pace slowed. His head stopped pounding with all his negative thoughts, and a weird kind of calm washed over him. Nicole's death was a tragic accident. Their argument definitely hadn't helped, but it wasn't to blame for the accident itself.

He counted himself lucky for the good times he'd spent with Nicole before everything went wrong. If he wanted any chance of finding love again, and happiness with it, he would have to deal with the guilt he felt about Nicole's death, and with his fear of letting Lottie down, too. And Dr Bartin was willing to help him with that process. The only remaining question was whether he was strong enough to let her.

Lottie

Fran had invited Lottie and Thierry round for lunch as it was Saturday and everyone was free. As she picked out one of her wrap dresses to wear, Lottie was excited to be going somewhere different and was looking forward to seeing Fran, Didier and little Chlöe. She took more time than usual over getting dressed and putting on some make-up, enjoying the chance to indulge herself for once. But Thierry had been waiting for her downstairs for ages, so she finally popped in a pair of drop earrings and made her way to join him.

At the sound of her footsteps on the stairs, Thierry glanced up from his book. The look he sent her gave her a warm feeling right in the pit of her stomach.

'You look amazing,' he said, coming to meet her. He leaned in to kiss her on the cheek and her skin heated at his touch.

'You look pretty handsome yourself.' She rested her hands on his forearms. He was wearing a pale blue button-down shirt, open at the neck, a dark pair of chinos and his worn leather jacket. He looked gorgeous, and all at once her desire for him was rekindled. From the look in his eyes, he felt the same. It was time they showed each other how much they still wanted one another, but for now, that would have to wait.

Thierry helped her with her coat and they left shortly afterwards. As they walked up the slope, Lottie was delighted to see the difference in the hedgerows, with so many more green leaves visible, and the rustle from the inner depths suggested wildlife was getting busy, as well. She spotted a squirrel dashing across the pathway and it made her laugh.

'It's good to hear you laughing, Lottie,' Thierry said as the squirrel disappeared up a tree.

'I'm so happy to be outside enjoying the fresh air, and I'm looking forward to doing something with you today. I hardly see you in the week.'

He nodded. 'I'm sorry. I need to do something about that.'

No sooner had they arrived outside the cottage than the front door was flung open and Chlöe dashed out to greet them. Ruby, the family dog, joined them too, her tail wagging furiously.

'*Salut,* Lottie *et* Thierry,' Chlöe cried, rushing to each of them for a hug.

'*Salut*, Chlöe,' Lottie replied, smiling. 'Gosh, I think you've grown in the few weeks since I last saw you.'

'I'm nearly four now. I'll be one of the oldest children at nursery school in September.'

Lottie marvelled at the little girl's vocabulary. She really had changed from a toddler to a proper little girl now, ready for her last year at nursery.

'Come on in, both of you. It's lovely to see you.' Didier kissed Lottie on both cheeks and shook Thierry's hand.

'Would you like to play with me, Thierry?' Chlöe took his hand and pulled him to sit on the floor with her, where she was playing an elaborate game with her Lego. Didier joined them and soon they were embroiled in setting up a complicated escape scene from a castle, where Chlöe had trapped all her figures.

Lottie was glad to have a moment to chat with her sister, who was busy in the kitchen making lunch.

'Is there anything I can do to help?' she asked, leaning on the edge of the counter where Fran was busy preparing a salad.

'No, don't you worry. I think everything's fine. We've got lasagne in the oven and I'm preparing a salad to go with it. Didier and Chlöe made dessert earlier, so we're all sorted. How are you feeling now the due date's so close?'

'I'm torn between wanting it to happen, and being scared stiff about the reality of it.'

Fran smiled. 'I'll be with you on the day, like we've planned all the way along, and everything will be fine. Thierry will be there too, holding your hand, won't he?'

'I haven't asked him, to be honest. I didn't think he'd want to come when it's not his baby. Do you think I should ask him?'

'I would if I were you. I think he'll be hurt if you don't ask him.'

Lottie still wasn't sure whether Thierry would want to come with her, but now Fran and Sylvie had both suggested it, perhaps she should get round to asking him.

'How are things going with you?' Lottie didn't want to make too big a deal of Fran's struggle to get pregnant, but she didn't want her sister to think she didn't care, either.

'Well, you know. There's always hope at this stage of the month. Fingers crossed it all comes together this time.' Fran gave her a broad smile, but it was a front. 'And how are you and Thierry getting on now you're living together?'

'Not too badly. He was overprotective at first, and would make decisions without asking me, but things have improved a bit since then.' She didn't tell Fran her worries concerning how Thierry was ever going to get over losing Nicole – this wasn't the right time for that sort of discussion – but it had all been playing on her mind since finding him so upset.

She glanced over to see Thierry helping Chlöe reconstruct a Lego castle wall and she smiled. He would be a good dad himself one day. She had no idea what his future plans were as far as their relationship was concerned, or whether they might one day have a child together, but she had no worries about him getting on with the baby she was due to have very soon.

Lottie took a seat on the sofa and watched as Chlöe bossed the two men about in her role as leader of the game.

'This is all good preparation for when your baby comes along, Lottie,' Didier said.

'We've got a few years at least until we'll be playing with Lego.' Lottie laughed and Thierry joined her.

'We can keep all of this and pass it on to you when the time comes,' Fran said, causing Chlöe to look up in horror.

'You can't ever get rid of my Lego. I love it too much.' She pulled a face and then reconsidered. 'No, it's all right. I don't mind sharing it with your baby, Lottie.'

'That's kind of you, Chlöe,' Thierry told her, and she came over to sit on his lap. He wrapped his arms around her and gave her a hug.

Lottie realised he would have known Chlöe since she was born, when Didier was still married to her mum, Isabelle. The two of them made a lovely picture together, and she wondered whether he and Nicole had planned to have children together.

The oven timer beeped. Fran jumped up to go and sort out the food, while Didier directed everyone to the table. Chlöe helped Fran serve the meal, and Didier and Thierry spent a moment tasting the wine before serving everyone.

'This pinot noir gets better every year, don't you think?' Didier asked.

'We've been lucky with the past few vintages,' Thierry said, 'but I agree, it's fast becoming one of our bestsellers.'

'I look forward to tasting some at some point,' Lottie said, lifting her glass of water.

'I'll save a bottle just for you,' Didier told her with a grin.

'How's Sylvie settling in at Frédéric's?' Lottie asked, once they all had their food and drinks.

'Now the cottage has sold and she knows she's staying at Frédéric's permanently, it's helped her relax,' Didier replied.

'I think she's enjoying it more than she lets on, you know,' Fran added. 'He does everything for her and she loves it, despite herself.'

Thierry raised his eyebrows subtly at Lottie from his place across the table and she stifled a laugh.

'And I can go and stay over too, which is great,' Chlöe said. 'I was sad when I couldn't stay before, but I know you needed your own room, Lottie.'

Chlöe was so grown up, Lottie couldn't get over it. 'I'm glad you can visit your grandma again. In fact, I expect that's helped her get better so much faster, too.'

Lottie was sure then she'd made the right decision to take Thierry up on his offer, and she was glad for Sylvie's sake, and for Chlöe's, that everything had worked out. Now she just needed to keep working with Thierry to strengthen the trust between them before the baby came.

Thierry

By the time they left the cottage, it was getting dark. Thierry took Lottie's hand and tucked it through his arm for the short walk down the slope back to his house.

'It's been a lovely day, hasn't it?' he asked as they wended their way down the path with only the vines for company.

'I really enjoyed it, yes. I'm glad they're so happy together, all of them. They make such a great family. I just hope another baby comes along for them soon.'

'It can only be a matter of time.' Even as Thierry said it, he couldn't be sure. He just hoped it would happen because they wanted it so much.

Lottie cleared her throat and he glanced down at her. 'Did you... Did you and Nicole ever think about having children?'

It was a perfectly natural question but it still caught him by surprise. This was the ideal opportunity for him to tell her the truth, but he couldn't. He didn't want to spoil what they had by bringing up the past yet again. There was time for that later.

'We talked about it, but we never got round to it.' It was as close to the truth as he could tell her without getting into everything.

They were soon back at home. Once Thierry had closed the door behind them, he turned to help Lottie take off her coat. As he did, the creamy pale skin at the nape of her neck was exposed and he bent to kiss it, causing her to sigh. He hung up her coat and his jacket before taking her hand and leading her to the stairs.

When they reached the bedroom, Lottie sat down on the bed to remove her shoes and her earrings. Thierry watched her movements, trying to gauge whether she wanted to make love as much as he did. He was so worried about hurting her now she was so close to her due date.

'Thierry.' She said his name softly, but the husky sound of her voice told him that she was as aroused as he was. She lifted her arms to him and he sat down next to her. The moment his lips touched hers, all his doubts fell away, and when she opened her mouth so that their tongues met, his desire for her only built further. He pulled back to undo her dress and let it slip from her shoulders, revealing a matching set of lacy underwear that set his heart racing.

'God, Lottie, you're so beautiful. Are you sure this is okay? I don't want to hurt you.'

'It's fine, Thierry. We'll take it slowly.' She undid the buttons on his shirt and ran her fingers over his chest giving him goosebumps at her touch. He stood to remove the rest of his clothes and his shoes, while Lottie removed her underwear and made herself comfortable on the bed. When he joined her again, she turned on her side and he kissed along her neck, delighting in the sensation of her skin against his.

'I've missed this, you know,' she told him and he could only agree.

Before long their bodies joined together and he took it slowly as she'd asked. If anything, that made the whole experience more thrilling, and he wasn't surprised when they both reached their climax shortly afterwards. It had been a while since they'd shared such intimacy and clearly, it was long overdue for both of them. He pulled Lottie gently closer and tucked her head underneath his chin.

'I love you, Lottie,' he whispered in her ear. He heard her sharp intake of breath in response. It was the first time he'd said those three words to her. He didn't expect anything from her in return, but he was ready to let her know his feelings.

She rolled over to face him.

'Do you mean that, Thierry?' Her face revealed all her vulnerability, making him even more determined to reassure her.

'I do. That's the one thing I know for sure right at this moment.'

She reached up and stroked his cheek and he bent to kiss her before wrapping his arms around her again. He waited to see if she would say anything else, but soon all he could hear was the soft rhythm of her breathing, telling him she'd fallen asleep. She still had trust issues after what had happened between her and Yiannis, but he hoped in time, she would come to trust him, and that she'd be able to say the words back to him that he longed to hear.

Unusually for Thierry, he found it difficult to fall asleep straight away after making love with Lottie. There was so much on his mind and his thoughts were buzzing around. He'd been so close to telling her about not wanting children with Nicole that evening. Now he wondered if it had been wrong of him not to say anything, after all. At least then he wouldn't be hiding any more secrets from her. But then she might have been furious with him, in which case they would never have gone on to make love.

He stared out of the window at the moonlit sky, admiring the array of stars on display. The sky was always so clear above the vineyard – it was one of the things he loved most about living there. As he struggled with his thoughts, the sight calmed him. He'd spent many nights on the veranda outside the house following an argument with Nicole, and had always found that looking at the stars was a good way of ordering the chaos in his mind.

Lottie turned onto her side and the sheet slipped away from her slumbering body. She was beautiful, and he counted himself so lucky to have this second chance after Nicole. He pulled the sheet up and tucked it gently around her, turning on his side as well to spoon his body next to hers. His final thought as he fell asleep was that he would do everything in his power not to muck things up this time, and to show Lottie he was worthy of her love.

CHAPTER FIVE

Lottie

Lottie was surprised to find Thierry still beside her the next morning. Even though it was a Sunday, he would normally have gone out to do his vineyard inspection regardless. She snuggled up next to his warm body – as close as she could get, anyway – delighted to have the opportunity to study him while he was asleep. She smiled at his gentle snoring, admiring his chest, with its light dusting of dark hair, as it rose and fell evenly with his breathing.

Thierry was a good man – she had no doubts about that – but when he'd told her he loved her, it had been the last thing she'd been expecting him to say. But no matter what her feelings for him, she wasn't ready to say it back to him yet. Yiannis had been the first man she'd given her heart to, and he had well and truly broken it. Not only that, but he'd left her with an evergreen reminder of him, in the form of their baby, and promptly left her to handle that life-changing situation all on her own.

So it wasn't going to be easy for her to fall in love again, especially with someone whose heart still belonged to his wife. And yet Thierry had said he loved her, and he had seemed so sincere. Was she being too hard on him in thinking he was still in love with his wife? She couldn't expect him to simply stop loving Nicole after all they'd shared together. But was it possible to love two people at the same time?

Thierry stirred and she reached out her hand to his chest, unable to resist touching him. Then he turned towards her and she felt the full force of his chocolate brown eyes studying her.

'Hey, how are you this morning?'

'I've been enjoying the chance to ogle you while you were asleep. I think it's the first time I've been able to since moving in.'

'You were due for a treat,' he said with a wink, pulling her gently towards him for a kiss. He stroked down her body to her hip and she heated at his touch. 'But now, I must get up.' He turned and jumped out of bed in a way she envied, given the huge size of her bump. A few minutes later, the shower came on, telling her that Thierry's superb work ethic had kicked in once again.

She rolled herself over slowly, slid her legs over the side of the bed, and sat up to pull on her gown and slip her feet into her slippers. Then she made her way downstairs to make some breakfast. She pulled a carton out of the fridge, planning to scramble some eggs, and put the filter coffee machine on for a change. If she kept herself busy, her mind wouldn't linger on what Thierry had told her last night, and what he might be expecting of her as a result.

'Mmm, that smells good,' Thierry said as he bounded down the stairs not long after. 'Thank you for getting breakfast ready.'

He gave her a quick kiss and they settled down at the table together. Silence fell and she wasn't sure if it was a comfortable one or not. Should she bring up the elephant in the room or would that only make things worse? She stifled a sigh and took the coward's way out.

'What are you up to today?' she asked him, avoiding eye contact as she spoke. She sensed him staring at her, but still didn't raise her eyes.

'I thought I might repaint the spare room today as there's not long to go now. I know we haven't talked about it again since I bought the paint, so if you don't want me to do it, that's fine.'

She finally looked up at him and found only love in his eyes. She hesitated for only a moment. 'If you're sure you don't mind, that would be great. Thank you. I might go and see Sylvie so I don't get in your way.'

'That's settled then. I'll get off and do my inspection now and then crack on with it.'

A minute later, he was gone, leaving her with her thoughts as she showered and got dressed. Even though he was overprotective at times – most of the time, in fact – he'd shown that he loved her. More than ever in the coming weeks, that was something she would need to hold on to.

She was still thinking about everything as she made her way slowly over to Sylvie's, and for once she didn't take in the scenery on her route. Instead, she found herself thinking of Yiannis and the moment when he'd told her he loved her. That had been after they'd made love too, only that time, she was so delighted that she'd actually cried.

'*Don't cry, my sweetheart. I mean it, I really do,*' he'd whispered as he held her in his arms. They were on the rickety double bed in her guest-house room, looking out over the tranquil sea in Almyrida. Lottie had thought all her dreams were coming true, until she'd found out she was pregnant.

'*No, no, no,*' he'd said when she'd told him, throwing his hands up at the news.

'*It will be okay, we'll manage together,*' she'd replied, thinking he needed time to get used to the idea, like she had. But she'd misunderstood – spectacularly, as it had turned out.

'*No,*' he said again. '*We won't. This isn't what I want for my life, Lottie. So, if you want this baby, you'll have to manage on your own.*'

It was as if he'd slapped her. She still reeled as she thought about it now. As she thought about the betrayal she'd felt at his hands, especially when he disappeared the following day without so much as a goodbye.

So, it was going to take her a while to trust Thierry's declaration of love, especially coming when it did. It probably didn't mean as much to him – just the usual words whispered after sex – so she shouldn't take it too seriously. She certainly shouldn't be worrying about saying it back, she told herself. Better to proceed cautiously and see what developed between them, especially as the baby was due any day now, and things might change completely between them after that.

Thierry

Thierry was in a great mood as he carried out his inspection that morning. Making love with Lottie the night before, and finding the courage to tell her he loved her, had restored his faith that they did have a future together.

And now she'd given him permission to repaint the second bedroom for the baby, it felt as though life couldn't get much better. It was less than a week until Lottie's due date, and he wanted to make sure the room was ready and the smell of paint didn't linger any longer than necessary.

By the time he got back home, Lottie had already gone out to see Sylvie over at Frédéric's house and so he had plenty of time to get his work done.

He went upstairs to survey the room before getting started. As he cast his eye around, his mind returned to the night Lottie had found him in tears, much to his embarrassment. Since then, he'd made a slow start on sorting out Nicole's things, knowing that he'd need to clear the room before painting. He'd recycled most of her clothes and shoes, throwing away a very few items, and putting even fewer aside to keep. It was her jewellery he was still struggling with, but he'd simply put the box in the wardrobe in his own room, planning to sort it out another day when he felt stronger.

He still hadn't told Lottie why he felt he'd let Nicole down. She would find it so difficult to understand why he hadn't wanted to have children back then, and he didn't have the courage to confess his secret to her yet. He was afraid once she knew, she would feel he'd let her down as well, and he wasn't sure he could take her disappointment. He hoped he could prove himself to her once the baby came so she'd know for sure he was worthy of her love, and that he could be a good father to her baby.

It only took him an hour to put the undercoat on and he decided to make himself a drink while he waited for it to dry. He glanced at the photo of Nicole on the mantelpiece as he made his way through to the kitchen. He was getting used to seeing it there and was glad Lottie had suggested it. It reminded him of all the other photos he had of their life together, and he mentally added them to his long list of things to sort out. He wasn't sure when he was ever going to get round to doing all these things.

He got back to his painting as soon as he'd finished his drink. He'd hoped keeping busy would take his mind off everything. Instead, the dull job left him hours to explore the deepest recesses of his mind in a way he didn't usually have time for. He tried to think about something else, but the only other thing his mind settled on was the fact that he was preparing this room for another man's child. He didn't have any problem with that – he wouldn't be with Lottie if he did – but against all his previous feelings, he found himself wishing it was his baby, and that he was going to be a father at last. And in no time, his thoughts returned to that fateful night.

'Is it that you don't want to have a baby, or is it that you don't want to have one with me?' Nicole had finally asked him that question on the night she died, and it had sent him into a tailspin, knowing how important his answer would be.

'I don't want to have a baby with anyone, for Christ's sake. Why does it all have to be about you?' He'd hated himself the minute the words were out of his mouth, and from the look on her face, she'd felt the same.

'*How dare you say that to me? I would do anything for you because I love you so much, but you can't do this one thing for me. Sometimes I wonder if you ever loved me at all. Well, now I guess I know.*' She'd grabbed her bag, slammed the door behind her as she left, and driven away. That was the last time he'd been able to talk to her properly, and he'd regretted their angry exchange ever since. How could they have said those things to each other when they loved one another so much?

Finally, it got too much for him being holed up in the house on his own with only his thoughts. He finished the first coat and went out for a walk across the vineyard.

Domaine des Montagnes had been his home for so long, he was like a member of Didier's family. Didier's father, Albert, had treated him well from the first moment he'd arrived at the estate, when he was as green as the shoots he was tending. At that point, he only had a few months' experience of vineyard management and winemaking, so the job had been a big step up for him – and a big risk for the estate. But with careful teaching by Albert, Thierry had learned quickly and now couldn't imagine working anywhere else. He missed Albert, but he was glad he got on so well with Sylvie and Didier; he never doubted their respect for him, and he never took it for granted, either.

'*Salut, Jean. Ça va aujourd'hui?*'

He greeted the workers as he walked through checking their progress with the final round of pruning. Most of the workers had been there longer than him and he'd learned a lot from them, too. They were a good team and the estate was thriving because of it. When he reached the far end of the vineyard, he turned and looked back at the whole estate. Even though it didn't belong to him, he was as proud as if it did. He was happy doing his work and didn't long for any more responsibility than that. All he wanted now was to be happy in his life, as well. He took in a few deep breaths, smelling the rich earth and the vineyard around him. It always made him feel good to be outside. He made his way back at last, knowing he still had one more coat of paint to finish before Lottie returned.

He waved at Ellie as he passed the château. She was leaning out of an upstairs window, cleaning the glass by the look of it. She'd done a good job of restoring the building to how it used to look in its glory days, and he was pleased to see someone taking care of it at last. It was good to see the whole estate flourishing and to see the changes being made all around him.

By the time he'd finished applying the last coat of paint, it was getting towards the end of the day. He was glad he'd managed to focus more on the job in hand after his walk, and to put his bad memories aside for a while. He hoped Lottie would be pleased with what he'd done. Now all he had to do was to persuade her to let him buy some of the furniture she would need for the baby.

Lottie

Lottie appraised the spare bedroom. Thierry had put the furniture back in it after decorating, and she smiled at what a good job he'd done. He was right about the room needing a fresh coat of paint, but it had been especially thoughtful of him to want to do it up before the baby came, and she could recognise that now. There was a lot less in the room than there had been before he'd decorated. She was proud of him for making a start on clearing Nicole's things and there was now no sign of them in the room. It must have been hard for him to do that, although he hadn't admitted that to her. She wondered what he'd done with it all.

Aside from the single bed, a wooden bedside table and a matching chest of drawers, there was a new Moses basket, which Lottie had purchased herself. She'd agreed with Thierry that he would help her buy a pushchair. Two of the drawers in the chest were full of baby clothes she'd been given as presents at the baby shower, and people had been kind enough to give her things like nappies, a changing bag and muslin squares, as well, which she might not even have thought of on her own. She'd never seen so many sleep-suits all in one place before, and she was so grateful for everyone's generosity.

Even though her due date had come and gone the day before without any fanfare, standing in this room made her very aware of how real this all was now. Soon she would be here with a baby in her arms, and the wait would be over.

'Is everything okay, Lottie?'

Thierry rested his chin on her shoulder and put his arms around her, snuggling against her in the doorway.

'Yes, I was admiring your handiwork and realising you were right to suggest this. Thank you.' She patted his hands resting on her stomach before turning to kiss him.

'I'm starving. Can we go and get breakfast?'

She laughed. He was always hungry after his vineyard inspection.

'Come on then. I've not eaten yet.'

They sat there a short while later enjoying their croissants, and Lottie was amazed at how well they were getting on together after such a short time. She only hoped things would continue like that after the baby was born. She finished her tea and stood up, turning awkwardly towards the sink to wash her cup out.

'Ow!' she cried, as she caught her side on the edge of the chair. 'Oh God.' She stepped away.

'Are you okay?' Thierry stood and held her arms as she felt the blood drain from her face.

'My waters have broken.' She swallowed and looked down in dismay at her now wet leggings.

'What do you need me to do?' Thierry asked, a panic-stricken look on his face.

'I need you to get Fran, please. She's my birth partner and she'll know what to do next. Can you give her a call while I go and get changed?'

She made her way slowly upstairs leaving Thierry to get on with that job, while she set about sorting herself out. She'd always expected her waters to break in a trickle rather than a gush. The midwife had been at pains to explain to her that that was what usually happened. She was suddenly frightened by the enormity of what was going to happen next and she wished Fran was there to reassure her.

'Lottie, there's no reply from her phone. I'll run over to the cottage. Will you be okay?'

'Yes, but hurry, please.'

Once she'd changed, Lottie began to make her way to the bed to lie down, but as she walked from the bathroom to the bedroom, she experienced a pain right across her body that she could only think was a contraction. She leaned against the wall and tried to take deep breaths to calm herself, knowing in her rational mind that it would pass in time. By the time she'd made it to the bed, she'd had to accept that this was the start of labour for her.

Just as she lay down, the door opened again downstairs, followed by footsteps running up the staircase. Fran appeared, her normally calm features all in disarray.

'Lottie, are you okay?' She was puffing having no doubt run the whole way.

'I'm okay, but my contractions have started. What do you think we should do?'

'When they're coming close together, that's the time to go to the hospital. Have you any idea how far apart they are right now?'

'I've only had the one so far.'

'I'll go and ring the midwife and see what she advises. Do you want anything?' Fran smoothed her sister's hair away from her hot face.

'Could you ask Thierry to come up, please?'

'I'll send him up with a cold flannel for your face.'

Thierry joined her shortly afterwards, sitting down on the edge of the bed and wiping her face gently. Another contraction washed over her and she took his hand, gripping it tightly as she tried to manage the pain.

'Oh my God, I hope this baby comes quickly. Those contractions are the worst thing ever.'

She looked up to find Thierry had paled and was looking uncomfortable.

'Will you drive us to the hospital, Thierry? I'll need Fran to help me on the way there.'

'I... I can't,' he stuttered.

She let go of his hand, stunned. 'Oh,' was all she could say.

Why hadn't she got round to asking him this important question before now? She was devastated, but didn't want to push him to come with them. Some men were no good in this kind of situation and she couldn't blame him. It wasn't his child, and despite all his declarations of love and promises to look after them both, he owed them nothing.

Thierry

Thierry slumped into the chair next to the bed, desperately trying to find the right words.

'I'm sorry, Lottie, I can't. It's complicated.'

'It's fine, I won't need your help. Fran will be with me and someone else can drive us.' Her tone was understandably frosty as he wrestled with his internal demons. How stupid was he not to have realised this day would come?

Another contraction overtook her and he held her hand instinctively. He thought she squeezed a bit tighter this time, pleased to be able to take her irritation out on him. He understood and was ready to take anything she needed to inflict on him. He hated himself for letting her down when she needed him most, like he'd done to Nicole. Why did he have to keep replaying this situation in his life? The awful thing was that even if he did go with Lottie to the hospital, he was afraid of letting her down there, too. So whatever he did, he couldn't win.

He remembered the day Nicole had died. He'd never seen so much blood. The stretcher they'd brought her in on after the accident was covered in it, and so was she. Sometimes when he closed his eyes, he could still see that awful image, especially during the night. The hospital was a terrible reminder of that evening for him, the one when his whole life came tumbling down around him and would never be the same again.

Thierry had never seen a baby being born, but he imagined there would be blood involved then too, and the thought of it filled him with dread. He couldn't say any of this to Lottie – she wouldn't understand, and he didn't have the right to expect her to.

Fran appeared in the doorway. 'The midwife said we should go to the hospital when the contractions are coming every five minutes and lasting for about a minute each time. What do you think? Is it time yet?'

'The contractions are about five minutes apart now,' Lottie confirmed. 'Is there someone who could drive us to the hospital?'

'But I thought...' Fran looked first at Thierry and then back to Lottie.

Lottie shook her head. 'Thierry can't do it, so we'll have to find someone else.'

Thierry stood up and began to pace up and down. He had to break this cycle and the only way to do it was by facing up to his fears.

'No, no, it's fine. I can do it.'

'Are you sure, Thierry? You look pale.' Fran reached out and squeezed his arm.

'I... I'm okay. It's just that it will be the first time I've been back to the hospital since Nicole...'

Lottie's face fell as the penny dropped. 'Oh Thierry, I'm so sorry. Look, you don't have to come. Fran will be with me, won't you?'

Fran nodded, but she didn't look like she was relishing the idea much, either.

'No, it's all right. I want to be with you, Lottie, and to look after you while you have the baby.'

He gave her a tentative smile, and this time when she squeezed his hand, it was for the right reasons.

'Okay, we need to get on our way. I've called Mum and Dad and they're going to meet us there.'

Thierry was grateful to Fran for focusing on the practical details and not letting him linger too much on what was going to happen once they got there. He helped Lottie up and encouraged her to lean on him as they followed Fran slowly downstairs. He gently eased her into the back of the car and Fran slipped in beside her for the short journey to the hospital.

As he drove, Thierry thought about how much more he'd have to discuss with Dr Bartin at his next counselling session. Despite overcoming his fear of returning to the hospital, he was still angry at himself for this latest slip-up, and he couldn't see how he would ever get past feeling like this. Nicole used to tell him not to beat himself up for things, but he'd never learned that skill. If something went wrong, it was always his fault, and he'd come so close to making yet another mistake. How was Lottie supposed to believe he loved her if he couldn't be with her at a time like this?

He shook his head, trying to dispel his negative thoughts as Dr Bartin had been encouraging him to do. Now was his chance to prove himself to Lottie. He'd taken his first step towards doing that by not giving in to his bad memories. That was something for him to be proud of, he reminded himself. He would be there with her to make sure everything went well for her, and that the baby was delivered safely into her arms. After that, he would help her to get on with the rest of her life and to provide her baby with the life she wanted them to have.

More than anything, he wanted to be a part of that life, too. Their relationship was his future and he was clinging on to it, hoping that it would free him from his past. Lottie was right about that, but she had no idea how frightened he was that if he told her everything that had happened between him and Nicole, she might never want to see him again.

CHAPTER SIX

Lottie

Lottie's contractions were coming every few minutes now and when they did, the cramping pain was almost unbearable. She distracted herself from it by thinking how proud she was of Thierry for facing his fears and telling her the truth. She'd never been so grateful to both him and Fran for being there to support her.

'Are you okay, Lottie?' Fran asked, after Lottie had been quiet for a while.

'When the contractions aren't coming, yes.'

She turned to look out of the window again, but was immediately engulfed by another contraction, her abdomen becoming rock hard as the pain moved through her, and she had to grab Fran's hand to help her through.

'It's not far, now, Lottie. Everything will be okay.'

At the hospital, Lottie checked in at the front desk with Fran, before they made their way slowly to the maternity unit where Thierry joined them after parking the car. Her parents arrived minutes later, both of them looking anxious.

'How are you feeling, love?' her mum asked as soon as she saw her, coming round to her other side to support her with Fran.

'I'm okay, but the contractions are definitely getting stronger.'

They didn't have to wait long before a nurse came out to guide Lottie to a room where she could settle in before being examined.

'I only need Fran to come in with me. Will you be okay to wait out here, all of you?' Lottie asked. Thierry still looked pale, and she was worried about him, so it was for the best for him to wait outside during the birth.

Before anyone could reply, Fran intervened. 'Lottie, I think it might be a good idea if Mum comes in, as well. She's the only one of us who's had a baby, after all.' Fran laughed, but her laughter didn't quite reach her eyes.

'What's this about, Fran? You're not backing out on me, are you?' Lottie frowned at her sister, trying to work out what was going on.

Fran's eyes filled with tears. 'I'm feeling a bit emotional myself, that's all. I think it would be good if Mum could be there to back me up if I need it.'

'Okay,' Lottie replied uncertainly. Fran picked up Lottie's bag, gave her dad and Thierry a tearful smile, and set off with Lottie after the nurse. When she reached the side room, Lottie sat down on the bed to fill in a form the nurse had given her. The pale green walls of the room reminded her that this was a hospital, and that she was about to embark on the most significant event of her life so far.

'Can you help your sister change into a gown when she's finished, please? The doctor will be along in a minute to do an examination, and then we can see where we are with this baby.' The nurse gave Fran a brisk smile before leaving the room.

Her mum entered the room and took a seat in one of the uncomfortable-looking plastic chairs while they waited for Lottie to finish with the form.

By the time the doctor arrived, they'd just managed to get Lottie into the hospital gown and to work out how to tie up the various ribbons at the back. After a short but thorough examination, the doctor pulled off her gloves and turned to include them all.

'So, Lottie, you are well dilated but not fully yet, so there will still be some time to go. Your contractions are coming regularly, but you seem to be managing them well. It might be an idea to have a warm bath to see if that will help move the contractions along, and then you can settle down for what may well turn out to be a long night. I'll be back again to see you soon.'

'How does a bath sound, Lottie?' her mum asked.

'If it helps with the pain, that sounds like a good idea. Listen, Fran, if you're not feeling up to this, you don't have to stay. Is everything okay?'

Fran's face crumpled and her mum rushed to put her arms around her older daughter. 'It's just that... I found out I'm not pregnant again this morning. And it's hard having to put a brave face on it all the time.'

'Oh my darling, I'm so sorry.' Her mum drew her in for a hug.

Fran looked over her mum's shoulder at Lottie. 'I'm sorry, Lottie, but this is all too much for me, to be honest. I just wasn't expecting you to go into labour today.'

Lottie reached out and took her hand. 'Don't worry. You go and sit with Dad and Thierry. Mum will look after me, won't you?'

'Yes, of course, sweetheart.'

Fran left the room and Lottie's spirits plummeted. She understood how awful this must all be for Fran, but even though her mum would be with her, it wouldn't be quite the same. Fran had been with her every step of the way, willing her to get to this point, and now she was worried she wouldn't be able to do all this without her.

'Everything's going to be fine, Lottie, don't worry,' her mum told her. 'You've been so brave and you can do this. I'll be here for you, I promise.'

Lottie smiled at her, grateful for her calming words. 'Thanks, Mum. It's just so daunting now it's really time, but I'm glad you're here with me.'

'Are you about ready for that bath now?' her mum asked, as another contraction came to an end.

Lottie nodded, her breath all used up on dealing with the pain from the contraction, while her mum held her hand until it was completely finished. She took some deep breaths and stood up to move to the bathroom with her mum's assistance.

'Have you thought of any names, Lottie?' her mum asked as they made their way haltingly across the room. Lottie was thankful for the distraction but her mind had gone blank. They weren't kidding with that baby brain stuff.

'Not really. It's so hard when I don't know if it's a boy or a girl. There are some names I like, but to be honest, I'm hoping I'll know the right name when I see my baby for the first time.'

Lottie took her mum's hand and eased herself gently into the bath. The warm water lapped against her enormous stomach and the baby started to kick inside her.

'God, did you see that, Mum? That kick was enormous.' Her eyes widened at the sight of her skin moving, and she was half expecting to see the baby's foot appear.

Her mum chuckled. 'I did see that. It's been such a long time since I had you that I've almost forgotten what that was like.'

Another contraction gripped her and she held on tight to the sides of the bath while her mum wiped her forehead with a cold flannel. The heat of the water was making her feel sick now, and she wished she hadn't decided to get in. Then the contraction was over and the nausea passed.

'Are you okay, love?'

'I'm just not sure having a bath was such a good idea. Would you mind helping me out again?'

Her mum held her as she stood and then stepped carefully out of the tub. She wrapped herself in the towel her mum handed her and took in a few deep breaths to calm herself.

By the time they returned to the main room, the contractions were coming more regularly, and Lottie was beginning to dread each new one. She walked around as much as she could in the gaps between them and tried to practise the deep breathing she'd learned with Fran. After a few hours, the nurse came back to check on her.

'How are you feeling, Lottie? Would you like any pain relief now the contractions are coming more often?'

'I'm okay at the moment. I'd like to go as long as I can without it.'

'Okay. I'll get the doctor to come back and check on you, but as the contractions are building now, you're obviously getting closer.'

The doctor came again shortly afterwards but Lottie's heart sank at the news she gave her.

'You're still only 5 cm dilated, I'm afraid, and we need you to be at 10 cm so there are still a few more hours to go yet. At that point, you'll feel the urge to push, which is perfectly normal. You're doing really well so far.'

Then she was gone. The intensity of the contractions just kept building as the hours dragged by. Lottie was finding that bending over the bed during the contractions made them slightly easier to deal with, and her mum was by her side the whole time.

'You will get through this, Lottie, I promise,' she soothed, after what felt like the hundredth contraction tore its way through her body.

'Are you sure?' she growled.

'I am, sweetheart. And I promise I'll look after you.'

'You might find some pain relief helpful now,' the nurse told Lottie when she returned for her next examination. Lottie nodded and the nurse showed her how to use the gas and air mask as the next contraction came.

Tears pricked at Lottie's eyes as the reality of her circumstances hit her hard. In that moment, she hated Yiannis for getting her pregnant and leaving her to face this all on her own. Even though her mum was with her, Lottie was the one having this baby – no-one else could do it for her.

A primal scream erupted from her then as another contraction hit and she released all her feelings. And with that one, came the need to push.

The doctor came back seconds later and did another examination.

'Okay, Lottie, you're fully dilated now, which means it's time to start pushing when you get the contractions, so that your baby starts to move down the birth canal.'

She turned on her side, trying to find some comfort, and breathed through the next contraction holding her mum's hand all the while. But the next time there was no urge to push and it took a moment for her to realise there was still a long way to go.

After what seemed like forever, the doctor came back, this time with a midwife.

'Okay, Lottie, you're going into the final stages now,' said the midwife, 'and I'm going to stay with you to see you through. You need to do a few more pushes until we can see the baby's head and then we'll switch to panting so the baby comes out nice and slowly. Are you comfortable lying on your side or do you want to switch positions?'

Lottie turned onto her back in time for the next contraction.

'Push now, Lottie,' encouraged the midwife. 'Oh, I can see the head.'

Lottie looked over at her mum and they smiled at each other, even though Lottie was exhausted.

'I think you're almost there now. Keep going, Lottie. It won't be much longer.'

And she was right. With the next contraction, she felt the baby's head move down and the midwife told her to pant because the head was outside her body. Lottie took her mum's hand again after she'd wiped her forehead one more time, and even though she was squeezing hard, her mum didn't once complain.

'Oh my God, I can feel the baby coming now,' she cried, as the next contraction took over, and finally, at the next one, Lottie's baby was born with a huge cry.

'Congratulations, Lottie. It's a girl!'

Minutes later, the midwife was placing her baby on her chest and she was staring down at her daughter.

'Oh, my darling, well done,' her mum said, through her tears. 'I'm so proud of you.'

Lottie shed a few tears herself then, proud and relieved at the same time that she had been able to get through the birth and that her baby was safe. When everything was over, the nurse came back to clean the baby and wrap her in a blanket.

As she stared down at her beautiful daughter, Lottie realised with a jolt that she was now a mother, and responsible for her own child. She was delighted but also frightened about what the future held for them both.

Thierry

Thierry had already spent several hours at the hospital, taking it in turns with Joseph, Lottie's dad, and Fran, to pace the corridor while they waited for the baby to be born. In the end, one of the nurses told them it would be a good few more hours before the baby came, so they might as well go home and rest. Joseph said he would stay to give Lottie and Christine moral support if they needed it, but Fran decided to go home.

'You will let me know as soon as there's any news, won't you, Dad?'

'Of course I will, sweetheart. You go home now and you can come back in the morning to relieve me.' He chuckled as he hugged her goodbye.

It was around eight in the evening when Fran left, but Thierry hung on, wanting to be there as soon as the baby was born. He'd lost count of how many times he'd swiped his hands through his hair, desperate to know how things were going, yet certain at the same time that he wasn't brave enough to go into the delivery room and see for himself. Still, the whole experience had been much better than he'd been expecting, and he was relieved about that.

'You should go home and get some rest, Thierry,' Joseph said at last. 'You'll be more help to Lottie and the baby tomorrow if you do.'

'You're right, but I can't. I'd like to be here when she has the baby so I can congratulate her and know everything's okay.'

At that moment, a baby's cry rang out from Lottie's room. Both men stood up and approached the door, just as a frazzled but happy-looking Christine appeared.

'It's a girl,' she told them, 'and Lottie and baby are both fine.'

'Can we see her?' asked Thierry.

'The nurse has said you can see her for a minute, but then she must rest. She's been at it for hours.'

Christine left the room, taking Joseph's arm, and allowed Thierry a few minutes on his own with Lottie. He swallowed nervously as he went in.

'Hey. Come and meet the baby.' Lottie looked exhausted but happy.

Thierry stepped closer but didn't go right up. 'Are you and the baby okay, Lottie? Did everything go all right?' He glanced from her to the baby and back again.

'It all went well, thank goodness. Come closer. It's okay, she won't bite.' Lottie chuckled and reached out to Thierry.

'She's so tiny,' he said. 'And look at her hair. She's perfect.' Thierry smiled but still retained a hint of nervousness.

'She looks it now but she didn't feel it when I was pushing her out.' Lottie laughed and Thierry joined in.

'I'm so proud of you, and so glad everything went okay. Is there anything you need me to bring from home? The nurse said you need rest, so I'll get off now.'

Lottie asked him to bring a few things and he turned to leave.

Then he changed his mind and took a step closer to kiss her goodbye. His lips settled on hers and it felt like everything was right with the world. He was as proud of Lottie as if he were the father of her baby.

'See you tomorrow,' he whispered, not wanting to wake the sleeping baby.

The next day, after a glorious night's sleep, Thierry was up and out early checking the state of the vines, which was especially important as rain was forecast for today. He'd expected to meet Didier on his rounds so he could share the news, but there was no sign of him as yet, so he made his way back home to get some breakfast.

He'd sent several messages to both Fran and Didier that morning already, but he hadn't heard anything in reply. He was about to leave the house again to go up to the office in case Didier was there, when his phone beeped. He let Didier in a few moments later, and poured him a black coffee from the pot.

'Thanks.' Didier accepted the drink and warmed his hands on the cup. 'I must have been over on the other side of the château to have missed you this morning. And I didn't have any signal, but Joseph texted Fran the good news anyway.'

'It's great news, isn't it?' Thierry beamed at his friend and sank onto a stool at the breakfast bar.

'You look relieved. You must have been worried about her.'

'I was. I care so much about her. And I almost ruined everything because, at first, I didn't think I had it in me to go with her to the hospital.'

'But you overcame that fear and went anyway. So you can be proud of yourself.' Didier understood how bad it had all been for him when Nicole had died.

'I'm glad I was there to see her after the baby was born. It was so hard what with all the waiting, but it was wonderful to go and see her and the baby.'

'I remember when Chlöe was born. It was such an amazing feeling.'

Thierry smiled at his friend. 'Yes, even though it's not my baby, I felt a protective instinct kick in, which was really strange.'

Didier sighed. 'I hope I get to experience that feeling again with Fran before too much longer.'

'It will happen for you both, I feel sure of it. It's just that it takes time. It must be hard for the two of you.'

Didier finished his coffee, pushed to his feet, and picked up his coat. 'Give Lottie our love, won't you? I'm sure Fran will pop in to see her later today.'

He gave Thierry a rueful smile and disappeared out of the front door, shutting it noisily behind him. Thierry wished with all his heart there was something he could do to help his friend, but things would have to happen in their own time.

He went to gather the things Lottie had asked for and was soon on his way back to the hospital to see her and her new baby.

Lottie

Lottie had managed to get some sleep during the night between feeding the baby and listening to all the noises in the hospital. She'd been awake for a while. One of the nurses passed the baby to her after one of the routine checks, and then she was glad to have some time on her own to appreciate her new daughter.

She looked down at the baby in her arms, full of wonder that she'd created another human being. As soon as they'd told her she'd had a girl, the name Marie popped into her head, and now that she'd had some time to mull it over, she felt it suited her completely. She stroked her daughter's dark hair and studied her clear blue eyes, obsessing over all the tiny details of her appearance.

'You are so precious, little one, and I'm so glad to have you in my life,' she cooed as her little girl studied her face.

She was relieved to have gone through the birth without any real problems, although she'd had no idea that giving birth could take quite that long. She'd been so grateful to her mum for being there with her and for supporting her throughout. It had brought them closer together, and for that she would always be thankful. As if she knew Lottie was thinking about her, the door opened and her mum appeared, closely followed by her dad.

'Hello, darling. How are you both?' her mum asked. 'Did you get any sleep?'

'Some, yes. I feel much better now.'

'She's so beautiful, sweetheart,' her dad said, coming up and kissing her on the cheek. 'I'm so proud of my little granddaughter, and of you.'

'I've decided on a name for your granddaughter,' she said, smiling at them both. 'I'm going to call her Marie.'

'Oh, that's a lovely name. It suits her, I think.' Her mum reached out and squeezed Lottie's hand.

'Thanks for everything, Mum. I couldn't have done it without you. And if I was grumpy with you, I'm sorry.' She grinned sheepishly and her mum laughed.

'You're entitled to be grumpy with your mum when you're giving birth, I think.'

The door to her room opened again and Lottie looked up to see Thierry on the threshold.

'Come on in,' she said smiling at him. 'You don't need to hover.'

Thierry deposited her bag next to the bed and approached tentatively. He was still nervous around Marie and she wanted to put him at ease.

'This is Marie,' she said. 'I settled on her name during the night.'

'That's beautiful, just like her. How are you feeling today?'

'Not too bad. I was just telling Mum and Dad that I did manage to get some sleep. Hopefully, I'll be able to go home today. I'll sleep better there, I think.'

'Today? That's quite soon, isn't it?'

'As long as the baby's feeding okay and there are no complications, they don't let you hang around. They need the bed for someone else.'

'I'm going to need to speak to Fran about borrowing her car seat, then, because we don't have one yet.'

'You're right. I completely forgot about that. I would prefer for Marie to have a new one, but there's nothing we can do about that now.'

'I'll send Fran a text to ask her if she can bring it with her when she comes to see you today.'

'Thanks, Thierry.' She was grateful for his support when she had so much else on her mind.

'If you do go home today, would you like me to stay on for a bit longer while you get used to everything?' her mum asked.

'That would be great, Mum, if you're sure you can spare the time.' Lottie had no idea how everything would go once she left the hospital; the prospect of being completely responsible for her new baby was terrifying right now, so it would be good to have her mum on hand to help out.

'I've taken a few more days' holiday from work so I can stay and help.'

Thierry returned to her side. 'That's all sorted. Fran should be here in a while, but she and Didier both send their love to you and Marie.'

'Has anyone told Ellie yet? I'm sure she'd want to know, and Sylvie, as well.'

'Didier will have told Sylvie and Fran has probably told Ellie,' her mum reassured her.

'Have you seen Fran, Mum? Was she okay yesterday?'

'We went straight back to the guest house after we left here last night. How did she seem to you, Joe, when she was outside with you?'

Her dad looked at Thierry. 'I think she was all right, just anxious about you, Lottie, like we were.'

Thierry nodded. 'I saw Didier this morning, and it was clear how much he wants to have another baby with Fran.'

'It will happen for them in time, I'm sure of it,' Joseph said. 'But for now, we can focus on our first granddaughter. I can't believe we're grandparents already.'

They all laughed, and Lottie was pleased to have this time with her parents and Thierry.

'Do you want to hold her, Dad?'

Her dad came closer and she lifted Marie towards him, placing her carefully into his arms. He took Marie as if he'd been holding babies all his life, which he had in a way. She looked at her dad's face and the love she saw in it for herself and her daughter brought tears to her eyes. Her mum took a photo as her dad turned to her with his baby granddaughter in his arms.

Thierry was staring at Lottie's dad, but she couldn't make out how he was feeling from his face. She reached out to take his hand, breaking the spell, and he gave her a wobbly smile.

'You can hold her next if you like?'

'No, no. She's fine with your dad.'

Lottie didn't know what to make of that statement. Maybe Thierry was frightened because he'd had so little experience with babies, or perhaps he didn't want to hold her because she wasn't his daughter. That thought made her heart sink. It was bound to take some time for him to bond with Marie. She stole a look at him again, trying to work out what he was thinking, but she came up blank.

CHAPTER SEVEN

Thierry

It was only a few days since Lottie had come home with Marie, and already Thierry was at his wits' end. When they'd returned from the hospital, Lottie had decided to move into the nursery with Marie straight away because she didn't want to disturb him during the night. While he understood the reason behind that decision, and was grateful for her thoughtfulness, he also felt shut out. Lottie was taking sole care of the baby during the night, and for a large part of the daytime. It would soon be taking its toll on her. But no matter how many times he offered to share looking after Marie, Lottie just said no. She was so stubborn, it was driving him mad.

This morning, he was up a bit later than usual because he was going to be tasting some of the young wines from the previous year's vintage with Didier. He was looking forward to having something to take his mind off Lottie. He thought about making her a drink and taking it up before he left, but he didn't want to wake her if she was asleep, and he couldn't face another rejection if she was awake. He needed to get out for some fresh air.

He opened the front door to set off for the wine-tasting rooms, only to find Fran about to knock.

'Fran, what brings you here this early?'

'I wanted a chat with you. Are you off out on your inspection?' She looked him up and down as if she was trying to decide whether he was dressed for outdoor weather or not.

'No, I'm meeting Didier for a tasting first today. Do you want to walk with me?' At Fran's nod, Thierry closed the door behind him and they set off together up the hill to the main office building.

'I love this time of year, seeing all the vines preparing to grow again and the leaves begin to shoot, but it's still quite cold first thing, isn't it?' Fran pulled her woollen jacket closer around her and tucked her chin inside her scarf.

'Deceptively so. We'll need to keep an eye on those temperatures so the young vines don't get damaged when they do appear.' Thierry cast his eye across the rows of vines and made a mental note to check with the vineyard team about the overnight temperatures expected for the coming week.

'Anyway, I wanted to talk to you about Lottie. Mum and I are both worried she's doing too much herself and won't let anyone else help her.'

'I'm worried about that too, but no matter how many times I offer, she won't let me in.' Thierry threw his hands up. 'God, but your sister has to be the most frustrating woman on the planet.'

Fran laughed. 'Didier might have something to say about that. Seriously, I think Lottie could do with someone to talk all this over with. I know you and Mum have been bearing the brunt of it all, so maybe it should be me. I have no idea if I'll have any more luck with persuading her than you've had, but it's important to try. Mum will have to go home soon, so Lottie won't be able to turn to her for much longer.'

'It's a good idea for you to try talking to her. I'm so worried she's going to make herself ill. I don't think she can be getting much sleep and then she's on call all day, as well.' Thierry sighed helplessly. 'Thanks for coming to see me and talking to me about all this, Fran. I appreciate being able to talk it over with you.'

'No problem. I know you love her as much as we all do.'

Thierry blushed and she smiled.

'How are things with you these days, anyway?' Fran glanced at him before returning her gaze to the path ahead.

Thierry didn't know what Didier had told Fran about Nicole, but she was easy to talk to. 'I still find it hard to deal with my grief, even this long after my wife's death, but things are getting better. I'm trying hard for Lottie's sake.'

'Everyone has their own way of dealing with grief, Thierry, so you shouldn't be so hard on yourself, if you don't mind me saying. Losing your wife is a terrible loss, and you're going to need time.'

'Thanks, Fran. I appreciate that. I'm hardest on myself because of how it all happened, but with time, I hope it will get easier to deal with.'

He couldn't bring himself to tell her the rest. He was still too ashamed. Acknowledging his shame made him feel better on the one hand, but on the other hand, he was overwhelmed at the prospect of having to deal with his shame for some time to come.

'I might try to pop down and see Lottie later while you're doing the tasting with Didier, if that's okay with you.'

'Of course. I hope you get on all right.'

Fran unlocked the door to the office and Thierry followed her in. 'I'm sure you know Lottie well enough by now to know she never takes the easy route. She's hard on herself, but if we try to corner her, we'll get nowhere. She has to feel that whatever we're suggesting has come from her.'

'Goodness knows how we're going to do that.' Thierry frowned at the thought. He hadn't managed to win many arguments with Lottie so far.

Fran busied herself putting the coffee machine on and setting cups out for drinks. 'I'd offer you a coffee but as you're going to be tasting, you probably don't want one, do you?' she asked, raising her eyebrows.

Thierry shook his head. 'You will let me know how you get on when you've been to see Lottie, won't you? And if you think I need to try a different approach, I'd be glad of your advice.'

He admired Lottie so much for her determination to look after Marie on her own – she was strong and brave, and had obviously bonded with her daughter – but she couldn't keep up this single-handed approach forever. Despite his lack of experience with babies, he did want to help. All he needed was for her to let him.

Lottie

It had been a long few days for Lottie after coming home from the hospital with baby Marie. There was such a lot to get used to, what with breastfeeding, trying to get the baby to sleep, and everything else in between. Thierry fussed over them both constantly, and her mum popped in every day, too. Sylvie and Ellie had also paid them a visit. Lottie's parents were staying at a guest house nearby, and although she was thankful for her mum's support, she was also desperate to resume control of her own life. She ought to let Thierry help her, but she was still worried about how he felt towards Marie, and she hadn't found the strength to ask him yet.

She was finishing giving Marie her morning feed when there was a knock on the front door. It couldn't be her mum or Thierry because they'd let themselves in. Lottie checked Marie was safe in her rocker and walked out to the hallway to see who it was. She was delighted to see Fran there.

'Morning, Lottie. How are you?' Fran stepped inside and embraced her.

'I'm okay. It's been two whole days since you last came to see me,' she complained, turning back towards the front room.

'I'm sorry. I wanted to give you time to settle in, and Mum was coming every day, so I didn't want to crowd you. Mum has been giving me updates in between, as well.'

As Fran entered the front room, she saw Marie in the rocker and smiled. 'Can I have a cuddle?'

Lottie lifted Marie out gently and passed her over.

'How have you been, then?' Fran asked, stroking Marie's tiny face.

'To tell you the truth, Fran, I'm exhausted. I'm up so many times in the night and then looking after Marie all day, as well. I don't know how much longer I can keep it up.'

'You don't have to. We're all here to help you. Thierry particularly wants to help make things easier for you.'

Lottie studied her hands. 'I do want to let you all help, but I'm frightened to hand over control when she's my responsibility.' She couldn't tell Fran about her worries to do with Thierry – that wouldn't be fair – but she would have loved to have talked it over with her sister.

'That's understandable, Lottie. You're her mum and you don't want anything to happen to her. But we all love her too, and we want to help you. No-one wants to take over. We just want to help.'

Lottie watched Fran as she cooed over her niece and considered what she'd said. A moment later the front door opened again. It would be her mum this time.

'Hello, my darlings. What a wonderful sight.' Christine beamed at them all, and put her hands out towards Marie, desperate to have her own cuddle. Fran handed the baby to her, and went into the kitchen to make them all a drink.

'How did you sleep last night?' her mum asked.

'Not too bad. She's waking up every couple of hours, but the feeds go quite quickly and she settles down again. Most of the time, I drop straight off to sleep again, so it's okay. But I would love a full night's sleep, I can't lie.'

'Why don't you ask Thierry to help? I'm sure he'd be happy to.'

'I know he would, he's offered several times already. But he has no experience of babies, and I'd worry. Marie's not his daughter, after all.'

'You need to teach him then, Lottie. Show him how to give her a bottle of your milk. Wake him up during the night, so he sees what you do. He'll learn over time and you'll get some sleep.' Her mum's worry was etched all over her face, despite her effort to hide it.

'I'll think about it. Mum, is it okay if I go for a shower as you're here?'

'Of course. We can take care of Marie.'

Her mum had been such a godsend, but Lottie couldn't rely on her forever. By the time she was dressed and had made her way downstairs, Marie was looking about ready for another feed.

'Thanks, *Maman*.' Lottie smiled at the sight of her mum rocking Marie to and fro. Marie still had the mass of dark hair and bright blue eyes she'd been born with. She couldn't have looked more different to her grandma, with her blonde hair and hazel eyes. But her grandma was besotted with her, as was everyone. Marie had a lovely, calm manner, and she studied everyone who held her with an intensity special to newborn babies.

'Are you still feeling sore, love?' her mum asked, as Lottie sat down gingerly at the kitchen table.

Lottie blushed. She was recovering from a small tear which had occurred during delivery. It was uncomfortable, but the midwife had said it would heal quite quickly. 'It's better, Mum, thanks.'

'Isn't the nurse coming to visit today?'

Lottie was sure her mum had confirmed this with her only yesterday. She had to stop herself from rolling her eyes. 'Yes, I think we talked about it yesterday, didn't we?'

'I wanted to be sure, that's all.'

'I'm going to ask her when we can start getting out and about. I think we could both do with some fresh air, after a week indoors.'

Her mum gasped.

'Are you sure you're both ready for that, Lottie?' It was Fran who intervened this time.

'I don't know, but we can't stay indoors forever, and I've got to get used to it some time. You can't keep us wrapped up in cotton wool.'

'We're only looking out for you, and giving you our advice,' her mum replied kindly.

'I wouldn't want to go out for long. I could give her a feed and change her, and then go for a short walk round the village, maybe. Anyway, I'll ask the nurse when she comes and see what she thinks before I make up my mind.'

She went to look out of the window, putting an end to the debate. She was fed up with the same four walls and the same company. She released a large sigh.

'There's plenty of time to get outside in the coming weeks, you know, Lottie. There's no rush.' Her mum came up to her and passed Marie over. It was time for her next feed. Lottie smiled down at her daughter and her heart filled with love.

'I'm going upstairs to feed Marie.'

She made her way carefully up the staircase to the room she was now sharing with her daughter and quietly shut the door behind her. She relished these moments of peace and quiet on her own with her baby, and no-one else's opinions. They were few and far between, with her mum and Thierry always around her. Still, if she wanted their help, she supposed she would have to accept their opinions, as well.

When Marie fell asleep full of her milk a short while later, she laid her gently in her Moses basket, closed the door to, and went back downstairs to wait for the nurse.

'Ah, Lottie, we're going to make a move now as you've got the nurse coming to visit.' Fran smiled at her. 'But I'll come back soon, and don't forget what I said. You can always call me.'

'Listen, Lottie, your dad and I will have to be going back home soon, as well. I hope that's okay, but we have to get back to work, and I can see you're settled here now with Thierry.'

Now that her mum had told her she was leaving, Lottie suddenly realised how much she'd miss her. Her eyes filled with tears as she went to her mum for a hug.

'Thanks for everything, *Maman*. We'll come and visit soon.' Lottie had no idea how, but she'd manage it somehow. She would have to talk to Thierry about whether he could help. He'd done everything he could to be there for her, and perhaps now was the time to trust him and let him do what he'd been offering to do for so long.

Thierry

After finishing the tasting of the young wines, Thierry put the glasses he and Didier had used in the dishwasher. They left the tasting room and walked back towards the office. As they reached the car park, they found Henri striding in the other direction towards his car. When he saw them, he stopped and turned back.

'How's everything been in the office this morning?' Didier asked.

'Fine, no problems,' he said, although his flustered look suggested otherwise. 'Listen, I might be gone a while. I've had a call from Ellie to say her mother has died, and obviously she wants to go back to the UK as soon as possible. I've offered to go with her, but she's telling me to stay here. I'm going home to try to persuade her it will be better if I go with her.'

'Of course.' Didier's face reflected how well he understood dealing with the death of a parent. 'Tell her I'm sorry to hear the news, and if you need time to go back with her, that won't be a problem.'

'Thanks, Didier, I appreciate it. But you know how stubborn she is. Sometimes, I feel like I'm the last person she wants to confide in. It's hard when she shuts me out like this.'

'I'm not the best qualified to give you advice, but maybe let her talk when you get home and see what she's feeling, rather than telling her what you want to do. She might appreciate that approach more.'

'Yeah, maybe you're right. I'll give it a go and see what happens. Wish me luck.' He climbed into his car and drove off, leaving them both watching him go.

'I wonder if Ellie's told Fran this news yet. I'd better go and see if I can find her. I'll see you later, Thierry.'

Thierry retraced his steps towards his house, planning to get some lunch before spending the afternoon touring the vineyard. He needed to check on what was happening with all the different grape varieties. The team had confirmed they were still covering the vines at night to protect from possible frost, and he wanted to check how that was working out. The young vines were so fragile at this time of year, and it was important to keep a close eye on them.

By the time he reached his house, the sun had disappeared and there were dark clouds overhead threatening a downpour. He would have to cover himself in waterproofs when he went out later. The house was unexpectedly quiet, and he experienced a sense of panic.

'Lottie?'

When there was no reply, he took the stairs two at a time to see if she was still upstairs. As he reached the landing, he met the community nurse leaving the nursery. He remembered then that she had come to give Lottie a check-up.

'Is everything okay?' he asked.

'Oh, yes. Lottie's healing nicely and the baby's doing well. See you next time.'

He made his way along the corridor and tapped softly on the door.

'Come in,' Lottie called out.

He found her pulling her clothes straight after the nurse's examination. She had a smile for him though, and that lifted his spirits.

'I was going to make some lunch. Will you join me?'

'That would be lovely. I'm starving. I'll put Marie down for her nap and I'll see you downstairs in a minute.'

It was the first time she'd agreed to have lunch with him since coming home from the hospital. She'd been keeping herself hidden away with the baby, making herself a sandwich and taking it back upstairs for the most part, so this was a welcome development. He wanted to talk everything over with her but didn't even know where to start. He had no idea what she was even thinking these days.

He caught sight of Nicole's picture again as he came into the front room. He remembered then how she'd always said how hard she found it to know what he was thinking, despite having known him for several years. It was true – he'd never given much of himself away, even to her. His family had lived by the edict that children should be seen and not heard, so he'd learned early on to keep his thoughts to himself. And he'd found it a hard habit to break, much to his wife's frustration at times. Now he and Lottie were in danger of losing one another through their lack of communication.

He picked up the photograph from the mantelpiece and studied his wife. He'd loved everything about her, from her wavy red hair to the sprinkling of freckles on her skin. When she smiled, her whole face lit up and bathed you in its warmth. The ache of missing her overwhelmed him again, and he fell onto the sofa with his arms wrapped around the picture frame. He'd always kept such a tight hold on his emotions, afraid to let anyone see his innermost feelings. Talking to the counsellor was helping, but he still had a long way to go.

He suspected Lottie felt the same a lot of the time and because he understood that, he found it difficult to push her to open up. But something had to give between them if they were to move forward together. He heard her coming down the stairs and quickly moved to put the photo back on the mantelpiece. He went to the kitchen to see what there was to eat in the fridge.

'How does an omelette sound? There's still some fresh bread too, from this morning.'

'That sounds great, thank you. It's been a busy morning, what with Mum, Fran, and the nurse coming today.'

'You must have been glad to see Fran.' He cracked the eggs into a bowl and started whisking them, trying to look suitably surprised, even though he'd known Fran was going to visit.

'I was. Mum told me she's going to have to go home now, so it's time for me to accept your help if you're still prepared to give it.' She gave him an awkward smile and he beamed right back at her.

'Nothing would give me greater pleasure.'

'I'm sorry I haven't asked sooner. I was worried about how you might feel towards Marie.'

He glanced up. 'What do you mean?'

'When you didn't want to hold Marie at the hospital, I wondered if that was because she's not your daughter.'

Thierry stared at her before putting down the bowl he was holding and coming round the counter. He took her gently by the arms. 'I have no experience with babies, it's true, and that's why I was a bit nervous around Marie to start with. But I want to learn, Lottie, and I want to help. I just need you to show me what to do. I certainly don't hold anything against your baby because she's not mine. I promise you I will take care of her just like you do.'

Lottie leaned forward and kissed him and he pulled her in for a hug. Thank goodness she'd told him what was on her mind. It was time they both started being more honest with each other.

Lottie

The nurse had advised Lottie to wait until Marie was two weeks old before venturing outside with her, and she was fed up with being stuck indoors while everyone else went about their daily lives. But while she longed to go out, she was also afraid of trying to do too much too soon, and then regretting it afterwards. She was at least communicating better with Thierry and they were meeting up for lunch every day, which gave her a chance to talk things over with him when she was worried. Fran had also been popping in, but the days still felt long, despite Lottie enjoying every minute she was spending with her daughter.

She reached out to tickle Marie's little pink foot as she lay on the bed next to her, and laughed as her little girl instinctively moved it away.

'Oh, Marie, why is it so hard to make all these decisions?'

Marie could only gurgle in reply.

Her mum had phoned since returning home, but Lottie really missed her, even though she knew her mum and dad couldn't stay with her forever. It was time for her to stop moping around and to accept her situation.

Once she'd finished getting Marie dressed, she scooped her up, wrapped the shawl Sylvie had knitted around her, and made her way carefully downstairs. She installed Marie in her rocker and went to get her bag from the front room. She was planning to go for a short walk with Marie in her pushchair, to get her used to being outside. Lottie was definitely ready for some fresh air herself, and now her stitches were healing, she should be okay to walk a short distance.

She'd checked the weather forecast before she got dressed and she prepared to bundle Marie up against the cold. Thierry hadn't liked the idea one bit when she'd told him at breakfast.

'Are you sure you're both ready for this, Lottie?' he'd pressed her.

'I want to give it a go, Thierry. We've been cooped up indoors now for the last two weeks. We both need some fresh air and some space.'

'What if it starts to rain?'

'Rain's not forecast today, but if it does rain, I'll have to come home again.'

'Do you want me to come with you?'

'No!'

Thierry pursed his lips.

'No, sorry, I didn't mean to shout,' she went on, 'but I'd like to spend some time with Marie on my own.'

He turned away then, and Lottie worried that she'd upset him. That was the last thing she wanted to do. But she did want to get out on her own, and there didn't seem to be an easy way of reassuring him she would be okay.

Finally, Marie was bundled up in a sleepsuit with a padded all-in-one outer suit on top. She fitted a blanket around her in the rocker and lifted her onto the pushchair outside. Then she attached the pushchair cover, put on her own coat, and set off slowly up the hill.

She couldn't believe how good it felt to be out of the house after so long. There was a cool breeze, but the sun was also shining, and Lottie was glad she'd made the effort. At the top of the hill she made the decision to continue on into the village. She used the path to skirt the gravelled courtyard and was soon on the track towards the main square. There were brightly coloured tulips nodding gently in the flowerbeds, together with clumps of daffodils at the foot of some of the trees. Lottie loved spring, and it was lifting her spirits no end to see these welcome signs of the season. She'd been chatting to Marie as they walked, but the next time she looked down at her, she was fast asleep.

As she reached the furthest corner of the square, she felt the first drop of rain. She looked up at the sky. The sunshine had disappeared and in its place there was now only cloud. She couldn't decide whether it would be a few spots, or whether a downpour was on the way. She stopped and bent down to get the rain cover from the pushchair's basket, but there was no sign of it.

'Damn, I must have left that at home.'

Two more drops of rain fell, and she realised that not only did she not have the rain cover but she hadn't brought the changing bag with her, either. Marie woke as more spots of rain fell, and she began to cry.

'Shh, sweetheart. It's only some rain, it won't hurt you.'

But Marie thought otherwise and her crying became more demanding. Reluctantly, Lottie turned the pushchair round and hurried back to Thierry's house. By the time they reached the front door, the raindrops had turned into a shower. Marie had stayed mostly dry inside the pushchair with the hood pulled up, but Lottie was soaked.

Thierry appeared as she opened the front door and took Marie from her. She lifted the pushchair awkwardly inside, wincing in discomfort at her still tender nether regions. She had to admit to herself that perhaps she'd tried to do too much for her first trip out. Not only that, but she hadn't been prepared for the rain, or for any other eventualities with a young baby in tow. Thierry was sure to waste no time in confirming this for her.

She hung her dripping coat in the utility room and dried her wet hair on the towel from the downstairs bathroom before going back in to face the music.

'Marie's fine, Lottie. She was hardly wet at all, just surprised by it all, probably. If you want to feed her, I can make you a hot drink if you like.'

Lottie stared into Thierry's kind face and found only under-standing there, not judgment. She was so grateful for him not saying, 'I told you so'.

'Thank you, Thierry. A hot drink would be lovely. I don't know where the rain came from. It certainly wasn't forecast.'

'Well, living near the mountains as we do, I suppose we have to be prepared for everything. Where did you go on your walk?'

As she settled down to feed the baby and tell Thierry about their first trip out, Lottie remembered the first signs of spring she'd seen, and how good it had felt to get outside. Still, she hadn't thought every-thing through, and so she felt like she'd failed at the first hurdle. On impulse, she decided to ask Thierry for his help.

'I'd like to have a bath once I put Marie down. Would you be able to keep an eye on her for me?'

'Sure, there should be plenty of hot water. You take as long as you like.' He looked pleased to have been asked and she was glad she'd made the effort.

Lying in the rose-scented water a short while later with bubbles all around her, Lottie reflected on her morning. She shouldn't be too hard on herself – she'd given it a go and they'd survived it. Thierry was obviously happy to help her, so she would start teaching him how to feed Marie and how to look after her so he could feel he was more a part of things.

CHAPTER EIGHT

<u>Thierry</u>

Lottie wanted to see Ellie before she left for London, and so she'd finally asked Thierry to look after Marie while she went out. It was the first time he'd been completely alone with the baby, and while he would never admit it to Lottie, he was nervous. Although she'd now started teaching him some basics, he was still worried he would get something wrong without her there telling him what to do. Still, if he wanted to prove himself to Lottie, there was no better way than showing her that he could look after Marie on his own.

Marie was on the floor in her little bouncy seat, a new gift from Lottie's parents, and she was gurgling away to herself as he sat across from her. She still had her dark hair and contrasting blue eyes. She was a beautiful baby, there was no doubt about that. He sat down on the floor next to her and took her little chubby hand in his. When she grabbed onto one of his fingers, he smiled. Even though she was another man's child, he was beginning to develop an affection for her, and that surprised him. The quiet moments he was spending feeding and changing her during the night, now that Lottie had asked him to share that responsibility, were transforming his views about children in general, but this child in particular.

He bounced the seat gently with his other hand and started chatting to Marie as he sometimes did during the night, and she gurgled and cooed at him in reply. With no brothers or sisters of his own, his experience of babies was limited. The only child he'd ever really known was Chlöe, but of course he hadn't spent as much time with her when she was a newborn. This experience was much more real to him. He wished he could turn back the clock and say yes to Nicole's desire for a baby, now he knew what was involved. He sighed. Maybe that was the point. He hadn't known, and he hadn't been ready back then.

The gentle movement of the bouncer had made Marie's eyes heavy, and she was beginning to doze. He eased his finger gently out of her hand and went to warm up her milk. She commented on his absence as he walked away, and he glanced back to see her eyes wide open. He was learning about the sixth sense babies have for knowing when they've been left alone, even for a minute. After testing the warmed milk on the back of his hand, Thierry rested the bottle on the coffee table and scooped Marie out of the bouncer and onto his lap. She took the milk easily, holding the bottle with one hand and his jumper with the other. As he studied her features again, he thought how lucky he was to be able to share Lottie's baby with her. He never imagined finding himself in this position after what had happened to Nicole.

Marie was virtually asleep by the time she'd finished her bottle, so he lifted her carefully onto his shoulder to burp her and then made his way upstairs to lay her down in her Moses basket.

He was downstairs doing some washing-up when Lottie returned.

As soon as she walked into the kitchen, a flicker of concern crossed her face when she couldn't see Marie. 'Is everything okay?' she asked.

'Yes, all fine. Marie's asleep upstairs after having her milk.'

'I'll pop up and check on her.' She smiled at him. 'Thank you so much for looking after her for me.'

She was back a few minutes later. 'It turns out Ellie has agreed to let Henri go with her to London.'

'Really? From what he said, I thought she'd be determined to go on her own.'

'She said she'd realised it would be good to have him with her to face her family. She's not that close to them and she fell out with her mum a few years ago, so having Henri there to hold her hand will be a comfort for her. That's why she hasn't gone sooner, and why they'll only be over there for a few days.'

Thierry wiped his hands on a tea towel, and put the kettle on. 'Did you know that this will only be the second time that Henri's been out of Alsace?'

Her eyes widened. 'I didn't know that.'

'He went to visit Ellie in London for the weekend when she was still living there, but apart from that, he's never travelled anywhere else. It'll be interesting to hear what he thinks of London this time and how he finds travelling out of France. He's always been a real homebody.' Thierry chuckled.

'I can't even imagine not wanting to travel,' Lottie said. 'There's so much more world to see out there beyond Alsace.'

'I've travelled a bit more than Henri, but I still haven't travelled outside of France.'

'Why not?'

'I didn't want to, I guess, especially once I settled here.' He shrugged, only really thinking about it for the first time.

Lottie looked dubious. 'So you've not been on holiday since you started working here?'

'No. I love it here.' He passed her a drink.

'But you can love your home and still enjoy travelling. I only travelled around Europe before I had to come home again, but I'd love to travel further afield.'

'Was Greece the furthest you went?' he asked.

'Yes, to Crete. It was so beautiful, Thierry. The sea was so clear and such a beautiful shade of green. And there's so much history there, too. It was amazing.'

'It must have been really hot there. I'm not sure I would have liked that.'

'It was hot, but we had siestas in the afternoon and then got ourselves going again.'

Lottie was so different to him and so fearless. 'Where do you think you get all this spirit of adventure from?' he asked.

'I don't know. Fran's the same, but our parents aren't great travellers. I know my granddad travelled a lot when he was young, so perhaps he passed it on to us. What about your parents? Do they like to travel?'

She'd never asked him about his family before and the question surprised him. 'Not as far as I remember. I haven't seen them for a long time. I left home when I was sixteen and I haven't been back since.'

Lottie looked like she wanted to ask a million questions, and if she did, he'd be honest with her, but he hoped she wouldn't ask them right now. He wasn't sure he was up to telling her that long story from his past.

Lottie

Despite having an awful night with Marie, Lottie got up at the normal time because she was trying to get herself and the baby into some kind of routine. She was now putting her down at the same time every night and getting her up at the same time in the morning. She could so easily have gone against her plan this morning, having been up several times in the night feeding and changing, but she wanted to be consistent. Lottie was desperate for Marie to sleep through the night, but she had no idea when she might expect her to do that when she was still only three weeks old.

After that first trip outside, they'd gone out several more times, and Lottie was now prepared for almost every eventuality. Today, she was going to visit Fran to see how she was doing. When Fran had last been to see her and the baby, she hadn't looked at all well, and Lottie was concerned about her sister's welfare since she'd been trying to get pregnant.

'I'm going to take Marie over to see Fran this morning, Thierry.'

'Shall we still meet for lunch as usual?'

'I should be back by then. I'll text you if anything changes.'

It was only a short walk to the courtyard where the vineyard estate's office was located, but as it was all uphill, Lottie took her time. The birds were singing as they walked alongside the rows of vines and Lottie felt tired but happy. She would feel even better once she'd spoken to Fran, and she quickened her pace at the thought.

By the time they reached the courtyard, little Marie had fallen asleep, so Lottie was able to leave her undisturbed while she went into the office in search of Fran. She knocked first and then opened the door to the hub of the vineyard estate. Fran was at her desk, but there was no sign of Didier. Henri had left for London with Ellie that morning.

'Lottie! What are you doing here?' Fran frowned and Lottie wasn't sure if she was glad to see her or not.

'I've brought Marie to see you. She's asleep in her pushchair, so I wondered if you could take a break for a coffee with me at the cottage.'

'I wish you'd told me you were coming. I'm really busy, what with Henri having gone with Ellie to London.' Her sister was unusually abrupt, which Lottie put down to the pressure she was under.

'Come on, Fran. It will do you good to get out and you can see your niece, as well. I'm sure the office can survive without you for a bit.'

'Okay, but I can't stay long.' Fran grabbed her coat, whistled to Ruby, her canine companion, who was sleeping peacefully on the floor alongside her, and followed Lottie back outside, where Marie was still fast asleep.

'How are things, Fran?' Lottie glanced at her sister as they walked, wondering if she would be honest enough to tell her how she was really feeling.

'Fine, fine. You know. I'm keeping busy.'

'That's good, but I hope you're looking after yourself, as well.'

'What do you mean?' Fran's tone was sharp, but Lottie wasn't afraid of that.

'You look like you've lost some weight, so I hope you're not forgetting to eat.'

Fran opened the door to the cottage and Lottie lifted the rocker off the pushchair to bring Marie inside. Fran put some water down in the kitchen for Ruby before straightening up and turning back to Lottie. 'Ooh, it's cold in here without the wood burner on. I'll get that sorted if you want to make the drinks.'

Lottie was coming back with the tea when Marie stirred. Fran's face lit up as she picked the baby up for a cuddle, her delight obvious. She would be a wonderful mother one day.

'She's getting so big, Lottie. She's already grown such a lot in a couple of weeks. I've missed seeing her these last few days.'

'I know it must be hard for you, Fran, with all you and Didier are going through, but don't let that put you off coming to see us. You can come and cry if you want, we won't mind.'

Tears sprang to Fran's eyes and she buried her face in Marie's outdoor sleepsuit. When she lifted her head again her eyes were watery, but she looked better.

'Let's get you out of this suit, sweetheart. You probably need a change and some milk, don't you?' Fran fussed over Marie as she changed her, and Lottie relaxed as she watched her sister interact with her niece.

Once Marie was feeding and settled, Lottie turned the conversation back to Fran.

'So have you and Didier decided what to do from here?'

'We can't agree. I want to keep trying for a baby of our own, but Didier wants to stop because it's causing me so much stress.' Fran bit her lip, her face darkening with worry.

'Oh God, that's hard. I know how much you want a baby, but I can also see Didier's point of view. You don't want to make yourself ill over it.'

'No, and I don't want to drive Didier away by becoming obsessed with getting pregnant, either. It doesn't make for a spontaneous love life, that's for sure.' Fran laughed and for a moment looked more like her old self.

'Oh, Fran, it seems so unfair for you to be struggling when you and Didier want a baby together so badly.'

'I know, but at least I can enjoy your beautiful Marie while I wait for my own baby to come. I think it will be the making of you becoming a mum. And hopefully it's only a matter of time for me and Didier.'

'I'm sure it is, but I know how hard it must be for you waiting to see each month.'

'It is hard. There's nothing quite like it for the rollercoaster of emotions you go through. I keep trying to tell myself it's only been six months or so, but when so many people fall pregnant straight away, it's so hard to keep being positive.'

'What does the doctor say?'

'They just tell us to give it more time.' Fran sighed and Lottie's heart ached for her sister.

Thierry

Nicole's parents had been in touch with Thierry regularly since she'd died, but it always unnerved him when they called. She was the only thing they'd ever had in common, and with her death, he longed to break those ties. Her parents were hurting as much as him following their daughter's death, but seeing them only brought it all back for him.

This time when he'd received their voicemail, things were different. He wanted to meet them and finally tell them the truth about what had happened and why so that they could all move on. He was dreading it, but at the same time he was desperate to get everything off his chest. They'd left him in no doubt since that night that he should have taken better care of Nicole, and he didn't disagree. They didn't know how much he was to blame. Once he'd told them, there would be no going back, so he had to be sure that this was the right thing to do. He couldn't say he was certain about it, but he was still determined to tell them.

He pulled up outside the restaurant near their house where they'd chosen to meet. They lived in a suburb of Strasbourg on the banks of the River Ill. It was pretty in places but a mostly industrial area, which he'd never enjoyed visiting when Nicole was alive.

'*Bonjour*, Thierry.' Nicole's mum, Nadine, kissed him formally on both cheeks and stood back while he shook hands with Pierre, her husband. They were even less warm towards him now.

'How is everything?' Pierre began once Thierry had sat down.

'I'm having counselling now, and it's been helpful.'

'That's good. I'm sure it will help you over the long term, as well.' Nadine gave him a tearful smile, and he wondered if she could do with some counselling too, although he would never dare tell her his thoughts.

Once the waiter had taken their drinks order, Thierry took a deep breath.

'There's still a lot I haven't told you about the day Nicole died. In fact, the counsellor is the first person I've been strong enough to tell the whole story to.'

Pierre took Nadine's hand, and for a long moment, Thierry could only look at their fingers entwined together, unable to speak for emotion at seeing their closeness. It underlined how alone he felt, even now, nearly two years after Nicole had passed away.

He cleared his throat. 'The thing is, as you know, Nicole wanted us to have a baby, but I didn't feel ready.'

The waiter appeared with their drinks, and Thierry waited for him to leave before speaking again.

'Nicole was determined to make me change my mind, and we argued about it a lot.'

'Why didn't you want to have a child, Thierry?' Pierre asked the one question he didn't want to answer, but it was time for him to be honest now.

'I was selfish, I suppose. I wanted us to have more time to ourselves, without having to worry about children. And I thought it would be better to wait until we had more money.'

Nadine dabbed at her eyes. 'Nicole wanted to have a child with you so much, Thierry, and it nearly broke her when you kept saying no.'

'I know that, Nadine. And I've spent the last couple of years regretting not giving her what she wanted.'

The waiter returned to take their food order. Thierry chose something from the menu, even though he wasn't sure he felt like eating any more.

'So, what happened on the day she died?' Pierre asked once the waiter had gone.

'Nicole raised the subject again, and we argued. We both said some... hurtful things, and she stormed out and took off in her car.'

'And you let her go? You didn't follow her?' Pierre's face twitched, and Thierry sensed his father-in-law's despair.

'We were both angry. I let her go so we could both cool off. I didn't know bad weather was coming in, or that she would have an accident with a crazy driver.' Thierry looked at Pierre and tried desperately to keep calm.

'She must have been so upset, and not thinking straight. Oh, my darling girl.' Nadine burst into full-on tears this time and Thierry's heart constricted with the pain he felt, both for himself and for them.

'Our daughter died after a pointless argument with you, Thierry, and if you hadn't had that argument, maybe she would be alive today.'

'If you're looking for someone to blame, go ahead and blame me. Believe me, there's nothing you can say to me that I haven't already said to myself. But the truth is that I'm not to blame. It was a tragic accident, and one I will regret till the day I die, but it wasn't my fault.'

Pierre put his arm round Nadine and pulled her close. 'We don't want bad feeling with you, Thierry, but you can see how this feels to us. We've lost our daughter, and we can never recover. We appreciate you telling us the truth, but it's probably best if we don't see each other any more.'

'I agree. It will be easier for us all to move on if we break that link between us now. I loved Nicole more than you will ever know, but these meetings only bring it all back for me, and perhaps for you, too.'

'I think it's best if we go now, Thierry.' He put some notes down on the table, and then they left without looking back.

Thierry asked the waiter to take their meals away before paying the bill and returning to his car. Telling Nicole's parents had been awful, but it needed to be done. Now they knew everything, maybe they would be able to start the healing process, and he would be able to start grieving for his lost wife properly.

Lottie

The house was unnaturally quiet as Lottie lay in bed a couple of days later. Thierry had offered to take Marie with him while he did his tour of the vineyard that morning, and Lottie had finally agreed. It was the first time anyone else had taken Marie out, and Lottie had been nervous about it. But she was coming to realise she would need to accept help if she was ever going to have any time to herself, and Thierry had already proved himself capable.

'You need to trust me to look after the baby perfectly well on my own,' he'd said and she'd known he was right, however hard it was for her to accept it. So she'd prepared the changing bag for Thierry to take with him, and she'd also agreed not to keep texting him for updates all the time.

Lottie had gone back to bed and dozed since they'd left, but she didn't want to waste the whole day. At the same time, she had no idea what to do with her free time now that she had it. Maybe she should try to relax and not feel the need to be busy. She would start with a long bath and see what time it was after that.

The bath proved too boring, though, and she soon dressed and went downstairs to eat a late breakfast. When her phone buzzed with a message, she pounced on it with childlike glee.

Just wanted to let you know everything is fine. We've been round the vineyard and we're popping over to the office now. See you later.

She released a long sigh as she pondered the prospect of more time to fill until they returned. She tried to read but found she couldn't concentrate, and watching the television made her feel the same. She turned it off and threw down the remote in disgust. She needed to feel useful, and it was only looking after Marie or doing her job that gave her a sense of purpose. She'd already had over two months' maternity leave from the nursery, and she could go back whenever she was ready. As she wasn't getting paid, it would be better for her to go back sooner rather than later. She hadn't heard from the nursery, so she decided to give them a call to arrange a meeting to discuss her return to work.

'*Allo, c'est Lottie Schell.* Could I speak to *Madame* Albert, please?'

'I'm sorry, she's in a meeting at the moment. Can I take a message for you?'

Lottie didn't recognise the person at the other end of the phone and decided they must be new. She wondered how many other changes might have happened in her absence. She left a message asking *Madame* Albert to call her about a meeting to discuss her return to work and then rang off. Now she was really in the doldrums. She had no friends, apart from her family and the people who worked on the vineyard, and she hadn't ventured out to the local group for new parents yet, either. If she wasn't careful, she would become isolated, and that was the last thing she needed.

A knock at the door interrupted her thoughts, and she found Fran waiting to come in.

'Is everything okay?'

Fran took off her coat and sat down. 'Yes, why? You look worried. What's the matter?'

'Thierry has gone out with Marie today to give me a break, and he messaged me to say he was going over to the office, so I didn't know if you were here to tell me that something had gone wrong.' Lottie fidgeted with her hair.

'Nothing's wrong, Lottie. When Thierry popped in with Marie, I thought I'd come and see you on your own for once. Have you had a good morning?'

'Not really. I've been miserable on my own and I haven't had anything to do.'

'Why didn't you go out?'

'Where would I go? I don't have any friends apart from you, and I don't drive, either. I don't have any sense of purpose without Marie.'

'Maybe next time we can plan to get together so you can make good use of your free time. Unless you want to go for lunch now? I'm free if you are, and it would do us both good to get out.'

Lottie hesitated for a moment but Fran didn't push her. 'Let me text Thierry to say we're going out. We can go somewhere in the village, can't we?'

'Yes, of course,' Fran replied, putting her coat back on.

A minute later they were walking into the village towards a nearby café, and Lottie felt happy for the first time all day.

'Well done for letting Thierry help you out like this. I can't imagine that was an easy decision for you.'

'It was hard at first, but then I had to accept that if I want any free time, I will have to let people help me. Thierry babysat for me last week, so I know he can do it. I just have to give him the chance to keep proving himself. Mind you, that was before I'd thought about what I'd actually do with all that free time.'

Fran laughed and tucked her arm through Lottie's as they made their way around the bustling village square. They took a seat in the window of the café and sipped on their coffees while they waited for their lunches to come.

'I did ring the nursery this morning to see if I could make an appointment to come in and discuss my return to work.'

Fran's eyes widened. 'Did you? Isn't it a bit early for that?'

'Not really. I've taken my mandatory maternity leave and as I've not been paid for it, I don't have much of my savings left now.'

'When are you going in?'

'I had to leave a message, but hopefully soon. It will be good to get back and to get into some sort of routine.'

'I know you need the money, but I wouldn't rush it. Wait and see what their advice is maybe.'

'I do need the money, but I also enjoy my work, and I think it will be good for me to get out of the house. Otherwise I'll be miserable in the long run.'

Fran nodded, but Lottie didn't think she was convinced. 'Have you spoken to Mum and Dad at all?'

'Not for a bit. I'd like to visit them, but I can't see how I can do that without a car. Trying to go on public transport is beyond me at the moment.'

'Any one of us could take you. We'd have to arrange it to fit round the vineyard, but we could do it.'

'That's the thing. You're all busy with your own lives, and I have to learn to fend for myself some of the time. I can't expect you all to help me out every time I get stuck.'

'Well, I'd ask Thierry about it first of all and see what he says. Henri will be back soon and that will make it easier for Thierry to take time off.'

CHAPTER NINE

<u>Thierry</u>

'How have you been since your last appointment? It was difficult for you, I know.' Dr Bartin gave Thierry her usual reassuring smile and he relaxed back into his armchair.

'I met with my in-laws and told them the truth about what happened.'

'How did they take it?' The counsellor made some notes as she listened, and he wondered what she'd written.

'They were upset, understandably, but I was glad to get it all off my chest. It's been a heavy weight, and although they said they don't want to see me any more, I was relieved not to be lying to them.'

'Did they blame you, as you thought they might?'

'They didn't say so in so many words, but that was definitely the impression they gave. You know, it's what I think myself. But I did say it was an accident and that I couldn't be blamed for that. I know that deep down, even if I do still feel guilty.'

'You should be proud of yourself for facing up to your feelings and telling them the truth. It sounds like it went as well as you might have expected. So, where do you go from here?'

'I don't know. I want to tell Lottie everything too, and I've made a start on that, which I think she appreciated, but I still haven't told her the whole truth about not wanting children with Nicole. She's letting me help her with the baby now, and I even took Marie out yesterday to give her some free time, so hopefully, she's beginning to trust me with sharing responsibility. I hope I'm also showing her I can be a good father to Marie, even though she's not my baby.'

'It sounds like you're making real progress now.' The counsellor tapped her chin with her pen. 'What's stopping you from telling Lottie you didn't want children before, but that you feel different now?'

'I want her to see for herself that I care for Marie, and hopefully that will soften the blow when I tell her the rest.'

'In my opinion, it would make more sense to tell her this now so it doesn't come as a surprise further down the line. She's just beginning to trust you. You don't want to spoil that by not telling her the truth.'

Thierry leaned forward, resting his arms on his knees. 'I'll have to give this some thought. I'm not sure if I'm ready for that yet.'

'And what about your feelings towards Nicole?'

'I already feel like I've turned a corner by talking to her parents, and I'm starting to accept that what happened was an accident. There are some other things I need to do which will help me move on, like finishing sorting out her things, but I'm not sure I can do all of that on my own.'

'There's no timetable for it, Thierry. You must do it when you feel ready and not let your conscience get in the way. There's no right or wrong when someone you love dies. Try to remember that and to be kind to yourself. They're your feelings at the end of the day, and that makes them valid. No-one else's opinion matters.'

'Thank you, Dr Bartin. I appreciate the chance to talk it all over with you.'

'And what about your family? Are you in touch with them at all?' The counsellor frowned, looking back through her notes.

'No, I haven't had any contact with my parents for years.'

'Why's that?'

'We just didn't get on and I couldn't wait to leave home. I haven't been back since and they haven't been in contact, either.'

'We're almost at the end of our time today, Thierry. Maybe we should try to talk more about the network of people around you next time. You're going to need people to support you as you move forward from here. Remember you're coming to see me to try to get past your grief over Nicole's death, and your guilt about not wanting children, so although it will be painful, it will also be to your advantage, I hope.'

Thierry nodded. As he was already discovering, Dr Bartin had an uncanny way of getting him to describe all his feelings and to confess all his secrets. Although it had been hard dealing with the difficult questions she asked, he was beginning to feel better for facing up to his past.

On the journey home, he thought about whether to tell Lottie about how he hadn't wanted children at the same time as Nicole. If he did tell her, he'd also have to tell her about the night Nicole died – and what if Lottie reacted in the same way his in-laws had? She might also think he should have gone after Nicole, and where would that leave them?

He parked in the courtyard and made his way back down to his house, where he fished out his key. He dug in his pocket for his phone at the same time, but couldn't find it. As he opened the door, Lottie was on the phone and the look she gave him made him uncertain as to her mood. She finished speaking and put the phone down.

'Hey. Who was that? Hardly anyone rings me on that line these days,' he said.

'It was Dr Bartin's office calling to say you'd left your phone there after your appointment.' She frowned at him. 'Why didn't you tell me you're seeing a doctor?'

Thierry's guilt reared its ugly head once again. He held her gaze for a minute, wondering what to say. In the end, he went for the truth. 'I didn't want anyone to know I'm having counselling. I'm not proud of the fact that I need help to deal with all my issues.' He braced himself, ready for her criticism.

'Counselling? How long have you been going?' she asked instead, looking relieved.

'For a couple of months. I'd been thinking about going for a while. Then when you told me you thought I still had a lot of grief and pent-up emotions to deal with, I knew the time was right to get some help. I'm sorry I didn't tell you about it.'

'Has it been helpful?' she asked, as they moved into the front room.

'Better than I was expecting, to be honest. The counsellor is understanding, and she had me talking in no time.' He laughed at how easily Dr Bartin had persuaded him to share all his burdens.

'Really? She must be good.' Lottie laughed with him, and some of his guilt lifted from his weary shoulders and disappeared.

'Is Marie asleep?'

She nodded. 'We went out for a long walk earlier and I think it tired her out.'

Thierry hesitated before asking his next question, then ploughed on. 'Would you be able to help me clear out the rest of Nicole's things? If you don't want to, I understand, but I thought I'd ask.'

Lottie reached for him, taking one of his hands in hers. 'Yes, of course.'

He drew her to him and her embrace revived his spirits. It was so good to know she was on his side.

Lottie

Lottie had been more surprised than she'd let on to Thierry about the fact that he'd been having counselling. She was proud of him for going but upset that he hadn't trusted her enough to tell her about it. But she didn't want to make too big a deal about him keeping it to himself, which was why she hadn't said anything.

Now, as she walked over to Ellie's house in the village, she drew in a deep breath and let it all out slowly. She would have to let this latest development with Thierry go for now and deal with it another time.

'Come on in, you two,' Ellie cried, opening the door to the house she shared with Henri. 'It's so good to see you both.'

'And you. It's been ages.' Lottie passed Marie over to Ellie, much to Ellie's surprise.

'Oh, my goodness, how do I hold her? I have no experience whatsoever with babies.'

Lottie showed her how to cradle Marie's head in her elbow and how to use her arm to support her back. She smiled at the sight of Ellie, who was practically allergic to babies, struggling to get used to holding one. Marie was happy enough and Lottie took off her coat and sat down on the sofa.

'Will she be okay if I sit down with her?' Ellie asked.

'Of course she will. You don't think I stand up all the time, do you?' Lottie laughed.

Ellie eased herself gently onto the sofa, never taking her eyes off her precious bundle, then glanced up at Lottie with delight when she managed to do it without upsetting her.

'She's gorgeous, Lottie, and she's grown so much since I last saw her.'

'I know. I can't believe she's almost a month old now.' Lottie paused to study her daughter, trying to commit to memory how she looked at this age before she grew any older. 'How did everything go when you went home?' she asked Ellie.

'The funeral went as well as could be expected, but my mum and I hadn't been close for years, so it wasn't emotional for me. It has given me some closure, at least, and allowed me to move on. And her heart attack was very sudden, so she died without suffering.' Despite her words, a look of deep sadness passed across Ellie's face.

Lottie would have liked to ask her why she hadn't been close to her mum, but she didn't want to pry. She'd wanted to ask Thierry the same, after he'd revealed that he didn't get on with his parents, either, but she hadn't wanted to push him to tell her more until he was ready. 'Shall I make us a drink, as you're holding the baby?'

'No, you're my guest. Let me pass her back to you now and I can finish getting things together for us. I got some nice cakes from the bakery this morning for a little treat.' She disappeared into the galley kitchen at the back of the house. Lottie followed with Marie in her arms and stood hovering at the doorway.

'So how does it feel to be back at work on the château?'

'Well, the downstairs is nearly finished, but there's all the upstairs work to get on with next. We did the plastering last year, but there's so much more to do still.'

Ellie put the tea things and the cakes onto a tray and led the way back to the living room.

'Have you enjoyed working on it?' Lottie asked once they'd sat down again. She picked up a lemon éclair from the pile of cakes Ellie had assembled on a plate.

'It's been great.' Ellie kicked off her shoes and tucked her feet up beneath her on the sofa. 'But I do have a confession to make, between you and me.'

'Go on, you know I'll keep it to myself.'

'Well, going home has only confirmed for me that I want to travel sooner rather than later. As much as I've enjoyed working on the château, I don't want it to hold me back. Fran asked me to stay around for their wedding, but I don't know when that will happen. So I want to leave to travel now, but I'm frightened what everyone's reaction will be, especially Henri's. We had such a good time travelling to London together, despite the funeral, and I'd like us to go away together for longer, but I'm not sure if he'd be up for it.'

'Would you come back here afterwards?'

'That would be my plan, as long as everyone still wanted me to. I could carry on working on the château then. It's just that I'm not ready to settle down yet, and all this talk of babies and marriage, although lovely, isn't for me right now.'

'You have to do what's right for you. Henri will understand that, I'm sure.'

'I just don't know what Fran and Didier will think if I disappear halfway through the job they gave me to do. And if Henri doesn't want to come with me, I don't know what that will mean for our relationship.'

'You'll have to talk to them all and see what they say. You need to discuss it with Henri first of all, don't you?'

Ellie nodded, but Lottie could see she was worried about how that conversation would go. She would have loved to talk over her situation with Thierry, but she didn't want to disclose any private matters to Ellie, so she kept it all to herself.

Marie fell straight asleep after they left Ellie's, and so Lottie took the opportunity to pop in and check on Fran on her way back, as well. The door to the office was ajar when she parked the pushchair, and as she was checking Marie was okay, Didier's deep voice sounded as he spoke to someone on the phone.

'That's right, there's not enough money to complete both the Visitors' Centre and the château, and the Visitors' Centre is more pressing right now. I think we'll have to put the château on hold for the time being. No, no-one else knows for the moment, so please keep that to yourself.'

Lottie turned the pushchair quietly round and continued on towards the archway without going in. Maybe that information would be the answer to one of Ellie's problems at least.

Thierry

Lottie was sitting at the kitchen table feeding Marie when Thierry came into the kitchen the next day.

'Morning,' he said, but she didn't reply. 'Hello to you, too,' he continued with a grin.

She had the decency to look shamefaced. 'Sorry, I've been trying to feed Marie for a while now. And she was awake a lot during the night, so I'm shattered to be honest.'

They'd been taking it in turns to get up during the night; when it was Lottie's turn, she slept in the spare room. Thierry was a deep sleeper, so he hadn't heard anything.

'Have you had any breakfast?' he asked, busying himself by putting the kettle on.

She shook her head and he worried she was trying to deal with everything on her own again.

'I can have a try at feeding her if you'd like a break,' he offered.

Lottie glanced up at him and frowned. 'That would be great, but...'

'But...' he pressed.

She swiped her hair out of her face. 'I just feel it's my job, that's all, as much as I appreciate your offer.'

'Why don't we give it a try? There's still some milk in the fridge from yesterday. I can use that.'

'Okay. I'll make us some breakfast.' She gave him a tired smile and he was relieved she'd agreed. He heated the milk before swapping places with her.

'I saw Fran yesterday afternoon, and she mentioned you'd like to take Marie home to visit your family. I was going to offer to take you, if you'd like me to.'

Lottie put some slices of bread and jam in front of him so that he could eat one-handed while he fed the baby.

'Oh, that's kind, but I couldn't put you to all that trouble.'

'It wouldn't be any trouble. I wouldn't have offered otherwise.'

'It's thoughtful of you, and I would be grateful for a lift. I would want to stay a few days, so I guess you'd have to drop me there and then I'd have to find someone else to bring me back.'

'I could stay, if you didn't mind? Then I could bring you back.'

Thierry was almost holding his breath, but was trying hard not to push her.

'I don't know. I'd have to think about it.'

He finished feeding Marie and stood up, lifting her gently onto his shoulder to burp her. Now he could look Lottie in the eye. 'Lottie, I think you might be reading too much into this. I want to help you, and I have a car, so I'm offering to drive you home and back again. There's no more to it than that.'

'We still don't have a car seat.' Her eyes lit up, as if she was pleased to have found an obstacle.

Thierry sighed. 'I'd completely forgotten about that, but I'm sure Fran and Didier would lend us theirs again.'

'Well, for a longer journey like this, I'd rather get Marie her own one, but there's no way I can afford that right now, so I think we'd better abandon this idea for the time being.'

Thierry bit his tongue. He moved Marie back into his arms and made his way to the front room to lull her to sleep, trying not to be infuriated. He'd only been trying to help, and still Lottie was determined to be independent.

'You can trust me, you know,' he ventured to her, after a couple of minutes' silence. 'I know you've been let down before and you're wary, but I'm not Yiannis. I will be here for you.'

She looked up at him from the sofa as he paced up and down. 'I do trust you, but I don't want to be dependent on you. I can do things for myself. And this has got nothing to do with Yiannis.'

He tried not to roll his eyes, knowing full well that it had everything to do with Yiannis. 'I know you can do things for yourself and I'm not trying to undermine you in any way. I only want to help because I care for you and because I can.'

'Thierry, look—' she began. He turned around, Marie fast asleep in his arms. 'It's not that I don't want your help... It's just I find it hard to accept it. I'm sorry. I know you're on my side.' She gave him a wobbly smile and he came across the room to her.

'I know it's hard. We're both learning.' He passed the baby to her before kissing her on both cheeks. 'I'll see you at lunchtime, okay?'

As he left the house, he made a quick phone call. He was soon driving on the *autoroute* back to Strasbourg, intent on putting his idea into action. If she didn't want to borrow a second-hand car seat, he would get her a brand-new one.

It took him longer than he'd expected to choose a seat from the vast array of items available, but with some help from one of the shop assistants, he finally found the right one and was on his way home again half an hour later.

He worried Lottie would find some reason not to accept it, but it was too late to dither about that now. He hadn't asked her permission, but what else was he to do if he wanted to help her? He couldn't stand by and always let her put him off. Still, doubt niggled at him and it only increased on the journey home.

By the time he got back to the vineyard, his earlier optimism had disappeared, leaving him deflated. He'd planned to take the car seat straight indoors to show Lottie so she could see that he'd solved her problem, but in the end, he didn't have the courage to discuss it with her again. He'd have to leave it for another day and hope she was in a more flexible mood. In the meantime, he left the car seat in the boot. He'd set it up at some point when he had a bit more time available.

Lottie

At last Lottie had managed to make an appointment to discuss her return to work with *Madame* Albert, the nursery manager. Fran had offered to babysit for her and she had accepted. It was Fran's first time looking after Marie, and Lottie was a little worried about her ability to handle everything, but Fran was determined.

'This won't be a problem for me. I've seen you do everything plenty of times, and I've had lots of experience looking after Chlöe.'

'Well, Chlöe's quite a bit older than Marie. You will call me if you have any problems, won't you? And did you read the checklist I gave you?'

'Lottie, you're going to be late for your meeting if you keep fussing. Now, off you go, and don't worry, we'll be fine. I'm looking forward to hearing all about how it goes when you come back.'

Lottie gave Marie a little hug, took one last look at herself in the mirror, and set off for the short walk into the village. The rain of the previous few days had now disappeared, and the sun was out again, but it was still quite cold, and she pulled her coat tighter around her. As she made her way into the village, she admired the colourful crocuses and tulips on display in the gardens bordering the path and was delighted spring was now in full swing.

'Hello, Pascale, how are you? I was worried you might have left. I spoke to someone else here on the phone the other day.'

'No, I'm still here. I must have been at lunch.' Pascale came out from behind the reception desk and gave Lottie a hug. 'It's great to see you. How's the baby?'

'She's really well, and growing fast. She's coming up to five weeks old now.'

'Goodness, that time has flown. Anyway, you're here to see *Madame*, aren't you? I'll let her know you've arrived.'

Lottie went over to the window to watch the children at play, giving Chlöe a little wave when she spotted her with her friends. She'd missed seeing them and was looking forward to spending some of her time here again. She wanted to come back part-time at first, and hoped *Madame* would be amenable to that idea.

'You can go on in now, Lottie. She's ready for you. Come out and have a chat afterwards, won't you?'

Lottie nodded before making her way along the corridor to *Madame* Albert's imposing office. She knocked lightly on the door.

'Ah, Lottie, come in. It's good to see you. How are you?' *Madame* Albert gestured to her to take a seat opposite the desk.

'I'm fine, thank you, *Madame*.' She looked up into the older woman's kindly face. *Madame* Albert was immaculately dressed in a formal suit, and not a hair was out of place, just as Lottie remembered her.

'And the baby?'

'Yes, she's well and growing fast.'

'They do have a habit of doing that. You must treasure these early days with her. They're gone before you know it.'

'I'm looking forward to coming back to work, though. I was watching the children out of the window and they made me realise how much I've missed being here.'

'That was why I wanted to see you face to face today. I'm afraid I have bad news on that front, Lottie.' *Madame* sank into her chair as if she had the weight of the world on her shoulders. 'You see, our intake has dropped, and with it our funding, so we can't afford to take you back on. I'm so sorry.'

Lottie felt short of breath. 'What? I can't believe this. How has this happened?'

'We don't have the money to pay you, or the work for you to do. Our numbers do go up and down, due to the change in the birth rate and people moving in and out of the area.'

'But *Madame*, I need this job. Where else will I get a job in such a small village?'

'I'm sorry, Lottie. I know it will be hard. It would be hard for any of the staff and I truly regret having to do this. As you'd only been with us a little while, it was fairest to let you go. I will make sure you receive some money in redundancy, although it won't be much, as we're not obliged to pay you and the board wasn't keen.'

Lottie found herself standing up in a trance.

'Take care, Lottie, and once again, I'm sorry.'

She left the office and wandered back towards reception.

'Is everything okay?' Pascale asked when she reappeared. 'You look like you've seen a ghost.'

'I've lost my job.'

'Oh no, Lottie. I'm so sorry. I had no idea.'

'No, me neither. I'm sorry, Pascale. I'm going to have to go.'

Lottie wandered aimlessly around the village square for a while, unable to face the thought of having to tell Fran and Thierry she'd lost her job. Once she told everyone, they'd all start telling her what to do, what was best for her, what was best for Marie. She didn't know if she could take all that well-meaning advice about how she should live her life.

She still had some money put by, but the little money she did have wouldn't last her and Marie much longer. She could have cried at the unfairness of it all. She would have to look for another job as soon as possible, but to do that she might need to call on family and friends to babysit more often, and she wasn't sure she could ask that much of them. The nursery job had been perfect in every way. She was sure to find it difficult to find another job quite as convenient for her situation, especially when she didn't drive.

Lottie stopped in the middle of the street, as she was completing her third circuit of the square. What was she thinking? She needed to be proactive rather than letting this get her down. It was rotten news and she would need some time to get over the shock of it all, but she would survive. She had to for Marie's sake.

She lifted her head up and made her way back home, determined to find a way. She would come up with a plan first, and then she would tell everyone what had happened.

CHAPTER TEN

Thierry

On the Friday night of that week, Thierry went out with Didier and Henri to Michel's bistro and wine bar in the village. The place was heaving but they managed to find a free table right in the back corner.

'God, I really need this,' Didier said, as they chinked glasses before taking a long sip of the pinot blanc before them.

'It's felt like a long week, hasn't it?' agreed Henri. 'It was good to get away with Ellie to England for a few days, despite it being for the funeral, but no sooner did we get home than she told me she wants to be off on her travels again.'

'Really?' Didier's eyebrows shot up. 'Are you going to go with her?'

'I'm not sure. I've said no for the moment – that's why it's been such a long week. We haven't talked much to each other at home since. I couldn't have been more surprised when she told me. Going to her mum's funeral has made her think more about how she's getting older, and how she doesn't want to miss her chance before she has to settle down. That was how she put it. But I love my life here and I honestly don't have any great desire to go and see other places. She told me I was boring, and that there was so much more to see outside of France.' Henri shook his head, obviously finding it hard to fathom her enthusiasm.

'Well, if you change your mind, you know it won't be a problem for you to take some time off, don't you?' Didier reminded him. Henri nodded, and Didier went on. 'How long does Ellie want to go for?'

Henri put his empty glass down on the table and waited for Thierry to fill it back up. 'She's talking about going for six months. That seems like an eternity to be apart to me, but she said she'll come back here afterwards.'

'Well, if you love her, you should think seriously about going with her,' Thierry advised.

'Is that what you'd do if it was Lottie?' Henri asked, narrowing his eyes.

'Well...'

'Exactly. You wouldn't want to give up your life here any more than I do.'

'But you wouldn't be giving up your life, would you? You'd be taking a sabbatical. And maybe it would do you good to travel and see the world while you're young and free of any responsibilities.'

Henri still looked sceptical. 'Do you wish you'd done that?'

'Listening to Lottie talk about her travels one night when we were chatting made me realise what a sheltered life I've led,' Thierry replied.

'And how are things going between you two?' Didier asked. 'Better, from the sounds of it.'

'Well, better in many ways, but Lottie can still be awkward when she wants to be. I'm doing my best to ask her what she wants and to listen to her, and sometimes it works, sometimes it doesn't.' Thierry shrugged.

They fell silent for a moment, each of them considering his own struggles.

'And how's everything with you and Fran, Didier?' Thierry asked.

'We've put the wedding on hold because trying to get pregnant has taken over for the moment. It's all Fran thinks about, and I'm worried it's going to make her ill. It's so up and down all the time. We wait for good news every month, only to have our hopes dashed. I don't think I can keep putting myself through it, but I don't want her to feel like we've failed.'

'Ellie told me part of the reason she wants to get away is that all the talk about babies and marriages is making her feel trapped.' Henri looked so downcast, Thierry couldn't think of what to say to comfort him.

'Christ, that was blunt. Do you want to get married to Ellie?'

'Of course, but I daren't suggest it now, even though I've been thinking about proposing to her for a while.'

'I have to admit that now might be a good time for her to go,' said Didier.

'What do you mean?' Henri asked sharply.

Didier held up his hands. 'I don't mean it against Ellie. She's been brilliant at taking over the restoration of the château since she moved here. It's just that I don't think we're going to have enough money to finish both the Visitors' Centre and the upstairs floor of the château for some time. If we were to concentrate on the centre while Ellie's away, we might be able to go back to the château when she returns.'

'Well, that's not exactly reassuring, but I understand managing your budget is your main concern.' Henri sniffed, looking decidedly put out.

'From what you've said, Henri, it doesn't sound like Ellie's going to change her mind about going anyway,' Thierry said.

Henri slumped in his chair. 'No, you're probably right. Nothing I've said so far has made any difference.'

'For what it's worth, I've never been anywhere outside France,' said Thierry. 'I left Paris to do some of my training in Bordeaux and the Bourgogne, but apart from that, I did all my studying here.'

'Same here with my training. And I travelled to see Isabelle when she was on location occasionally, but that was always in France so it wouldn't disrupt Chlöe too much. Do you think we're narrow-minded because we've never been outside France?'

'I imagine Fran, Lottie, and Ellie might give a different answer to that question than we would,' Thierry replied, and they all laughed. 'Time for some more wine, I think.'

While they waited for their waiter to come over, Thierry thought about his lack of desire to travel and wondered if it had narrowed his outlook on life. Nicole had never mentioned wanting to, so it had never been an issue between them. But it might have benefitted them to travel when they were younger. It would be great for Henri to go with Ellie now and put off settling down for a while. If he had his time again, that's what he would do.

Lottie

Lottie had had her first unbroken night's sleep with Marie and was hopeful that she might have a few more in the coming weeks. She'd even managed to get ready before Thierry left to do his inspection, and to spend some time with him at breakfast. Once she'd fed Marie and popped her in her bouncer, she decided it would be a good time to give her mum a call and catch up.

'*Maman*, hi, it's Lottie. How are you?'

'I'm better for hearing your voice, sweetheart. How are you?'

'I'm fine, and so is Marie. I'm sorry I haven't called for a while.'

'Don't worry. I know there's a lot to do when you have a young baby. How have things been?'

Lottie told her all about Marie having slept through the night and the way she was growing so fast. 'I was hoping to bring Marie home to see you and Dad, and also to introduce her to *Papi*, but it's tricky transport-wise.'

'Couldn't Thierry bring you home? I'm sure he wouldn't mind.'

'Thierry did offer to bring me, actually, and it was only the fact that we still haven't got a car seat that got in the way. I can't afford to get one at the moment and I'd rather Marie has a new one. I know it's probably not necessary, but I worry about using a second-hand one, especially on longer journeys.'

'Oh, Thierry hasn't told you then?'

'Told me what?' Lottie bristled.

'Well, he called the other day and asked our advice about getting a new car seat. *Papi* was here at the time, and he offered to pay for it as a gift to you and Marie. So I think Thierry went and bought one after that. I presumed he'd spoken to you, or given it to you since then.'

'No, he hasn't, probably because he thinks I'll be mad with him about it. I'm grateful to *Papi* for saying that he'd buy it for us, but I wish Thierry would talk things over with me before making decisions like that, you know.'

'The trouble is that you're both quite single-minded and neither of you wants to give in.'

'I don't see how I'm being single-minded when all I want is for him to let me make my own decisions. He makes me cross even when he's doing me a good deed.'

'Try not to be too hard on him. He only wants to help you come and visit and it would be lovely to see you all. I know *Papi* would love to meet Marie.'

'I'd love that, too. I'll speak to Thierry and see what we can sort out.'

Lottie rang off, pleased she'd made an effort to call her mum and determined to get down to visit them as soon as she could. She hadn't seen her granddad in ages and it would be good to see him again. It had been too long since she'd been home, and she regretted how stubborn she'd been when Thierry had suggested taking her.

On an impulse, she decided she'd go and find him. She scooped Marie out of her bouncer and onto her changing mat, chatting to her all the while to distract her, and then she popped her into her sleepsuit. It was drizzling with rain as she set off down the slope towards the château, and that meant she would be sure to find him outside, inspecting the vines. She should have thought about how difficult it might be to access the vineyard with a pushchair in tow. As she reached the first rows of vines, though, Thierry appeared in the distance and she gave him a wave to get his attention. He was covered from head to toe in waterproofs and wellies.

'What are you doing here?' he asked, approaching.

'I was coming to see you, of course.'

'I'm sorry. I wasn't expecting you, that's all. I'm about to go and do an inspection. This blasted weather.' He raised his eyes to study the dark clouds gathering.

'I thought you would be. It's fine, I won't keep you long. I was just speaking to my mum and I was wondering if I could take you up on your offer to take me home this weekend, if that would work for you?'

Thierry looked sheepish. 'She told you about the car seat, didn't she?'

Lottie nodded, with a grin.

'I'm sorry I didn't tell you before.'

'It's all right. I'm not annoyed – well, only a bit because you didn't ask me about it first. I'm just pleased I can go home and visit everyone. So what do you think?'

Thierry blew out a sigh of obvious relief and she wondered if she was so awful that he hadn't been able to bring himself to tell her the good thing he'd done.

'That should be okay,' he said. 'I'd need to check with Didier that he's going to be around. How long did you plan to be away? How about if we went on Saturday morning and came back Sunday evening?'

'That would be great, thank you. Are you sure it's still okay? I don't want to give you problems at work.'

'You won't. I'll tell you later, when I've spoken to Didier.'

'Okay, I'll let you go. I hope the vines are all right.'

Thierry grimaced. 'Thanks for coming to see me. It was good to see you so unexpectedly. And thanks for being so understanding about my latest faux pas.' He grinned, and she laughed.

Lottie decided to go up to the office rather than going straight home again. She opened the door, and Didier helped her carry the pushchair inside. Fran came round her desk to help her with Marie, before Didier disappeared off to join Thierry to check on the vines.

Fran laid Marie along her thighs, delighting in chatting to her niece, giving Lottie a chance to talk to Henri. She took off her wet coat and gratefully accepted the hot drink he offered her.

'How's everything with you and Ellie?' Lottie asked. 'I haven't seen her for a few days.'

'She's busy over at the château. To be honest, I've hardly seen myself since we came back from England.'

Lottie wasn't sure if she should bring up the subject of Ellie's desire to travel, so she waited for him to carry on.

'She's told me she wants to travel now. Did she tell you that?'

'She did mention that she was thinking about it, yes.'

'What do you think of the idea?'

'Well, as someone who couldn't wait to travel myself, I understand her feelings. It's something you have to get out of your system while you're still young enough to do it, I think. There's plenty of time to settle down later.' She wanted to encourage him to go with Ellie but didn't feel it was her place. She just hoped he would come to the right decision on his own.

Thierry

Thierry cast his eye around the emerging Visitors' Centre. The walls were all plastered now but looked like they still needed a final coat of paint; there was no flooring in place, and lighting and furniture had yet to be installed. Clearly, there was still a long way to go, and he could see why Didier was worried about not having enough money to complete both the project he'd employed Fran to oversee and the upstairs of the château. Fran had invited him in to help her decide what they'd need to install for the wine tastings at the end of the tours, but that was all still quite a long way off.

At that moment, Fran appeared from round a corner, where she'd been talking to one of the builders. She gave him a quick wave. He smiled in return and carried on his inspection while he waited for her, making a list in his notebook of all the things that still needed doing.

Thierry wanted to have racks installed all the way round the shop area to display all their wines, as well as bins with special offers dotted here and there. He also wanted a tasting counter where wines could be poured out for visitors at the end of a tour, and also for people who came into the shop and wanted to taste a particular wine or selection of wines. There would need to be fridges too, and a special smaller room for the more expensive wines.

'Thierry, I'm so sorry to keep you waiting,' Fran said, arriving a few minutes later.

'No problem at all. I've been having a look around and a think about what we'll need to finish the area off. How long do you think it will be before we can start choosing furniture and installing the equipment we'll need?'

'About another month. That's what I was discussing with the builder. Our original plan was to open in the spring, so we're a bit behind schedule, but not much. We only need to finish off the painting and then install the flooring and the wine racks.'

'Are you still happy to go with a tasting counter? And we'll need special fridges to keep the wines cool. I know they're not cheap.'

'I still want all the things we originally discussed, but as you probably know, we have to be very careful with the budget, what with needing to finish the château, as well.'

'It's a delicate balancing act, I know.'

'We'll also need a reception counter and till area, and I'd like an area for the more expensive wines, but that might have to wait for phase two. The most expensive element so far has been the air conditioning we've had to install to keep the whole room at the right temperature. That was much more than we were expecting.'

'Okay, well, maybe we should focus on doing the priorities for phase one, as you've suggested, and leave some things for phase two once we have some money coming in from the organised tours.'

'That sounds like a sensible plan. Thanks, Thierry. I've been pulling my hair out over it all lately. I don't seem to have enough time to do everything.'

They discussed the practicalities of the tastings after the half-hour tour of the winery, including the number of wines they would offer visitors and how much they should charge. They were hoping to make their money from wine sales in the shop after the tour. A lot was riding on making a success of the Visitors' Centre to improve their cash flow and enable them to get back on with restoring the château after Ellie returned from her travels.

'That all sounds good,' Thierry said. 'How many people were you planning to have on a tour? If lots of people turn up at the tastings counter at once, it could be too much for the staff to handle.'

'Good point. I think we'd keep to a maximum of ten people per tour and space the tours out to one every two hours at first. We'd probably fit in two in the morning and two in the afternoon.'

'That sounds reasonable. Once we know how it all works out, we can always add in more.'

'Well, that's enough to be going on with. Why don't we meet again in a couple of weeks' time to see where we are then?'

Thierry nodded and turned towards the entrance and Fran fell in alongside him to make her way back to the office.

'I hear you and Lottie are going home to visit my parents this weekend,' she said.

'Well, as long as Didier's okay with me being away.'

'I'm sure it will be fine. You don't have enough time off, as far as I'm concerned. Nor does Henri. I want him to go travelling with Ellie, but I have no idea how I'd manage without him if he did.'

'We'll be fine, whatever happens. We always muck in together when we need to.' He smiled.

'That's true, even if it would be a shame for them to be gone for so long. But as Lottie was saying the other day, it's best to do these things when you're young and free of responsibilities. That's what I did, and I loved every minute of living in London. Well, mostly,' she added as an afterthought.

Thierry knew Didier was supposed to have travelled with her, but had been unable to go because his father had passed away. In the intervening years, they'd both got together with other people, until fate had given them a second chance. And thank heaven for those.

'I'm glad you and Didier found your way back to each other in the end,' Thierry said.

'Me, too,' she said. 'I wish we hadn't wasted all those years apart, though.'

'Do you ever wonder whether things happen the way they do for a reason? I mean, I wouldn't have met Lottie if you hadn't come back here to work on the vineyard.'

'And I wouldn't have met Didier again if my ex hadn't cheated on me,' Fran said. 'You're right in some ways, but there are some things we all regret happening, even so.'

He wished with all his heart that Nicole hadn't died, but what would their relationship be like now if she was still alive? He didn't want to dwell on that too much, given how much they'd been arguing at the time of her death.

Lottie

Lottie was delighted to receive a call from Sylvie the next morning. She wanted to come and visit her and Marie that afternoon after picking Chlöe up from nursery. Sylvie had visited her briefly the week after she came out of hospital, but to Lottie's shame, she hadn't seen her since then, and Marie had changed so much during that time.

She'd been to the *boulangerie* to get some cakes and was now eagerly awaiting their arrival. She'd had a good night's sleep the night before; Thierry had been on duty and she hadn't even heard him get up. The day had gone well so far, too. Now that Marie was getting a bit older, things were settling down, at least a little.

She'd just put the kettle on when there was a knock at the door.

'Come on in,' she said, kissing them both hello.

Chlöe made a beeline for Marie and plopped herself down in front of her so that they could catch up.

'She's so much bigger now,' she said.

'You're right, she is,' said Sylvie. 'Babies grow so quickly, don't they?'

Lottie brought over drinks for everyone, setting Sylvie's down next to her on the coffee table beside her chair.

'How are you, Sylvie? I'm sorry it's been so long since we've seen you.'

'It has been a long time, but that's been down to me, too. I do find it harder now I'm living that bit further away, but I'm trying to stay in touch with everyone. I can't drive and it's a bit too far to walk, so it has been difficult. Frédéric dropped me at the nursery and he's off tasting wine with Didier now.'

'I saw you when you came to the nursery,' Chlöe piped up, and Lottie's heart sank. Now there would be questions.

'Yes, that's right, you did.' She tapped Chlöe lightly on the nose.

'Will you be coming back to work at the nursery soon? We miss you.'

'I miss you all, too. I'm not sure when I'll be coming back. I have to look after Marie because she's still so little.'

'Have you enquired about going back?' Sylvie asked.

'Yes, that's why I was there that day.' Lottie bit her lip, not wanting to continue this conversation in front of Chlöe. Marie started grizzling at just the right moment. Lottie glanced at the clock.

'Ooh, she's hungry. Time for her feed,' she told Chlöe.

She lifted Marie out of her bouncer and onto her lap to feed her. Chlöe provided a rapt audience, having never seen a baby being fed before.

'Does Marie eat food as well as milk?' she asked.

'No, not yet. She's still too young, but she will do soon.'

'What will she eat? Could she have lasagne?'

Lottie laughed. 'Not till she has some teeth.'

'When will she get those?' Chlöe asked, wide-eyed.

'Not for a few months yet.'

Chlöe pulled a face. 'It must be boring having milk all the time. Won't your milk run out?'

'No, it keeps coming while she wants it for now. Once she has teeth and can start to eat proper food, I'll stop feeding her milk then.'

'When will Marie be able to play with me?'

'Quite soon,' Lottie reassured her. 'When she can sit up on her own, she'll be able to do more, but that won't be for a few months yet, either, I'm afraid.'

Chlöe went off to her bag to get some of her toys to play with. Lottie was afraid she'd grown bored with Marie already. She came back and sat down in front of her with the toys, though, so perhaps not.

'Have you heard about Ellie wanting to travel?' Lottie asked Sylvie.

'Yes, Fran did mention something about that. It will do her good, I should think, after all she's been through recently. Is Henri going to go with her? They'll miss each other terribly if he doesn't.'

'She's asked him, but he's a bit unsure about leaving Alsace and the vineyard.'

'Oh, that boy. He's so loyal to us, but he could benefit from seeing other places, too. I'll encourage him to go with her when I next see him. Fran and Didier will have a lot of extra work on their hands without them, won't they?' Sylvie frowned, knowing how much work was involved in keeping the vineyard running every day.

Lottie didn't know how much to say about the finances. Maybe Didier had decided not to tell his mum. 'Well, I think the plan may be to stop work on the château until Ellie gets back, but if Henri goes as well, there will be a big gap in the team.' And that's when it hit her – she could be the one to fill that gap, if only she could get up the courage to ask Fran.

'Yes, indeed. I must speak to Didier about that, as well.'

'Don't you go worrying about it all, Sylvie. You need to look after yourself most of all.'

Chlöe looked up then. 'That's what Frédéric is always telling you, *Mémé.*'

Sylvie and Lottie both laughed.

'Thierry's taking Marie and me home this weekend to see my family, and she'll meet my granddad for the first time then.'

'Oh, how lovely. Your parents will be happy to see you again. It will be nice for you to see your granddad too, and to introduce him to Thierry, won't it?'

Lottie nodded. 'Yes, I haven't seen him in ages. Not since I first found out I was pregnant, actually, before I came to live here with Fran.'

'I remember that. You lived with Fran in the cottage, didn't you?'

'That's right.' You couldn't get anything past Chlöe.

Chlöe jumped up to go and look at the picture of Thierry with Nicole. 'Are you married to Thierry now, Lottie?'

Lottie flashed a look of concern at Sylvie, but Sylvie smiled back reassuringly.

'No, we're not married, Chlöe. That's Thierry and his wife in the picture, but she passed away some time ago.'

'Oh, that's sad for Thierry. I'm glad he has you and Marie to look after him now.'

And with that statement, Chlöe sat back down on the floor and got back to the business of playing with her toys.

CHAPTER ELEVEN

Thierry

Looking forward to his weekend away with Lottie and Marie, Thierry woke up bright and early to set about getting everything ready for their journey. He wanted to make things as smooth as possible. All he had left to do was to put in the new car seat for Marie. He dutifully laid out the instructions on the back seat of the car and read them through, then went back to the beginning again to see if he could make any sense of them. Feeling none the wiser after the second reading, he decided to have a go at putting the seat in the car using his common sense. How hard could it be?

Half an hour later, he was sweating like a pig and issuing expletives at an alarming rate. And still the car seat was no closer to being fixed safely. He had to admit defeat and call on Didier.

'You mean a simple old car seat got the better of you, Thierry?' Didier laughed into his phone as he left the cottage and made his way down to Thierry's house.

'Don't start on me. I've been wrangling with this thing for almost an hour now and I still have no clue how to do it.' Thierry blew out a long breath and tried to relax, hoping Lottie wouldn't come out and ask what was happening.

Didier took one look at the seat and fixed it firmly in place in less than five minutes. He clapped Thierry on the back, grinning at his stunned expression. 'It all comes with experience, *mon brave*.'

There were no words for Thierry's frustration. He managed to grind out a thank you before going back inside to collect Lottie and Marie, annoyed he was now running late.

'What's taken you so long?' Lottie demanded. She looked like she'd been dealing with the car seat herself, and his heart sank at the thought of them both trying to keep their tempers on the way there.

'I couldn't work out how to put the car seat in and had to ask Didier to help me.' He gave her a smile, but it didn't seem to make much difference.

Lottie picked up Marie and Thierry brought their bags. Within no time, they were on their way, and a fragile silence filled the air.

'Did you have a bad night?' he asked, after they'd been travelling for a few minutes. It had been Lottie's turn to get up last night and she was such a light sleeper. Perhaps the lack of sleep was getting to her.

'No more so than usual. Why?'

'Well, you seem annoyed about something and I wondered if that was it.'

'You annoyed me by taking so long. You were so particular about when we were going to leave, and then you were late yourself.' She crossed her arms and stared out of the window.

'I did say I was sorry, but you seemed like you were annoyed long before I came back in.'

There was a brief silence before she spoke again. 'I'm worried about going, that's all.'

'I thought you were looking forward to seeing your family.'

'I was until I remembered how, when we're all together, I always revert to being the baby of the family. The one who makes all the wrong decisions, compared to Fran.' She twisted the end of a length of hair before flinging it back over her shoulder.

'I don't know what to say to that. I genuinely believe your family love you. And for what it's worth, I don't think they favour Fran over you for one minute. In fact, I envy you the closeness you share with them.'

She didn't say another word for the rest of the journey, and he wondered what had got her in such a state. As they arrived in Colmar, Thierry tried one more time to reassure her.

'Listen, whatever happens, I'm on your side, you know. Try to keep calm. You're a mum yourself now, and you're making good decisions every day.'

'It certainly doesn't feel that way sometimes. Take that next left turn up ahead.'

The rest of the journey was spent with her directing him to the family house. He had the briefest chance to take in some of the views, but where Lottie's parents lived was on the outskirts of Colmar, and much like any other town with its industrial areas and shopping centres.

He pulled onto the gravel driveway a couple of minutes later and got out to stretch his legs, taking in the neatly kept front garden and the typical half-timbered Alsatian farmhouse. Lottie lifted Marie out. She was still dozy after falling asleep on the way. She glanced at him and he gave her what he hoped was an encouraging smile. Lottie's mum appeared at the door, followed by her dad, and an older man Thierry assumed must be her granddad.

'Oh, Lottie, it's marvellous to see you! And Marie – hasn't she grown?' Her mum cooed over them both, and Lottie handed Marie over to her while she hugged her dad and granddad.

'*Papi*, this is Thierry.'

Her granddad put out his hand. 'I'm glad to meet you at last, Thierry. Thank you for bringing Lottie and Marie here to visit this weekend. I don't travel so much any more.'

'Good to see you again, Thierry.' Lottie's dad, Joseph, shook his hand too, and clapped him on the back. 'How are those wines looking this year?'

They went inside and gathered in the kitchen while Joseph made everyone a drink.

'I'll pass Marie back to you, Lottie. I'm sure you want to give her a feed now.'

'She'll let me know when she's hungry, Mum.' Lottie's jaw was tight and her reply to her mum was clipped.

Thierry tried not to hold his breath as tension filled the air.

'Could someone point me in the direction of the bathroom, please?' he asked, in an effort at distracting them all from Lottie's obvious irritation.

'I'll show you where it is,' Lottie replied, and he followed her as she led him out of the kitchen and down a long corridor towards the other end of the house.

'I've been here five minutes,' she muttered, 'and she's already telling me what to do.'

Lottie

Why did this happen every time she met up with her mum? She took everything her mum said the wrong way, and without fail, she ended up full of resentment. She'd even taken her miserable mood out on Thierry and he'd done nothing to deserve it. Partly, she was still upset after finding out that she had no job to return to, and desperate to talk it over with someone, but she couldn't bear the thought of having to tell them all about it and dealing with their pity – or worse their criticism.

She set up the Moses basket in her old bedroom, and after feeding Marie, she laid her down for a nap. Then she escaped to the back garden for a moment to think. It would only be a moment's escape – someone else was sure to come along and ask her how she was. In the fields behind the house was the footpath to the vineyards, where she and Fran had wandered as children. She stared out at it and tried to calm herself.

'Are you all right, *ma petite*?' *Papi* came alongside and put his arm round her.

'I'm cross with myself for being cross with *Maman*, but she does know how to get my back up.'

'That's what you think she's trying to do, but I promise you, she's not. We all regret the way we say things sometimes, and she really is only trying to help you and Marie.'

'I know that, *Papi*, of course I do. I don't want to be resentful all the time, but I wish she would trust me to look after Marie myself.'

'It's just as hard for her, you know. Maybe now you're a mum, you'll start to see things more from her point of view.' He laughed at the expression of amazement on Lottie's face. 'Or maybe not yet!'

'I know I need to be more mature about everything and not fly off the handle so often. I don't know how to stop myself from being so annoyed so much of the time. I've been hard on Thierry today, as well, and I feel guilty about that now, too.'

'He's strong enough to deal with it, I think. He seems to really care for you, and for Marie. How are you getting along with each other?'

'Pretty well for the most part, but he has a lot of past history to deal with still. And he's so protective of me, which is a good thing most of the time but can get annoying, too.'

'Hmm, it sounds like you've still got a lot to talk about before you can move on with each other, if that's what you want to do.'

'I do want to move on with him, *Papi* – I love him, although I've not told him that yet – but there's so much going on in both our lives right now.'

'And how are you managing financially? Things must be tight when you're not working.'

To Lottie's total embarrassment, tears sprang to her eyes. She swiped furiously at her face but *Papi* was too quick for her, and he pulled her in for a hug. She let herself be comforted by her granddad's strong arms as she breathed in the familiar smell of his old-fashioned cologne.

'It's so hard, *Papi*. I do have some savings, and of course I'm lucky in that I don't have to pay any rent, but I need to get back to work.'

'All in good time, sweetheart. I think you're worrying about so many things, but you have yourself and your new baby to worry about most importantly.' He pulled back and looked her in the eye. She stared up into his wise old face. 'I want to give you some money to help you out.' He put up his hand to silence the protest she tried to make. 'I gave Fran some money to put towards her wedding when that happens, and I want to do the same for you. If it helps to tide you over a bit longer until you can go back to work, it will be a weight off my mind.'

'Thank you, *Papi*. I'd be so grateful.'

Thierry appeared on the patio and looked out across the garden until he spotted them and waved.

'Let's go and join everyone, and remember, deep breaths when things annoy you. You will get through this, I promise.' *Papi* kissed her on the cheek and took her hand, and they ambled slowly across the lawn to where Thierry was waiting for them.

'Everything okay?' he asked as they got nearer. Lottie nodded. 'Your mum has offered to babysit Marie so we can go out tonight and spend some time together. Would you like to do that? You can show me the town.' He laughed and Lottie joined in.

'That sounds like a good night out,' *Papi* agreed. 'Your mum would be fine looking after Marie,' he added, sensing Lottie's hesitation.

'That does sound lovely, and I know Mum will be fine, but I'd worry about being apart from her for that long.'

'If you take your phone, your mum can get in touch with you if there's a problem,' Thierry said. 'And we can come straight back, I promise.'

'I'd better go and talk to Mum first, but I would like to go out if we can.' She gave Thierry a little smile as she passed him to go back inside.

'Did Thierry tell you about my idea?' her mum asked, as she entered the kitchen.

'Yes, thanks for offering. Are you sure you'd be all right if we went out all evening?'

'Of course. If you express some milk before you leave, I should be all set.'

'Well, I'll talk you through her bedtime routine as well, so you know what we normally do.'

Her mum studied her face as if she was about to say something, but then she changed her mind. 'Okay, that will be fine.'

Marie's cry sounded from upstairs and Lottie turned to go and get her. 'I'll be back in a minute and we can talk some more,' Lottie said. 'I'm sorry about earlier.' She gave her mum a small smile. She had to let go at some point, and her mum was the best person to help with that.

***

Thierry

It was a small victory to get Lottie to leave Marie with her mum and persuade her out of the house, but Thierry was glad about it, all the same.

'She'll be okay, you know, I'm sure of it, and if there's a problem of any kind, they'll be in touch.' He reached out and squeezed her hand.

Thierry was driving them into town for a meal at a little restaurant Lottie's dad had recommended, and as they got closer to the centre, he began to take in the abundance of flowers everywhere. No wonder Colmar was known as a *ville fleurie*. Geraniums of all types spilled out of flower boxes on bridges, on houses, even at the side of the road, making the town very bright alongside the pastel-coloured timber houses.

'I know Marie will be fine in my heart of hearts, but I'm still worried every time I leave her with someone else. If anything happens to her while she's not in my care, I'll never be able to forgive myself for not being there for her.'

'They all love her as much as you do, and they wouldn't let anything bad happen to her. But I understand how that must feel. It must be hard for you to relax completely, and to put your trust in others when she's so precious to you.'

'I do find it hard, yes, and it's harder still because her dad's not on the scene to share the responsibility. Thanks for being so understanding about it all. You of all people must know how I feel.'

'What do you mean?' He frowned as he glanced over at her, taking his eyes off the road for a split second.

'I think you find it hard to trust people, too. You haven't trusted me enough yet to tell me about your family, for example. I'm not pushing you, but it's the sort of thing we should be sharing with each other.'

Thierry blew out a long breath, surprised by the turn the conversation was taking. 'I told you I'm not close to them, and that's it, there's no more to tell.'

'This is exactly what I mean, Thierry,' she replied, warming to her theme. 'You don't trust me enough to tell me the whole story, but I sense there's much more to it than that. I want to know you more, but you're always holding something back.'

Thierry flexed his fingers on the steering wheel. 'It's not that I don't trust you. It's just that I haven't talked about my family in years. I left home such a long time ago, and it hardly seems worth bringing it all up again now.'

'Wouldn't you think it was odd if I didn't want to talk to you about my family?'

'I suppose, but your relationship with your family is very different to mine.' He sighed, but didn't say any more until they reached the town and he'd parked the car. 'I don't want to talk about this here, or in the restaurant, to be honest. I wanted to give you a good night out, not get bogged down in my miserable past.'

He studied her face for signs that she might change her mind, and let him off the hook, but she remained doggedly silent.

Here goes nothing, he thought. 'I'm an only child. My parents both had high-flying jobs in Paris, so I was brought up by a succession of nannies, none of whose names I can even remember. My parents hardly spent any time with me at home, preferring to spend their time at work or travelling without me. It wasn't that they were unkind; it was more like indifference. I never felt they loved me or wanted me. And as I grew up, after they'd packed me off to boarding school, I knew I had to get out of there as soon as I could, so that's what I did.'

'Have you really not seen them since you were sixteen?' She looked pained at the thought of it.

He shook his head. 'They were my parents in name only. I don't feel any attachment to them at all.'

'But what about when you and Nicole got married? Didn't they come?'

'I didn't ask them. Nicole didn't understand it, either, but she accepted that was how I felt.' He shrugged as if it was all perfectly normal, because to him, it was. He didn't want his parents to take any part in his life.

Lottie took his hand, and he looked up at her in surprise. 'I'm so sorry, Thierry, for what you went through. I must seem so childish to you when I've been complaining about my family. I didn't realise how lucky I was.'

'We all take what we've got for granted, Lottie. I can't pretend I've been any better at that than you.' He thought about Nicole again and briefly closed his eyes.

Lottie seemed to accept that answer and he breathed a sigh of relief, but he'd have to tell her everything else at some point. Still, he was hoping he would have redeemed himself by then.

'Don't you get lonely sometimes without family to call on? It must have been so hard for you when Nicole died, to have to face it all alone.'

'I've always been a loner, but my family's made up of everyone at the vineyard now. They've always looked out for me, and Sylvie took me under her wing when I first came to work here. And I would really like to make things work with you.'

She leaned over and kissed him then. A light brush of her lips on his, but it was so intimate after all the struggles that had gone before. He settled one hand on her lower back and the other at the back of her neck and pulled her gently towards him, and the kiss deepened. The warmth of her lips against his sent tingles down his spine, and he wished there was more space for him to press his body against hers.

All too soon, she pulled away, and he was left wanting, wondering when they might have the chance to kiss again.

Lottie

Lottie was proud of Thierry for finally sharing more of his past with her. It had taken a lot of trust on his part to tell her, but he was a good man, and she wanted him to stop beating himself up about everything that had happened to him.

They were seated at a table in the window of the busy restaurant, and waiting for their starters to come, when Lottie's phone buzzed with a text.

'Everything okay?' Thierry asked, a worried frown on his face.

'Yes, Mum was letting me know that Marie's asleep and everything's good.' She put her phone away and concentrated on her starter, which had just arrived.

'It was nice meeting your granddad at last after hearing you talk so much about him.'

'He's lovely, but he's always been closer to Fran, so it was good to spend time with him and to have him to myself.'

'Did you and Fran get on when you were young?'

'Most of the time. I missed her so much when she left home to go to university, and then when she went on to London. Colmar was never enough for me, not back then, anyway.'

'You didn't want to study yourself?'

Lottie scoffed at the thought of it. 'No, I'm not academic like Fran. I was always getting into trouble at school. All I wanted to do was to travel and see the world. I didn't quite get that far, but I saw a lot of Europe, at least.'

'Where did you go?'

'To Spain, Italy, and down through Croatia to Greece. It was wonderful, until I found out I was pregnant and had to come home again to face the music.'

'Do you mean your family?'

She nodded. 'To be fair, they were much more supportive than I thought they would be. I was such a wild child, and I thought they would be upset with me for being so reckless.'

Lottie ate the last of her salmon starter as Thierry absorbed her words.

'I liked travelling when I was studying to be a winemaker,' he said, 'but my heart's here in Alsace. I don't have any yearning to travel. I feel for Henri. It's going to hit him hard if Ellie goes and he doesn't.'

'I don't understand why he wouldn't want to go with her. Anyone can see how much he loves her.'

Thierry shrugged. 'We're all different, I suppose, but it will be difficult for him without her.'

'It's what she wants to do at this time in her life though, and he has to respect that.'

'Just as she has to accept that travelling might not be for him. But if they want to be together, one of them will have to compromise.'

Lottie was thoughtful for a moment. 'That's what you've done with me. I'm so grateful to you, and proud of you as well, for telling me what happened between you and Nicole, and about your family. I know I kept pushing you, and I'm sorry for that.'

'You were right, though. If we're going to have a future together, you need to be able to trust me, and in the end, that's what gave me the courage to tell you.'

Lottie had just finished eating her main dish of *spaetzle* when her phone buzzed again. This time she read the text from her mum out to Thierry:

Marie just woke up and she has a bit of a temperature. What do you want me to do?

'What do you want to do, Lottie?'

'I think I'd rather go home now. I'll ask her to keep an eye on her temperature, but I feel worried about being so far from home if she's not well.'

Thierry called for the bill straight away and they made their way back to the car.

Lottie was quiet on the way home, checking her phone constantly for updates from her mum and relaying the messages to Thierry.

'She's rocking her back to sleep now, Dad says.'

'I'm sure she'll be fine. Try not to worry,' he finished, laying his hand on hers.

'Honestly, sometimes I feel so overwhelmed by the responsibility of having a whole new life to take care of. I love her so much and I don't want anything to happen to her.'

'Of course, and it won't. You're a great mum.'

Lottie's heart warmed at his words. She hoped she was a good mum, even though the learning curve was enormous.

The minute they arrived back at the farmhouse, she jumped out and ran straight indoors, with Thierry close on her heels.

'Is everything all right, Mum?'

'Yes, darling, she's fine. She's fast asleep now. I'm so sorry. I didn't mean for you to cut your evening short.'

'I'd rather come home and be sure she's okay. I'll pop up and see her.'

Lottie pushed the door to her bedroom open and approached the Moses basket as quietly as she could. Marie was flat on her back and sound asleep, her little chest rising and falling in perfect rhythm. Lottie reached out and stroked her daughter's cheek, releasing a sigh of relief. Her mum and dad had done a great job while she was out, and she was grateful. She shut the door quietly behind her and padded back downstairs to the living room.

'Thanks for looking after her, both of you. She seems fine now.' Lottie worried at her thumbnail even as she said it, feeling guilty for having gone out.

Her mum came over to give her a hug. 'She *is* fine, Lottie. Please don't blame yourself for going out.'

'Did you manage to have a nice evening at least?' her dad asked.

She looked over at Thierry fondly, pushing her struggle with her guilt away. 'It was nice to get out on our own after so long, wasn't it?'

Thierry nodded and smiled back at her. They'd turned a corner today, she thought to herself, and she was relieved. At last they could move on and continue with their relationship, and maybe she could finally find the courage to tell him how much she loved him. It was time to put the past behind them, and to see if they could make a future together. And for her, that meant perhaps she should learn to depend on him more so she could do other things, even if that did leave her feeling guilty some of the time.

CHAPTER TWELVE

Thierry

Thierry lay in the narrow single bed in the spare room the following morning, listening to the sounds of the countryside. A cockerel crowed loudly on one of the neighbouring farms – a stronger alarm call than any electronic device – followed by the church bells ringing seven o'clock. Then silence fell again. It was a rare thing for Thierry to have a lie-in – not something he yearned for when on the vineyard – and he found himself enjoying some time to think before getting up and facing the day.

With Lottie's fiery temper and freedom with her opinions, he hadn't expected her to be so understanding when he'd told her about his family. It had made him regret not having told her sooner. Now he was wondering who else he should have been more open with. Didier and Sylvie, for a start, although they'd never resented him for keeping himself to himself. He regretted that he still hadn't told Lottie everything and he wasn't sure that she would be as sympathetic next time.

He sighed and swung his legs over the edge of the bed. It was still only 7.30 and he didn't want to wake anyone. He walked to the door and opened it a crack to see if there were any signs of life.

'*Bonjour*, Thierry!' Lottie's mum came bustling along the corridor, fully dressed and with a look on her face that told him she was ready for business. 'Did you sleep well?'

'Yes, very well, thank you, Christine.' He ducked behind the door so that only his head was poking out, not wanting Lottie's mum to see him in his boxers. 'I'm going to pop in the shower if that's okay, and I'll be down in a minute.'

'Of course. I'm going down to get breakfast on.'

Thierry re-emerged fifteen minutes later, bumping into Lottie and Marie on the landing this time.

'Morning, you look well-rested,' he said, bending to kiss her cheek. 'Did you two have a good night?'

'We did. I think it must be the difference in the air here or something, but Marie slept straight through. And there's no sign of a temperature this morning, thank goodness.'

'So, Thierry,' Lottie's dad began, as soon as they'd sat down at the breakfast table that was now heaving with homemade pancakes and blueberries, 'I know you're on a break from work, but *Papi* and I wondered if you'd like to visit one of the local vineyards with us this morning, and taste some of the wines here. Lottie and her mum can spend some time together then, as well.'

'You mean we can do the cooking,' Lottie's mum interrupted with a laugh as she sat down at the table herself.

'You go if you want to,' Lottie replied, looking at Thierry with a reassuring smile.

'Are you sure you don't mind?'

'No, honestly.'

They were on their way shortly afterwards, but Thierry still wasn't sure whether Lottie had been happy for him to go. Nor was he entirely sure whether Joseph had an ulterior motive for inviting him out on his own.

'How are things going with you and Lottie?' he asked not long after they'd left.

Thierry's heart sank as his worst fears were realised. 'We're getting on very well.'

'And what are your plans?' her dad continued.

'I don't understand what you mean.'

'You've been seeing each other for quite a while now, as well as living together, and we wondered if you had any plans, you know, to get married.'

'Come on, Joseph. You're putting Thierry in a difficult position. Leave him alone.'

Thank goodness for *Papi*. Thierry had no idea what he would have said otherwise. He wasn't ready to get married again yet, and he didn't think it was Lottie's priority for the time being, either. He hoped it was something they could look forward to in the future, but there was plenty of time for all that.

They arrived at the vineyard for the wine tasting shortly afterwards, and Thierry was spared the embarrassment of any further questioning as they toured the facility. At the end of the tour, they found themselves in the tasting room and shop, and he seized the chance to compare the set-up with their plans for Domaine des Montagnes.

He was impressed with the vineyard's handling of the free tasting. They gave a gift card to each visitor, which was already loaded with a certain amount of money. Visitors then used the card against the wines they wanted to taste, which came in an automatic dispenser. It meant a minimal amount of effort for the staff, and let the visitors make their own choices about what they wanted to taste. They could even top up the card if they wanted to taste a more expensive wine. They left with a couple of bottles of wine each to take home, and Thierry made some mental notes to share with Fran on his return.

Back at the house, the food Lottie and her mum had been cooking smelled divine. Thierry guessed it was roast chicken and his stomach rumbled on cue as they entered the house.

'*Salut, Mesdames,*' Joseph called.

Lottie had a strained look on her face when they walked in, and Thierry worried how she'd got on with her mum in their absence.

'Hey, shall I take Marie? Is she due for a sleep soon?'

'Thanks. Yes, hopefully. Shall we walk round the garden for a few minutes before dinner, to see if that helps?'

Clearly she was desperate to get outside, and Thierry needed the break, too.

'How's it all gone this morning?'

'Mum keeps on telling me I should forget about going back to work and just concentrate on looking after Marie. No amount of telling her I'll need money to live on so that I can look after Marie will make her change her mind. I don't know where she thinks I'll get the money if I don't go out to work.'

'Your dad tried to grill me about what my intentions are towards you when we were out this morning. It's only because *Papi* intervened that I managed to get away without having to reply.'

'Oh my God, Thierry, I'm so sorry. How embarrassing.'

'It was awkward for him to be asking whether we were going to get married when that's the last thing on our minds right now.'

Lottie's face fell. 'We'd better go back in. Marie's fallen asleep already.'

Thierry followed Lottie back inside, surprised by the abrupt end to their discussion. What had he done wrong now?

Lottie

Lottie was quiet again on the journey home. It had been good to see her family, but she was still upset with both her parents when they left. And worse than that, she was hurt by Thierry's seeming lack of interest in a long-term future with her and Marie. She didn't want to get married to him, either, at the moment, but she wouldn't rule it out for the future. She'd thought he felt the same, but that wasn't the impression he'd given her.

'What are you thinking about, Lottie? You've gone quiet again. In fact, you've been off with me since we were in the garden.'

'That's not true at all. I've got a lot on my mind, that's all. And I wish Mum and Dad had more confidence that I'll do what's right for Marie and me, rather than encouraging me to depend on you for everything.'

'They mean well, Lottie, and they only want to help and to see you settled. And we're getting on okay as we are, aren't we?'

She chewed on her lip as she thought about the loss of her job. If she told any of them about that, it would only make everything worse, so she kept it to herself, even though bottling it up was only causing her to feel even more stressed.

'I'll admit I found it hard to accept help at first, but I understood pretty quickly that I wouldn't be able to manage completely on my own. Now I trust you, Sylvie, and Fran to look after Marie in the same way I would, and I'm grateful to Mum and Dad for babysitting this weekend, as well. But just because I'm accepting help, that shouldn't mean I can't think about going back to work. It makes me feel like a failure when Mum says that sort of thing, whether she means it or not. And asking you about our plans only makes me think that Dad thinks I need a man to look after me, too.' Her voice had risen while she was talking and she took a deep breath to try to calm her frustration.

'You don't need a man or anyone else to look after you, but I'm glad that you've let us help you. Your ability to trust others to look after Marie only makes me respect you more. You know you're doing a great job. Don't let others take that away from you. And you don't need to prove yourself to anyone.'

'Thank you.'

Lottie returned to looking out of the window at the vineyards they were passing. She was more confused than ever about Thierry's feelings towards her. He didn't want to marry her – he'd made that clear – but he was happy for her to live with him in his house, which meant he must have some long-term plan with regard to their relationship. For her part, she wanted them to pursue things to see where they might go, but until he confirmed what he was thinking, she wasn't prepared to confess her thoughts. She'd tried that once before with Marie's father and look where that had got her.

They reached the courtyard car park mid-afternoon, and Lottie felt happy to be back home again. They climbed out of the car and Thierry took the car seat out and lifted it onto the pushchair frame.

'I'll see you back at home later, after you've seen Fran,' he said, grabbing their bags.

'Thanks for taking me home this weekend.'

He leaned forward to kiss her and then pulled her into his arms for a brief, warm embrace, before bending down to kiss Marie as well. Lottie's heart warmed at how caring he was becoming towards her daughter. He would make a good dad himself one day, she was sure of it. Mind you, they'd never had that conversation, either, and so she didn't even know if that was something he'd want in the future.

She knocked on the door of the cottage a few minutes later. By the time she'd lifted Marie out of the pushchair there was still no answer, so she knocked again. She should have asked if it would be okay for her to pop in, but they were usually home on Sunday afternoons. She was surprised not to find them in.

As she was turning to put Marie back in her seat, the door opened and Didier appeared.

'My God, Didier, what happened? You look terrible.'

He gave her a tired smile. 'Fran's not been well this weekend, Lottie. I didn't know you were coming. I'm sorry I took a while to come to the door.'

'What's the matter? Is she okay now? Can I see her?'

'Look, come on in and I'll explain.'

'Have you had bad news on the pregnancy front again?' she asked, once they were inside.

He nodded. 'It was a week or so ago when she did the test, and I thought she was dealing with it okay, but it's hit her hard this weekend.'

'Can I see her?'

'Yes, she's upstairs. Chlöe's with my mum, so you can leave Marie with me.' He reached out to take the baby, and Lottie made her way upstairs, worried sick.

She tapped lightly on their bedroom door. 'Fran, it's me. Can I come in?'

She pushed the door gently open when Fran didn't reply. Her sister was lying on her bed, curled up on her side. Lottie wasn't even sure whether she'd heard her come in.

She sat down next to her. 'Fran, I'm so sorry.'

Fran's sobbing was the only sound in the room. Lottie reached for her sister and drew her into her arms, wishing there was something she could say to make her feel better.

'I'm sorry, Lottie. I don't want you to see me like this.' She sat back and wiped her face with a tissue.

'Don't be silly. I love you and you can always talk to me about anything. Didier said you found out a week or so ago. You can tell me when you're feeling low, you know. You don't always have to put on a front.'

'I'm trying not to keep going on about it. I must be driving Didier mad.' She tried to laugh but it came out as a sob.

'It's good for you to talk about it, Fran. Don't keep it all inside. That won't be good for you at all.' She patted Fran's hand, wishing she could make everything okay. Even though she hadn't planned to be a mum, she counted herself so lucky to have Marie. Lottie had spent much of her young life envying Fran for her achievements and her easy social skills, and yet here she was with the one thing her sister wanted more than anything else in the world. And she would give anything to make that wish come true for her.

Thierry

Thierry was up early the next morning and waiting in the office with Henri when Didier arrived.

'God, Didier, you don't look well enough to be here. Are you ill?' He frowned at his friend. Lottie had told him Fran wasn't well, but she hadn't said any more than that.

'No, it's just been a bit of a difficult weekend, and I haven't had a lot of sleep. We found out Fran's not pregnant again, and she sank into a complete depression. There wasn't anything I could say to make her feel better. Mum looked after Chlöe for us, and I spent the whole weekend taking care of Fran as best I could. She won't be in today for obvious reasons, and I'd be grateful if you didn't bring it up when she's back. She's going to be fragile for a while.'

'I'm so sorry, Didier.' Henri put a cup of hot coffee in front of him.

'I dropped Lottie off at yours last night because she wanted to see Fran. I hope that was okay.'

'I wasn't sure at first, and I did ask Lottie to keep it to herself, by the way, but then when Lottie went up to see her, I think it did help to cheer Fran up a little. I spent some time with Marie, as well, which did wonders for my spirits.'

'What will you do now?'

'I guess we're going to keep trying, but my main worry is that I don't know how all this is going to affect her mental health, if we keep chasing this dream. I know she wants a baby of her own and I understand that, but I don't think we should keep pursuing it at any cost, you know.'

Thierry and Henri nodded. Thierry hated to see his friend suffering in this way, let alone what it must be doing to Fran.

'I popped in early to tell Fran about some wine tastings we did at the weekend, but I can catch up with her another time.'

'Yes, I thought you were in the office early. Did you have a good weekend?'

'We did, yes, thanks.' He wanted to say that he and Lottie may have turned a corner in their relationship, but after their conversation in the garden and in the car, he wasn't sure any more.

Thierry said his goodbyes and went back outside to do his vineyard inspection. He tucked his scarf in around the neck of his jacket and pulled his gloves on. The ground wasn't so wet now, but he still wore his boots. There were only a few clouds in the bright blue sky this morning, but there was always a risk of early morning frost.

He said good morning to the workers, who were busy ploughing the soil beneath the vines, and carried out a quick check for any signs of disease on the new buds as he walked. With his eagle eye, he was used to spotting signs of mildew or other disease from a distance.

He had a lot of work still to do with last year's wines too, and this was now urgent, as soon he would have to spend more and more time outside working on the present year's harvest. He planned to spend the whole afternoon filtering wines from their sediment and readying those that needed a second fermentation to go into casks.

Lottie had told him she'd make something for lunch for them both, and by the time midday came round, he was starving.

'*Salut!*' he called, taking his boots off at the front door. 'How are you today?'

'We're fine. How are you?' Lottie asked, kissing him on both cheeks as he came into the kitchen.

'It was cold out there first thing, but it's turned into a nice spring day. Everything's going well in the vineyard, I think.'

Lottie handed Marie to him and he cooed over her while she finished putting things out on the table for lunch.

'I saw Didier in the office this morning and he told me the latest about Fran. How was she when you saw her last night?'

'Yes, I'm sorry I couldn't say much last night. He wanted to tell you himself, I think. Fran looked terrible, to be honest.' She frowned. 'It's hit her very hard, and I don't know how much longer she can take these disappointments.'

'Didier would be happy for them to stop trying now. He doesn't want her to be hurt any more than she already has been.'

'He can't protect her from that hurt though, can he?'

'No, but it doesn't mean he won't try. He loves her.' Thierry shrugged, as if that was all there was to it.

'He does, and that only makes it all the more difficult for him to keep seeing her so upset.'

They sat down to the warm quiche Lottie had made, along with some fresh coleslaw.

'This is delicious, Lottie. You're a great cook, you know.'

'Thanks.' She gave him a shy grin at his compliment. 'I do like cooking, I must admit, but I don't ever seem to have the time for it, especially now. Maybe I ought to give it more of a go.'

'Have you heard anything more from the nursery about going back to work?' He still didn't want her to go back, but he knew better than to tell her that.

Lottie hesitated for a moment, and Thierry wondered if there was something she wasn't telling him. 'No. I don't have a date for going back to work yet. I'm using my savings to keep me going.'

'You don't need to worry about money, Lottie. I can cover what you need.'

'I appreciate the offer, but I like to have my own money, so I'll need to get back to work soon,' she said firmly.

'I'm surprised they haven't been in touch with you already, if they want you to come back so much. Maybe you should give the nursery another ring to find out what their plans are.' He secretly hoped they didn't want to offer her her old job after all, and then she wouldn't have to go back to work.

'Yes, I might do that this afternoon,' she said without looking up from her plate.

There was something she wasn't telling him, he was sure of it, but if he pushed her, it would only lead to another argument.

Lottie

The wine bar was unusually quiet when Lottie arrived with Fran and Ellie, which made it easier for the three women to chat and bring each other up to date about their lives. Lottie had asked Thierry to babysit for her so she could go out with them, and although she was nervous about leaving Marie for the whole evening again, she was doing her best not to worry.

'I've been looking after Marie with you since the day she was born, so why should it be any different for me to babysit if you go out for the evening? You've expressed the milk I'll need, so I'm all set. I promise I'll let you know if there are any problems, but I'm sure there won't be.'

There was no getting past Thierry when he was that determined, so here she was, sitting in the wine bar sipping at a chilled glass of pinot blanc, and trying not to fret. She stopped thinking about Thierry and Marie and focused instead on what Fran was saying.

'It's been so difficult dealing with the stress of it all every month. You know, I feel constantly anxious once the ovulation period has passed and I'm waiting to see if I'm pregnant again. And last weekend, the sadness of it all was overwhelming. But then I bounce back again when I know that we have another chance at it.'

Lottie reached out to pat her hand. 'You look a hundred times better than when I saw you last week, and I'm relieved about that.' She smiled at her sister.

'Didier's been so good to me, and I know it's just as hard for him to deal with all the emotions involved. I honestly couldn't be doing all this without him.'

'Literally!' Ellie laughed, and Lottie and Fran joined in.

'How about you, Ellie? How are your travel plans going?' Fran asked.

'I'm almost ready to go. I'm just hanging on a bit longer to try to persuade Henri to come with me.'

'Well done for being bold and asking him,' Lottie said.

'I still don't know if he'll say yes. He's a home bird, by his own admission, so I don't know if he'll change his mind. I'll miss him so much if he decides not to come with me.'

'Of course you will,' Fran agreed.

'I know it's going to be difficult without me here to help you, and if Henri were to come with me, it would be even harder. He said Didier had told him he wouldn't mind if he came with me, though.'

'Did he?' Fran's surprise was evident, and Ellie reached out and patted her on the arm by way of apology, knowing how much extra work that would mean for her friend.

'We'll have to wait and see. I'm not holding my breath, to be honest, but I'm still going to go, regardless.'

'We're always busy, but recently I've been enjoying my work more,' Fran told them. 'And I think a lot of that's down to Thierry.'

'Really? Why's that?' Lottie was all ears.

'He's been advising me on how to decorate and furnish the new tasting room at the Visitors' Centre. This is based on research he's been doing visiting other places to see what their set-up is like. He told me he went to a vineyard with *Papi* and Dad while he was away with you, Lottie.'

'That's lovely of him, isn't it?' Ellie beamed at Lottie.

'Yes, it is. Thierry and I had a good weekend, and things were going well, but then he said he had no thoughts of marriage at the moment, and I didn't know how to take it. I'm not thinking about marriage yet, either, but I was looking at a more settled relationship. I wouldn't have moved in with him if I hadn't been sure he was in this for the long term.'

Fran frowned at her sister, confused. 'And you're already living with each other, so surely marriage is the next step.'

'Exactly.' Lottie sighed. 'Every time I think I know where I stand, something else happens and I end up confused.' She still hadn't told him she loved him, though, and that thought made her feel terrible. Maybe he thought she wasn't in it for the long term, either.

'Maybe you should ask him what his plans are,' Ellie offered.

'That would be the sensible thing to do, but you know me.' Lottie laughed, but her heart tightened once again at the thought that Thierry might not see a real future for them. She didn't want to go down that road, especially now she had Marie to think about.

'Time for another round of drinks, I think, and then Ellie can tell us where she's going to go on her travels.' Fran waved the waiter over to order more drinks and then disappeared off to the ladies.

'I feel selfish for adding to all Fran's woes by upping and leaving when she needs me most.' Ellie's face fell.

'Don't be silly. She knows you want to go, and perhaps now is the best time for you to go, while you've got no other commitments.' Lottie wasn't sure whether to reveal to Ellie that, anyway, there was no money in the budget for the rest of the work to be done on the château. She didn't even know if Fran knew about it.

'But Fran was probably hoping I'd be able to help with finishing off the Visitors' Centre and now she'll have to manage it all on her own.'

'What sort of thing would you have been doing at the Centre, then?'

'I've only been helping with admin so far because I've had the château to work on as well, but I think she's going to need someone to carry on doing the admin when I leave, as well as helping to run the tasting room and shop.'

'That sounds like a lot of work for Fran to do on her own, certainly, and if she does fall pregnant, it could all get too much for her. I suppose she'll advertise soon enough.'

Once again Lottie thought to herself that doing the admin would be the perfect job for her, and something she could do with Marie in tow, as well. But before she started to get her hopes up, she brought herself up sharp. She couldn't ask Fran to give her that job, not while Ellie was still here. How would that look to her friend? She frowned, then she groaned inwardly at her next thought: Fran might think she was using her to solve her problems, and she didn't want to put her in that situation.

CHAPTER THIRTEEN

Thierry

Thierry woke to dark, thunderous clouds and as soon as he'd left the house, he could feel that the air was heavy with rain. By the time he reached the château, persistent raindrops were already striking the ground, and his heart sank. If the new shoots were knocked off, the vines might never recover before the harvest in the autumn. Besides the size of the harvest, the quality of the resulting wine could also be affected, and this was something he and Didier had had to deal with before.

Didier's face was like granite when they met by the first rows of vines, and his tension matched Thierry's own. They didn't say a word to each other as they walked down the slope. When they reached the junction of the two fields, they split off, going their separate ways. Thierry followed the pinot noir vines, anxiously checking for rain damage, as well as for mildew or other diseases caused by the wet conditions. He walked up and down dozens of rows, concerned about how weighted down the foliage was by the rain – so much so the leaves were almost touching the stony soil – and was relieved when he reached the final row without having seen any sign of disease or damage. Didier had already moved on to the next plot of vines and Thierry did the same, this time inspecting the pinot blanc. They spent a full hour on their inspection before they met up at the bottom of the slope, having checked all the vines as best they could.

'How did it all look to you?' Didier asked, his features more relaxed now.

'I don't think there's any mildew or damage on the areas I inspected. You?'

'It was all clear for me, too. Depending on the weather tomorrow, we should do another inspection to check the buds.'

'Agreed.'

The rain had already begun to ease up as they made their way back to the courtyard.

'I met with Fran the other day to talk about how we're going to hold the wine tastings in the new Visitors' Centre,' Thierry said on the way.

'Yes, she said how well everything's coming together.'

'Have you spoken to her about stopping work on the château so that there's enough money to finish the centre? It would be such a weight off her mind to know that's what you're definitely going to do.'

'I know you're right, and we have discussed the options, but I haven't finally made my mind up yet. If we stop work on the château, where does that leave Ellie?'

'But Ellie wants to travel anyway, so surely if she knows there's no money in the budget, that would free her up to go, with no regrets.'

'And how will Henri view that, if he doesn't go with her? He'll think I'm pushing her away.' Didier sighed and Thierry appreciated his dilemma.

They went back to the office, which was now empty, as it was lunchtime. Thierry walked over to the sink to wash his hands.

'The reality is that the Visitors' Centre can start bringing in income almost straight away, so I don't think you've got a lot of choice about this,' he said.

'About what?' Henri asked, entering the main office from the back room.

Thierry and Didier stared at him, both men feeling awkward. Henri looked from one to the other, and when neither of them replied immediately, he shrugged and took a seat behind his desk.

'We were talking about the Visitors' Centre and the château, and the fact that there's not enough money to finish them both off right now,' Didier said finally.

'Are you going to go with finishing the Visitors' Centre, then?'

'I haven't decided yet. I don't want you or Ellie to feel under any pressure from me. But I have to be honest and agree that stopping work on the château until our funds improve does make more sense. I know this isn't what you want to hear, Henri. I'm sorry.'

Henri's downcast face was making Thierry feel guilty and the decision wasn't even anything to do with him, so goodness knows how Didier must be feeling.

'Once Ellie hears this, there'll be nothing to keep her here, which is why I've kept it to myself. I'm ready to settle down with her, but she's made it clear that's not the life she wants.'

'It may be that it's not the life she wants right at this moment, Henri, but she loves you and she'll come back. I have no doubt about that, and nor does Fran.'

'If she did love me, she'd stay.'

'That's not fair, Henri. You have to let her go and do what she wants to do, if you want any chance of her coming back to you.' Thierry understood his frustration but he was sure about this. 'If you stand in her way, you risk losing her altogether.'

Henri looked at Didier. 'When will you tell her?'

'I think it would be best coming from Fran, but I haven't confirmed it with her yet. She has enough to deal with at the moment.'

'This would be one less worry for her, though,' Thierry said.

'Yes, you're probably right. But I don't want her to feel we're pushing Ellie away. And it won't matter about the money if Fran feels she's lost her friend.'

'Maybe you should talk to Ellie first, then?'

Didier looked at Thierry as if he was mad. 'What, and leave Fran in the dark? She wouldn't thank me for that.'

'*Merde!* I don't know. I'm trying to come up with solutions. You're treading on eggshells, it seems to me. You know the truth of the situation, so tell them and leave them to handle it in their own way.'

'It's easy for you to say, but you won't be the one having to tell them the bad news, will you?'

'No, I accept that, but if it was me, I think I would rather know than be kept in the dark.'

Lottie

Thierry had left early that morning when Lottie was up feeding Marie, and she'd heard the heavy rain that followed his departure. It had been a terrible week for rain and he was worried about the vines. She'd managed to go back to sleep for a couple of hours until Marie's next cry and she was pleased to see the day was much brighter. They were going to see Sylvie, so she was glad to be up reasonably early.

After a quick breakfast, they were on their way to the village, stopping off only at the *boulangerie* to buy some lunch.

'Ah, Lottie and Marie, how wonderful to see you both,' Sylvie said, opening the door a few minutes later. Frédéric's house was similar to Sylvie's; it was painted a bright pastel colour in the Alsatian way and had the traditional timber frame, but it was much bigger than Sylvie's cottage, with plenty of room for Chlöe to come and stay. The small front garden was immaculate, with neat clipped hedges bordering a short path to the door and an abundance of spring flowers. Everywhere Lottie looked, there was colour: red and pink geraniums and petunias tumbling from pots, and tulips, irises, hyacinths, and delphiniums in the borders. The smell was heavenly.

'I was just admiring your garden,' she said, lifting Marie out of the pushchair. She passed her to Sylvie for a cuddle, then grabbed her bags and followed Sylvie inside.

'Thank you. Frédéric has put me in charge of the front garden only, for now, so I don't overdo it, and it's looking much better. I hope to be able to get out in the back garden eventually.'

Lottie walked over to the picture window at the back of the lounge which gave onto the back garden. 'Oh goodness, that's a much bigger garden for you to be tackling, but you'll get there in time.' She bent down to retrieve her parcel. 'I popped into the *boulangerie* and bought us some fresh tomato tarts for lunch.'

'That was kind of you. I'll look forward to that. So, how have you both been? Marie looks like she's going from strength to strength.'

Lottie took Marie from her so she could make drinks, giving her daughter a hug. Marie gurgled at her and grasped a lock of her hair gently. Lottie kissed her on the cheek before sitting down to feed her. 'She's doing really well. We had a good time with my parents and granddad the other weekend too, and Thierry's helping me with all her care now.'

'That is good to hear. And is there any news about you getting your old job back? It's only that I heard some gossip in the village and I wondered if it might affect you.'

Lottie's face fell. 'What have you heard, Sylvie?'

'That the nursery's been struggling. I heard they'd been considering laying people off to save money. I was worried you'd be one of the first to go, as you only started work there recently.'

'Well, that's exactly what has happened. I'm sorry I haven't told you myself, Sylvie. I was so mortified about losing my job, and I was embarrassed to admit it to everyone. I wanted to try to sort it out for myself. I hope you're not too cross with me.'

'You know I'm not cross, but I do wish you'd let us help you sometimes, rather than always trying to do everything yourself. Even being able to talk to someone about it might have helped.'

'I know, but what can anyone do? This is for me to sort out on my own.'

''What about talking to Fran and Didier to see if there's anything available at the domaine? With Ellie going, and maybe Henri, they're sure to need some help with all the work they currently have.'

'That has crossed my mind, but I don't want to bother them when they've got so much else to deal with right now. And I don't want them to give me a job because they feel they have to.'

'I don't think they would ever do that. If you don't mind me saying, you need to get over your pride and speak to your sister. If she doesn't even know you're looking for a job, how can she help you?'

Lottie pondered that for a moment. Could she summon up the courage to have a chat with Fran next time she saw her?

'I'll try, Sylvie. I need to do something soon because I've already had to dig into my savings. It's getting more and more urgent for me to find something.'

'It's such a shame about the nursery. You were so happy there and well-suited to the job, as well. Still, it's worth speaking to Fran, especially as I imagine you only want something part-time and in the village.'

'Yes, that's right. I couldn't rely on public transport to get me anywhere, and it would take me away from Marie for too long if I got a job elsewhere.' She sighed and popped Marie onto her shoulder.

'I have a good feeling this will all sort itself out for you.' Sylvie smiled. 'Shall we have some lunch now? You can tell me more about how you're getting on with Thierry.'

Frédéric joined them from the garden, where he'd obviously been beavering away, but Lottie's mind was on other things. She was still wondering whether she could speak to Fran about a job on the vineyard. She didn't want to get her hopes up too soon, but it would be so perfect for her and Marie, and it would sort out all her financial problems at the same time.

Thierry

Thierry was glad to see that Fran was looking much better when he arrived for the meeting with her, Didier, and Henri in the Visitors' Centre later that morning. He wanted so much for things to work out for her and Didier – they truly deserved it.

'Okay, everyone,' Fran began, 'let's make a start. First of all, I wanted to update you on where we are. Now we've stopped work on the château, we're making much faster progress with the centre, as you can see. The floor has been finished, and the builders have put some of the wine racks in already. The air conditioning is going in later this week, and after that, the equipment we ordered to chill wines or keep them at suitable temperatures will be arriving. Thanks to Thierry, we've also ordered some dispensers to deliver the wine directly to customers when they reach the tasting room after the tour.'

'When do you think we'll be ready to open?' Thierry asked, glad that Didier had obviously told Fran about the finances and that everything was now out in the open.

'Well, the centre should be finished by the end of this month at the latest, but I also need to think about staff. I'd wanted Ellie to continue helping me with the admin once the centre opened, so I'll need someone else for that now.' She paused to look apologetically at Henri. 'And I'll need people to help run the shop and tastings, as well.'

'I'll speak to *Maman* to see if she knows of anyone.' Didier smiled at Fran, and Thierry caught the look that passed between them. Their love was obvious for all to see and an unexpected stab of envy passed through him. Since coming back from her parents' house, he and Lottie hadn't been able to regain the closeness they'd been sharing before, and he missed it.

Fran tapped her finger against her chin. 'Is there anything else I haven't thought of?'

'I could organise the stock, manage the wine in the shop, and help with tastings sometimes.'

'That would be great, Thierry, thank you. Oh, and the photos we had taken of the vineyard will be arriving in their frames next week. So they'll just need hanging.'

'I think you've covered everything, Fran. You've done a great job getting it all off the ground. We never thought it would happen.' Henri gave her a little round of applause and she blushed.

'There is one other thing we need to consider about the business as a whole,' Fran continued.

'What's that?' Thierry asked. Was this yet another change he wasn't prepared for?

'We need to consider how we'd manage if Henri decides to go with Ellie.'

Henri's hands flew to his face. 'I can't believe she told you that when I haven't even given her my reply yet.'

'So she's asked you to go with her. Good for her.' Didier clapped Henri on the back. 'I've told you we can manage without you if you want to go.'

'I know, but I don't know what I'm going to do yet. I've hardly had time to think about it myself.'

'It will be hard for us to manage without you, for sure, but we will manage, Henri. Don't let your loyalty to the vineyard stop you from going with Ellie, if that's where you want to be.'

Fran stepped over to give him a hug, and silence fell in the room as they considered how everything was changing.

Thierry walked back towards the office with Henri after the meeting, leaving Fran and Didier to talk on their own in the Visitors' Centre.

'What would you do if you were me, Thierry?'

Thierry's heart sank at the thought of having to give Henri advice. 'I don't know. I'm not much of a travelling man myself, so I can understand how you don't want to go. But that's not the issue, is it?'

'No, Ellie's the issue, and I love her. It's as simple as that. I don't want to lose her by not going with her, but I also love my life here, and there doesn't seem to be any way for me to balance those two things.'

'You're going to have to compromise if you want to do that. Fran and Didier have given you the freedom to go, so if you love Ellie, you should tell her and go with her. That would be my advice. And it's only for six months, which isn't that long in the grand scheme of things. Everything here will carry on and we'll survive without you until you return.' Thierry wondered exactly how they would manage, but didn't tell Henri that.

Henri gave him a long look. 'Maybe you're right. It's time I stopped worrying about it and got on with it.'

As Henri set off in the direction of the château, Thierry made his way towards the vineyard, wondering what the future might hold for him and Lottie. They'd been getting on so well, but every time he thought that, something else happened to make him think she wasn't as ready for a long-term relationship as he was. Her parents obviously thought they were destined to stay together, and that was what he wanted, too. He couldn't fathom what Lottie wanted, and the more he asked her, the more she backed away. He still had to tell her the final piece of information about his past, but he wasn't going to put himself through all that if she wasn't interested in a proper future with him.

He'd advised Henri to talk to Ellie and to tell her his feelings, and perhaps that was what he should do with Lottie. Maybe it was time to ask her what she was looking for from him, and to tell her what his intentions were in return. At least then they would both know where they stood, rather than dancing around each other, wondering what the other one wanted. They'd been seeing each other for long enough now. It was time to make up their minds.

Lottie

'Hello?' Lottie was standing in the newly refurbished kitchen of the château, looking for Ellie. Marie wriggled in her arms, wanting to see everything, so she held on tight to her while turning circles to show her the sights.

'Coming!' Ellie called a moment later.

Lottie wandered into the main living room, hardly able to believe the transformation since she'd last been here. It had looked good then, but now it was fully restored to its former splendour. All the walls had been replastered and the ceilings had new decorative mouldings. The stone floors had all been repaired, and there were new painted wooden doors that were more in keeping with the original 18th-century building. Lottie kept noticing all the little details as she carried Marie through the rooms on the lower floor. Just as she reached the hallway, she heard Ellie coming down the stairs, and she and Marie both looked up. That's when Lottie gasped.

The wooden staircase and balustrade had been polished until they shone. The carpet had been removed for the time being because there was still work to be done upstairs, but the staircase looked magnificent.

'Wow, Ellie. You've done an amazing job here. You must be so pleased.'

'Thank you, I am. The builders have worked so hard, and it looks completely different, doesn't it?' Ellie chucked Marie under the chin, making the baby laugh.

'Shall we go and get some lunch?'

'I'll grab my coat. It's good to see you both. How are you doing?'

'We're pretty good.'

'And how's everything with you and Thierry since I last saw you?'

'It's about the same. I just don't know where we go from here. I need reassuring that his heart's really in this relationship.'

'He's always given me the impression he's head over heels for you.'

'I'm still not convinced about that.'

Lottie strapped Marie in the pushchair and joined Ellie on the path back up to the courtyard.

'I have some good news,' Ellie said, when they were halfway up the hill. She paused to look at Lottie, who raised her eyebrows. 'Henri told me yesterday that he's going to come with me when I go travelling. I still can't believe it.'

'Oh, my goodness, that's great news.' Lottie stopped the pushchair and threw her arms around her friend.

'Now he's told me, there's no reason to delay. Fran and Didier have diverted the rest of their budget from the château to finishing the Visitors' Centre, and my job is on hold. So we might as well get going as soon as we can.'

Ellie's face glowed with excitement, and Lottie felt a twinge of envy. She remembered that feeling of itchy feet all too well and had loved looking forward to discovering new places. But she wouldn't swap her new life for a moment. She looked down at Marie, who was dozing off, and her love for her daughter swelled inside her. There would be plenty of time to travel in the future.

'Where are you going to go first, do you think?'

'Paris. I've only ever travelled through on my way home, and Henri's never been. This time I want to explore it before we work our way around France and then down into Spain or Italy. I'd like to go even further than that, but with only six months to play with, we'll probably stick to Europe.'

'That all sounds wonderful, and Paris is especially lovely in the spring and summer.' Lottie had some wonderful memories of her previous visits to Paris before she'd met Yiannis, when her life was a lot less complicated.

Ellie looped her arm through hers. 'I hope you'll tell me all the best places to visit. You can be our travel guide and feel like you're doing it along with us.'

Lottie was glad she understood how she felt. 'I'll be happy to guide you, and you can tell me about any new places you think I should go when Marie's a bit older.'

'It's a deal. Anyway, you'll be going back to work soon, won't you? That'll take your mind off travelling.'

'Not at the nursery, no.'

Ellie stopped on the path and turned to her. 'What do you mean? I thought you went in to see them the other day to sort it all out.'

'I did, and that's when they told me they can't take me back. There's no work and no money to pay me with. I finally told Sylvie about it yesterday because she'd heard some gossip about the nursery in the village. I didn't want to admit to the others because they'll get on at me about what I should and shouldn't do next.'

'What *are* you going to do next?'

'I don't know. Thierry keeps telling me I don't need to work, that he'll support me. But I don't want to be dependent on him in that way. And besides, I like working.'

'You should tell Fran. With Henri and me leaving, she's going to need someone to help with the admin for the estate as well as running the new Visitors' Centre. You could do that part-time and they'd still be better off financially because they wouldn't be paying the two of us.'

'I have thought about it, but I don't want Fran to offer me a job out of pity, and I didn't want you to feel I was jumping into your shoes before you've even left.'

Ellie rolled her eyes. 'Stop worrying about it and do it. It makes absolute sense, and Fran would be delighted to be working with you.'

'Do you think so? I want her to do it for the right reasons, not because I'm her sister.'

'Stop being so hard on yourself. You'll be a great asset to the vineyard. Anyway, if you don't tell her, I will.' Ellie gave her a grin, and Lottie had to laugh at her friend's bold declaration. She was going to miss her while she was away.

CHAPTER FOURTEEN

<u>Thierry</u>

Dr Bartin looked at Thierry over her horn-rimmed glasses as he told her how things had gone since his last visit. She made a couple of notes as he spoke, but mostly she paid attention to what he was saying.

'We had a great trip to her parents, and when Lottie asked me about my family, I was honest with her.'

'And have you told Lottie the full story about what happened between you and Nicole yet?'

'No, I'm still afraid of how she might react to it. But we are talking more, and her positive reaction to everything has really helped me.'

'That's good news, then, for the most part. You should be proud of yourself for being more truthful with Lottie. That will allow her to trust you more and, in turn, your relationship will develop and deepen, if that's what you want to happen.'

'It is what I want to happen, definitely. But right now, I don't know where we stand.'

He told the counsellor about the way things had changed between them after her dad had asked him what his intentions were.

'And since then, I don't know how to get us back to where we were. On top of that, she still wants to go out to work, even though I've told her I can support her and Marie on my salary. But I don't know how to make her see sense on that issue, so I've kept quiet about it for now.'

Dr Bartin laughed. 'You still have a way to go on this, Thierry. It's very domineering when you describe it as 'making her see sense'. It sounds like you're only paying attention to what you want, rather than wondering why Lottie doesn't want to accept your offer. What is it she wants?'

'She's determined to go back to work. But surely it makes sense for me to help her when she's struggling right now.' He shrugged, genuinely confused about why Lottie didn't get his point of view on this issue.

The counsellor thought for a moment. 'Maybe Lottie doesn't want to be dependent on you. Perhaps she wants to prove herself capable of bringing her daughter up herself. So what's stopping her from doing that?'

'She's on maternity leave at the moment and living off her savings. I don't think she has much money left now, so she's trying to go back to work part-time.'

'My advice would be to support her in her efforts. Maybe you could offer to babysit for her while she's at work, for example, which would be a great weight off her mind.'

'Well, I'll give it some thought.'

Dr Bartin consulted her notes again. 'And how have you been getting on with the baby?'

Thierry's face lit up. 'Spending time with Lottie's daughter has made me realise I could be a good dad. I wasn't ready to be a father when Nicole pressed me about it, but now things have changed. I've changed.'

'How do you feel about having children of your own now?'

Thierry held his hands up. 'I'm coming round to it. It's likely that Lottie will want to have more children, but when I tell her how I was with Nicole, it could be a deal-breaker for her if she thinks I still feel the same way.'

'Wouldn't it be better to be completely honest with her?'

'I'll have to tell her at some point, but I'm worried she'll reject me completely then, and I'm not sure I can face it.'

'And how do you feel about having children with Lottie?'

'If Lottie can get past the way I treated Nicole, then I would be happy to have children with her. But telling Lottie the truth is the most important thing at the moment, and I don't know how to do it.'

'Isn't this what you want most of all? To move on from your past so that you can build a new life with Lottie and her baby? If it is, then you need to find a way to have this discussion so you both know where you stand.'

'But what if I tell her and she rejects me? How will I handle it?'

'I think it's time for you to be honest with yourself. If you love Lottie – and I think you do – she needs to know that you've moved on from your wife's death, and that you want to live a full life with her, including possibly having more children together. If you can show her honestly that that's how you feel, she'll respect you more for that. You just need to decide whether you can take the risk of rejection.'

Once again, Thierry's mind was overwhelmed when he left Dr Bartin's office. He'd been putting off having this honest discussion with Lottie since they'd come back from her parents, but Dr Bartin was right: he needed to tell her exactly how he felt.

Before he could do that, there was one more thing standing in his way – something that, once done, might allow him to forgive himself at last. He shuddered at the idea of confronting one of his remaining fears. He'd been avoiding it for nearly two years, but as the anniversary of Nicole's death was approaching, now was the right time for him to find the courage to do it at last.

Lottie

Lottie's day got off to a great start when she received a cheque from *Papi* in the post as promised. He'd been so generous and the money would help as a backup while she still wasn't working. She decided to call him straight away to thank him.

'*Allo, Papi, c'est* Lottie.'

'Ah, Lottie, it's great to hear from you. How are things?'

'Much better for me, as I just received your kind gift. Thank you.'

'It was my pleasure and I'm glad if it helps you. Is there any news on the job front?'

She still didn't want to tell her family until she'd spoken to Fran. 'Not yet, but there's something that might come off for me, so keep your fingers crossed.'

They chatted for a while longer, then she rang off just as Thierry was coming back in from his morning tour of the estate.

'*Bonjour*, Thierry.'

'*Ça va?*' He kissed her on both cheeks.

'Yes, all good today, thank you.'

Marie kicked her feet in her rocker as soon as she saw him and the smile that passed between them filled Lottie's heart with joy.

'So, what are you getting up to today?' he asked, once he had Marie in his arms.

'I want to go and see Fran, and I wondered if you might be able to look after Marie for me for a little while, please.'

'Okay, no worries. Take your time, we'll be fine.'

'There's milk in the fridge, and I should be back by lunchtime at the latest.'

Lottie hurried up the hill to the office and found Fran busy at her desk as always. This time she'd texted her beforehand so that she was expecting her.

'*Bonjour, tout le monde,*' she said, stepping inside.

'*Salut*, Lottie,' Fran replied. 'I'm going to pop out with Lottie for a short while, Henri. I'll have the phone with me.'

Henri nodded and returned to the pile of papers on his desk.

'How are you then, Lottie? Is everything okay? Your text sounded pretty urgent.'

'Everything's fine, but I did want to talk to you about something important.'

Fran let them into the cottage shortly afterwards and went to make a drink. Lottie sat down at the breakfast bar and collected her thoughts. By the time Fran turned round and gave her her full attention, she was ready.

'So, the first thing is that I've lost my job at the nursery.'

'Oh no! What happened?'

Lottie filled Fran in on the background, then added, 'The thing is, I've known for a while, but I've kept it to myself because I didn't want everyone giving me their opinion about what I should do next. I do want to work, although only part-time, so I don't have to be dependent on Thierry for everything. That's not how I want to live my life, but he doesn't agree with me, and I'm sure Mum would feel the same. Still, I'm determined to find something.'

'Okay, I can understand that. But where are you going to get another job?'

'That's where I'm hoping you might come in. I've held off asking you about this, because I didn't want to be insensitive about Ellie leaving, but she's insisted I talk to you about whether there's any chance of me helping you out when she goes travelling with Henri.' Lottie released the breath she didn't realise she'd been holding.

Fran's eyes widened. 'Is Henri definitely going away? She hasn't confirmed that with me.'

Lottie felt the blood drain from her face. 'Oh God. I thought she would have told you by now. She told me last week, so I thought you must know.'

'No, she hasn't told me yet, but listen, it's fine. I knew it was a possibility. If it was only Ellie going, I don't think there would be a job for you, but if Henri is going too, then I could do with some help, even if only part-time. I'll have to talk to Didier about it, so I can't promise it's a yes immediately, but I think he'll agree when he finds out about Henri.'

'Are you sure? I don't want you to feel obliged just because I'm your sister.'

'You know I wouldn't make a decision based on that, no matter how much I love you. But this will make sense. So let me speak to Didier and I'll get back to you.'

'Okay, thanks so much, Fran. I hope Thierry will be pleased for me when I tell him, and happy to babysit for me sometimes – but are you okay with me bringing Marie with me occasionally, too?'

'We can be flexible about how best to work around you. You could even work from home some of the time.'

Lottie reached out to embrace her sister. 'I can't tell you how much this means to me.'

'You'll be doing me a big favour yourself, so it's a win all round.'

They walked back to the courtyard and Lottie said goodbye to Fran with another hug before making her way home. She was so pleased with herself for having had the courage to speak to Fran, and hopeful that Didier would agree when she asked him. Now all she had to do was work out how she was going to tell Thierry once she'd got confirmation. He had to be pleased for her, surely. This way, she would feel independent to some degree and Thierry would be able to help her with Marie, as well. And they could finally start to look to the future together. Maybe this would be the push they needed to have the conversation they'd both been avoiding since they'd come home from her parents' as well.

Thierry

Everyone said that the first anniversaries were the hardest to get through after the death of someone you love. Thierry couldn't argue with that. Nicole's birthday and the anniversary of her death had been two of the hardest days of his life last year, and today, the second anniversary of her death, was turning out to be just as diffi-cult. The first anniversary had been a blur that he'd got through only by keeping himself mindlessly busy, but this time he'd been playing over the events of that final day in minute detail, and it was proving almost impossible to close himself off to that constant loop.

He'd given himself a specific job to do today, and he tried to concentrate on it to take his mind off the painful memories intruding into his thoughts. In the two years since Nicole's death, he'd never been back to the churchyard to visit her grave. This was one more thing to feel guilty about. He'd thought about going many times, but in the end, he'd never had the strength to follow through. But today was different. He wanted to honour her memory, to use this step to help him in his grieving process and help him find acceptance.

It was drizzling when he set off for the florist's in the village, but hardly enough for him to turn on his windscreen wipers. He hoped it would stop by the time he got to the church. He'd asked the florist to put together a bouquet of Nicole's favourite flowers, which he'd always bought her for her birthday.

'Ah, *Monsieur Bernard, un moment, s'il vous plaît.*'

He waited while the florist went out into her back room to collect the bouquet, fidgeting with his keys. She reappeared a few minutes later, bearing a bouquet of bright yellow freesias, mixed with some creamy roses and gypsophila. It was perfect and Nicole would have loved it. Thierry swallowed, trying to keep a hold on his emotions.

Once back in the car, he set the flowers carefully on the passenger seat and set off for the short drive back to the church where his wife was buried, near her parents' home. It was also the church where they'd been married five short years ago. He'd learned so much about himself in that time, and even more since Nicole's death.

He pulled up on the gravel alongside the outer wall of the Romanesque church and stared at the churchyard in front of him, and the ancient church building with its two towers beyond. At least

Nicole was buried in one of the few graveyards where the church was on the same land. Something told him she was more at peace here than she would have been in an anonymous cemetery on the outskirts of the village.

He sat for a few minutes, steeling himself to leave the car in the still drizzling rain and make his way to Nicole's grave on the other side of the church. Just being here was bringing back all the awful feelings he'd experienced on the day of her funeral, but had suppressed because he was in public. Nicole came from a small family so there weren't many people there, but it had been such a sombre day, made all the worse because she'd been so young at the time of her death.

Climbing out of the car at last, he walked round to the passenger side to collect the bouquet and then made his way to the wrought-iron gate at the entrance to the churchyard. He took the path to the right after closing the gate behind him, and followed it round towards the church door. He didn't want to go inside. He didn't want to engage with anyone else who might be there. He wanted to be on his own to grieve for his wife. He reached the door and turned right to cross the grass towards the grave, which was in the far corner.

Here lies Nicole Bernard, beloved wife and daughter, taken too soon.

As he contemplated the inscription, whose words he had composed, he felt all his restraint crumble under the weight of his unexpressed grief, and then the tears fell. He kneeled down to place the bouquet on the cold slab of dark grey marble and found he didn't have the strength to get back up again. His tears had turned into wretched sobs, and he reached into his pocket for his handkerchief.

'Oh, Nicole, I'm so sorry for arguing with you that day. I'd give anything to take back all the unkind things I said to you. I will always love you. I've never stopped loving you from that first day we met. Wherever you are now, I only hope you've found peace, my sweetheart.'

He finally stood up again, brushing the dirt from his knees. He looked at the inscription one last time before turning to go. As he followed the path round the church back towards the car park, he saw his in-laws arriving to pay their respects. He should have realised they would come to visit their daughter on this day as well, and he hoped his being there didn't cause a problem. He wiped his eyes one last time and approached the gate.

'Thierry, it's good to see you here. Are you okay?' Nadine seemed to see right into his soul and all his reserve went in the face of her scrutiny.

'I will be, thanks, Nadine.' His voice sounded croaky and he tried to clear his throat before speaking again. 'How are you both?'

'It's another difficult day for us all, but we'll get through it.' Pierre nodded briefly at him.

'Thierry, I know we probably won't see each other any more after this, but we don't want to fall out with you. We don't blame you for Nicole's death. We're coming to terms with everything you told us and trying to move on bit by bit. We hope you'll be able to do the same over time, and if we see each other, we hope we'll be able to talk kindly about our shared love for Nicole with you.'

Nadine gave Thierry a sad smile and he understood her pain. He nodded at them both and then made his way back to the car. The emptiness inside him had grown even larger as a result of visiting Nicole.

Lottie

Lottie had been desperate to tell Thierry about her job situation since Fran had confirmed Didier's agreement to her, but so far the timing hadn't been right. He'd been very quiet yesterday, so she hadn't wanted to bother him with it all, and today he'd left early again, making it impossible for her to speak to him at all.

She'd decided to take the plunge and attend the Parents and Babies session in the village. Marie was nearly two months old now, and she thought it would be good for both of them to socialise with other babies and their parents. She gathered all the things she needed for Marie's bag and popped it underneath the pushchair before lifting the rocker on.

When she arrived at the *Salle*, she found the door propped open with a chair, and a sign on it proclaiming the group open for visitors. She paused for a moment, steeling herself, and then took a deep breath before going through the door. The corridor was full of empty pushchairs and the odd pram, so she took her cue from them and parked hers in one of the last available places, before lifting Marie out and hooking her bag on her shoulder.

When she entered the room where the group was being held, she was sure every pair of eyes turned to examine her. She felt her face flush with embarrassment – this was her worst nightmare – but she kept her eyes on Marie until she sensed people losing interest. Then she looked up to see if there was a spot where she could settle. Most people were in groups with their friends, and she was pleased to see a good mix of mums and dads, and grandparents, too. She couldn't see anyone completely on their own, let alone anyone she recognised. Her stomach did a little somersault at the thought she might end up going home without having spoken to anyone.

She sat down on a piece of carpet that was free and laid Marie on a play mat while she searched for a suitable toy. She picked up a little zebra rattle and put it in Marie's hand, clasping hers around it to help her shake it.

'Hi there, I'm Yvette. Is this your first time here?'

She looked up into a young woman's friendly face and nodded. 'Yes, I'm Lottie.'

Yvette sat on the floor and placed her own baby boy in front of her. 'Nice to meet you. And who's this?' she asked, smiling at Marie. She introduced her own baby as Jean-Claude. 'He's reached six months now so he can sit up quite comfortably on his own, which makes a big difference to my life.'

She laughed, and Lottie warmed to her immediately. 'Marie's coming up to two months old now.'

They chatted back and forth and Lottie began to relax, wondering what she'd ever worried about in terms of visiting the group.

'I haven't lived in the village long, and my partner works quite long hours in Strasbourg, so it's nice to meet someone new. I've been coming for a couple of weeks and have chatted to a few people, but I still don't feel I know many new parents.'

'I only moved here last year, as well. I live on the vineyard near the church, and I used to work at the nursery till I had Marie, so I know a few people, but no new mums.'

'What does your partner do?'

'Marie's dad isn't with me. He left when he found out I was pregnant. But I'm living with my new partner now.'

'Oh, damn, I'm sorry about Marie's dad, that must be hard. It's good that you've got a new partner now and family nearby, as well. Would you like a cup of tea?'

Lottie gazed after Yvette as she walked off to get them drinks. She hadn't even reacted when she'd told her about being a single mum. Maybe some of the worry about that had just been in her head, after all.

The rest of the session flew by and soon Lottie was making her way back to the vineyard, hopeful of seeing Thierry at lunchtime and filling him in on all she'd been up to. When she got home, though, the house was empty, and there was no message from Thierry on her phone to say whether he would be coming home for lunch. She sent him a quick text to ask, but when he hadn't replied after ten minutes, she decided to go ahead and make some lunch for herself and not wait.

She fed Marie while she was waiting for her quiche to cook and laid her down for a nap after burping her. She sat quietly at the table, feeling lonely without Thierry there to talk to. It was unlike him not to let her know what he was doing and she worried something might have happened.

She was stacking her things in the dishwasher when he finally replied to tell her he was too busy to come for lunch. She put her phone down on the counter and stared out of the window. Something was up with him, but she had no idea what it was. She didn't want to wait all afternoon to find out, so she would wait for Marie to wake up and then she would go and find him.

CHAPTER FIFTEEN

Thierry

Thierry bumped into Sylvie unexpectedly as he was arriving back at the office after his morning inspection.

They kissed each other in greeting. 'How are you, Sylvie? I'm sorry it's been so long since we last saw each other.'

'I'm fine, Thierry. And don't worry, I know how busy you all are. I hear you and Lottie are getting on well together. She told me so when she last came over with Marie.'

Thierry was delighted to hear that, although it would be nice to hear it from Lottie herself sometimes. 'Yes, things are going pretty well. It's been good having them both at the house.'

'And isn't it great news about her new job? I told her she should speak to Fran when I saw her last, and now everything has worked out perfectly.'

Thierry's jaw tightened. 'What new job is that? As far as I knew, she was still waiting to hear back from the nursery.'

'Oh, *mon Dieu*. I didn't mean to put my foot in it. I'd best be quiet and let you speak to Lottie about it yourself.'

Thierry was so annoyed to find out this way that he stayed out in the vineyard through lunchtime and into the afternoon. He'd worked for hours training and tying up the vines, reasoning that the task would take his mind off Lottie, but it was a job that came like second nature to his practised hands, leaving his mind free to wander. All he wanted to do was look after her and Marie, and try as he might, he couldn't understand why this was such a big problem for her. And now she'd gone and got another job without even telling him about it first.

He paused for a moment, reproaching himself for thinking about 'looking after her'. She was perfectly capable of looking after herself. Still, he couldn't understand why she was so determined to provide for herself and Marie on her own. He wanted to talk it over with her, but the words would all come out wrong.

He didn't respond to Lottie's text until long after she'd sent it. He hated himself for being so irrational when he was just as bad at keeping things to himself, but it felt like she'd never even begun to trust him.

He focused on the vines again, reassured by his expertise in this task, if in nothing else in his life. He carried on with the job for another half an hour, and as he reached the end of the row, he put away his tools in his jacket, stretched his back, and turned to make his way towards his house. He hoped by the time he got there, he would have reached a decision about how to tackle this with Lottie.

'Hey, I was about to come and look for you,' Lottie said as he opened the front door. 'I was just waiting for Marie to wake up.' She looked unsure of him, and he felt guilty for avoiding her all afternoon.

'I've been busy with the vines.' He gestured at the estate behind him.

'I missed you at lunch, and I wondered if you were okay. You sounded annoyed in your text. You still do, in fact.'

He scoffed at that, and then everything tumbled out. 'I am annoyed, you're right. I thought things were going well between us, you know, Lottie,' he told her coming into the front room. 'I've tried hard to take a step back and not to push you. I've done my best to help you. I've even been seeing the counsellor to help me deal with my grief. So when I saw Sylvie this morning and she told me about you getting a 'new job', rather than you telling me yourself, I think I had a right to feel a bit annoyed.'

'Look, I only spoke to Fran on Monday. You were out all day yesterday and now it's Wednesday. I've been wanting to talk to you, but there was never a good time.'

He folded his arms and glared at her. 'But there's more to it than that, isn't there? How long have you known about losing your job at the nursery? Obviously you didn't feel you could trust me with that information. And all this time I've been telling you that you don't need a job, that I would support you, but you've been rejecting the idea. You could have told me the truth then.'

Lottie put her hands on her hips in response. 'I didn't tell you about losing my job precisely because I thought you would react like this. And now, instead of supporting me in my search for a new one, all you're doing is proving all my worst fears right by being angry with me.'

Thierry swallowed, trying to hide how much it hurt to hear her say those words. 'Maybe if you'd trusted me enough to tell me the truth as soon as you lost your job, we could have talked about it more openly then. As it is, I had to find out what was going on from someone else. I don't want you to get a job, it's true. I've always been ready to help with Marie, and in any other way you need.'

Lottie threw her hands up and stalked over to the window. 'Why is it so hard for you to understand that I want a job so I can be independent and not have to rely on you for everything?'

He took a deep breath. 'That's not fair. I do understand your need for independence. What I don't understand is why you won't depend on me just a little. Why put yourself through all this trouble? You have somewhere to stay and no rent to pay. You don't even need a job just yet.'

'And what if everything between us goes wrong, like it is now, and I have to leave? Where would I be then?'

His eyebrows shot up. 'When you say that, I can't help but think you're not committed to a relationship with me. That's what I've been thinking since we left your parents' house. The very idea of marriage to me sent you running for the hills.'

Lottie faltered for a moment, then regained control. 'What are you talking about? You were the one who said marriage was the furthest thing from your mind, which I took to mean you didn't want to marry *me*.'

'Well, that says it all.' He sighed as all the anger went out of him. 'We're just not on the same page with each other, even after all this time. All I want to do is help you, and all you seem to want to do is reject me. I can't carry on like this much longer.'

'Well, I was also going to ask if you could help me with babysitting when I start working for Fran, so it couldn't be further from the truth that I'm rejecting your help, could it?' She lifted her chin in that defiant way of hers that both irritated and delighted him.

He pushed his hands through his hair. 'I don't know how many times I've told you that I'm always happy to help you, especially with looking after Marie.'

Lottie's nostrils flared and he could see she was taking deep breaths to try to calm herself before speaking again. 'How I live my life is up to me. I thought you wanted to help Marie and me, and that you were beginning to understand me better, but obviously not.'

'Look, I don't want to argue with you any more. I need to take a shower.' He disappeared upstairs before she could say another word. They'd resolved nothing and he had no idea how they were going to sort things out between them.

Lottie

Lottie was still fuming about their argument the next day, after a sleepless night tossing and turning. How dare he keep telling her what to do? Well, she didn't need him, she could look after herself, just as she'd always known she could. She was up early, having slept in the nursery with Marie again, and she was determined to pack up her stuff and get right on with finding herself somewhere else to live. Then everything would be fine. She had no idea where that would be right now, but someone would take her in. She was sure of it.

Marie was settled and happy in her bouncer, so Lottie set about texting round to see if she could find somewhere to go. She was about to start with Fran when she realised that there was no room in their cottage – they only had two bedrooms. She could try Sylvie, but she had no idea whether she would be welcome at Frédéric's house. The only person who might be able to help was Ellie, especially as she and Henri were going away soon and their house would be free. She sent off a quick text, picked Marie up, and then went upstairs to start packing.

As she put their clothes into her suitcase, she worried for a second whether she was doing the right thing in leaving rather than talking everything over with Thierry. Then she told herself the time for talking was over. He never listened to her anyway. He didn't want her to get a job; he wanted her to be dependent on him for every penny. Well, that wasn't how she wanted to live her life, and she'd lost count of the number of times she'd told him so.

Ellie replied: *I'm on my way to the château. Shall I come over and see you?*

Lottie texted straight back and sat down to wait. She hoped Thierry didn't come back till much later so she could be gone before he returned. Ellie knocked on the door a few minutes later, and Lottie filled her in on some of what had happened.

'I'm sorry to ask you, but do you think we could come and stay with you?'

Ellie frowned. 'I don't have any problem with you coming to stay, but I'd have to speak to Henri about it first. It is his house and I wouldn't want to make things awkward between him and Thierry.'

'Of course.' Lottie bit her lip, knowing Ellie was right but still desperate to get away.

'I'll pop back to the office now and see if I can speak to Henri on my own. I'll let you know as soon as I can.'

Lottie had a feeling Henri might not agree to let her stay out of loyalty to Thierry. She understood that, but she was still hopeful. Then she heard Thierry's key in the door and her heart sank. She wasn't ready for another confrontation, but one was definitely coming.

He came into the living room a moment later, his face like thunder. 'Why is your suitcase in the hallway? And Marie's bags? You weren't being serious about moving out, were you?'

'That's you all over, Thierry. You never take what I say seriously. You always think you're in the right. I *was* serious and that's why our bags are there. I'm waiting for someone to come back to me.'

'But where will you go?'

'You don't need to worry about that. We're not your responsibility.'

'You are my responsibility, and I don't want you to go. I love you both and I don't want any harm to come to you. Please let's talk about this.'

'No. We've done lots of talking and we haven't got anywhere. I want my independence, and you don't understand that. I don't think you'll ever understand what it means to me, not to have to depend on a man ever again.' Her voice cracked, despite all her efforts to remain strong.

'But I'm not Yiannis. I've looked after you both and I always will. I do understand that you don't want to depend on me for everything, but surely we can discuss this, after all we've been through together.'

'You mean discuss my accepting that you don't want me to have a job? That's not going to happen, Thierry.'

Thierry's broad shoulders slumped and she worried again whether she was doing the right thing. 'Okay, maybe you're right,' he said. 'This isn't working out between us, is it? We seem to want different things. And no matter what I do, you reject me. Well, I don't want to take your independence away from you, Lottie, so if you need to leave, that's up to you.'

He turned abruptly and left, without even having taken his boots off, and she was suddenly bereft. Marie started to cry and Lottie felt a tear slip down her face. How had it all come to this? And why had Thierry just given up?

Henri says it's okay, but just to warn you, he's not happy about it. I've had to agree to him telling Thierry where you are. I'll be back in a minute to help you move your stuff.

Lottie wiped her face and calmed Marie before changing her and putting her into her pushchair. Apart from her suitcase of their clothes, she would just take the Moses basket for now and come back for anything else later.

As she rocked Marie in the pushchair, she looked around Thierry's house with sadness. They'd had some happy times together, but in the end they hadn't been compatible. It broke her heart for their relationship to end like this, with Thierry giving up so easily and not even being prepared to compromise on things with her. She needed some space to work out what she was going to do next and to mend her broken heart yet again.

Thierry

Thierry woke up the next day feeling like he'd made yet another awful mistake in his life. He missed Lottie so much, and his heart ached at the thought that he might never spend time with Marie again. He loved Lottie, and that's what was driving his need to protect her and Marie, but he hadn't told her that, and now it might all be too late for them.

For the first time since Nicole had died, he couldn't motivate himself to get up and out into the vineyard. He'd just come downstairs for some breakfast when there was a knock at the door. He was still in his pyjamas and embarrassed to reveal that to whoever might be calling this early, but he went to see who it was.

'*Bonjour*, Thierry,' Henri said, with an uncomfortable smile. 'How are you holding up?'

Thierry let him in and made his way back to the kitchen, knowing how much Henri liked his caffeine. 'Terrible is the only word for it. I miss them both so much, but I don't think I'll ever be able to persuade Lottie to come back now.'

Henri took the cup of coffee he passed him and sat down at the dining table. 'She misses you too, you know. There were lots of tears last night, so I wouldn't give up hope yet. I guess you're both going to have to decide whether you can compromise.'

'I don't know if we can. She wants to be independent all the time and I want her to depend on me some of the time. The fact that she doesn't want to makes me feel she doesn't trust me.'

'And yet you're one of the first people she turns to when she needs help. She trusts you to look after her daughter, the most precious person in her life. That says a great deal about how important you are to her, I would say.'

'But her actions tell a different story to her words, sometimes. I know she's wary after what happened to her in the past, but I've shown her I'm not like that. I've tried to show her that she can depend on me without me taking her freedom away, but she doesn't believe how important she is to me. I've also come to love Marie as if she were my own daughter, and I didn't think I would ever say that. I never wanted to have children with Nicole and now look at me.'

'Well, if you love them both, and I know you do, you're going to have to work out a way to fight to get them back.'

'I don't know if I've got that fight in me, Henri. All I want to do is help her, and yet at every turn, I seem to let her down. I don't know what I can do to prove myself to her.'

'You can come back from this with Lottie. You've made mistakes, but they're not irreversible. You've been there for her consistently through her pregnancy and since the birth. That should tell her a lot about your commitment to her and Marie.'

'But she knew all that before and still it wasn't enough.'

'You're going to have to accept that she wants to work and try to understand her reasons. They're not a reflection on you, so if you support her in her need to be independent, by offering to babysit for Marie while she goes out to work, for example, she'll see you're trying to change.'

'I can compromise by doing that, but what will she be doing?'

'I guess by accepting your help and coming back, she'll be compromising. Ironically, in order to be independent, she has to depend on you to help with looking after Marie. That's a massive step for her to take. So you won't be the only one who's taking a risk with their heart here.'

'I don't know, Henri. I'm still not sure. I haven't told her about not wanting children with Nicole, either. I know I should come clean about that too so there are no more secrets between us.'

'And are you worried she'll be upset about that?'

Thierry nodded. 'I was hoping to show her I could be a good dad to Marie before telling her about my past with Nicole. I'm worried she'll think I'm not worthy of her love or of being a dad to Marie.'

'I think now's the time for you to be completely honest and to see what she says.'

'I still think there's more to it than that for her. She's not been completely honest yet, either.'

'Well, you'll only know if you talk to her. I wouldn't leave it too long, either.'

Henri left shortly afterwards and Thierry went out to the vine-yard to do his inspection. By the time he reached the bottom of the hill, the vineyard had done its magic and he was feeling more hope-ful. Now that they were in June, the weather had really started to improve. The flowering of the vines was properly underway with the benefit of more sunshine, and soon they would have to give the foliage its first trim.

He looked out towards the majestic Vosges mountains in the distance and thanked goodness for the place he had chosen to live. Even though he hadn't been born in Alsace, it felt like home to him. He stared up at the sky, absorbing the sun's rays and taking deep breaths to help him think. He finally turned away from the view and began wending his way back up the hill, checking the vines as he went.

Henri was right about him needing to speak to Lottie, but too often, when they tried to talk, it descended into an argument. They were both so strong-willed and used to getting their own way. But that was how he'd been when Nicole was alive and he'd had to live with regrets ever since. So he needed to change.

Lottie had already shown him she was willing to depend on him by asking him to look after Marie. It wasn't financial dependence, although he was helping her financially in other ways, but she still needed him. And that was all he wanted, wasn't it? To feel needed. If she was willing to make that change, then he had to be prepared to change, too. But he would have to time his moment carefully and work hard to let Lottie have her say.

Lottie

Lottie arrived early at the wine bar, after leaving Marie with Ellie and Henri. She bought herself a glass of mineral water and found a table where she could keep an eye on the door. She wanted to see Thierry when he arrived so she would be prepared.

She'd been surprised to receive his text asking if they could meet and talk, but it was the right thing for them both to do if they were ever to move forward. And she hoped there was a way for them to do that.

She took a sip of her drink as she wondered what Thierry might have to say, and when she next looked up, he was coming through the door. She waved and he gave her a small smile before going to the bar himself. She studied his profile as he waited for his drink. His dark hair flopped over his forehead as usual and she smiled as he pushed it out of his eyes. He looked like he hadn't shaved for a couple of days, and she wondered if he'd had a lot going on at work. She'd missed seeing him every day. It was more than that, in fact. Her heart ached from not seeing him. It was only in the week since she'd left that she'd realised how much she loved him.

'Thank you for coming,' he said, as he reached the table. He set his glass down and leaned over to kiss her cheek.

'How are you?' she asked.

'I'm fine. How are you and Marie?'

'We're okay.'

They both fell silent, having got the pleasantries over with.

'So, what did you want to talk about?' Lottie asked, desperate to get the ball rolling and to end the awkward silence.

Thierry cleared his throat. 'There's something I need to tell you, but before I do, I want to explain why I'm doing so. I've really missed you and Marie since you've been gone, and I don't think I told you often enough when you were there how much I love you both. I don't want this to be another foolish mistake on my part. I want you both to be in my life, if you can forgive me for all my stupid behaviour.'

Lottie reached out and squeezed his hand. 'I've missed you so much too, and I know Marie misses being with you, as well.'

'The thing is, Lottie, there's something I've not told you, and I need to be honest with you about it so that you know everything before you decide whether to let me back into your life.'

Lottie didn't know what to make of that statement, so she just nodded and gripped her hands together in her lap.

'I told you how on the night Nicole died we had an argument, and when you asked me what the argument was about, I told you it didn't matter. But it did. It was an argument we had constantly; Nicole wanted to have children, but I didn't.'

Lottie couldn't help but gasp. 'Why didn't you want to have children with her?'

'It wasn't about Nicole, and it wasn't because I didn't like children. It was just that I wasn't ready. Selfishly, I wanted to keep her to myself for a bit longer. I wanted us to be free to do what we wanted, when we wanted, without having to worry about childcare, or the extra expense, or any of the other challenges having children would bring. And I suppose I didn't want to end up resenting a child in the way I felt my parents resented me. Nicole kept trying to persuade me to change my mind, and it's been one of my biggest regrets since she died that I wouldn't give her what she wanted.'

'So why did you start going out with me, when you knew from the start that I was pregnant?' She tried not to sound indignant, but she wasn't sure if she managed it.

He shrugged. 'There was a spark between us from the first time we met in the courtyard, when you arrived to help with the harvest. And by the time I found out you were pregnant, it didn't matter. I already liked you for who you were and I didn't want to let any obstacles stand in the way of our getting to know each other better.'

'Why are you only telling me this now? Don't you think it would have been better for me to know this sooner?'

'I should have told you before, I know, but I was afraid if I did tell you, it would mean the end for us. So instead, I tried to be a good partner to you and when Marie came along, I tried to show you that I could be a good father to her, that my view had changed.'

'You have been a good partner to me and you've been good to Marie, Thierry, but you're not her dad. I'll always want to be honest with her about who her real dad is.'

'I know that, and I respect that, but I hope, if we can get back together, that I can be the next best thing she'll have to her own father.'

'And how would you feel about having your own kids now?'

'So much has changed since I was having this discussion with Nicole. I know I've changed a lot since then – and I feel differently about having children now.'

'I've obviously seen how you are with Marie, and also with Chlöe, so I know that you're good with children, and I believe you when you say you've changed. My biggest concern is that you didn't trust me enough to tell me all this before. It feels like you're only telling me because we've reached a crisis point and you have no other choice.'

'I understand that, but you have to admit you've had trouble trusting me with information, too. Like not telling me when you lost your job at the nursery. It was awful having to find that out from Sylvie, and not from you.'

'I didn't tell you because I knew you'd say I didn't need a job, that you would look after me, blah, blah, blah.' She crossed her arms. 'I'm still not sure you understand why I want a job, but I need to be sure that you do before we can even think about getting back together.'

'After you'd gone, I thought a lot about what had happened between us. I realised you've already told me that you're prepared to depend on me to some extent by asking me to look after Marie when you go to work. That's your compromise, and mine is to accept your need to work. I understand now why you want to have your own income and I'm sorry it took me so long.'

'Well, that's good news, at least.' She raised her glass to toast that with him, but he didn't join in.

'There is something else, Lottie.'

Her heart sank. What was this about now?

'I've been honest enough to tell you my final secret, but I don't think you've told me all yours yet.'

CHAPTER SIXTEEN

Thierry

'What do you mean? I don't have any secrets.'

This might be the final straw for Lottie, but Thierry had to ask her anyway. 'I still think there's something on your mind that's stopping you from committing completely to me.'

Lottie swallowed and looked down at her lap, confirming for him that he was right. She took a few moments to look up again. 'I'm worried about losing my independence, and I think there will be many more arguments about that down the line for us. I still feel fragile after what Yiannis did to me, and that makes it hard for me to trust you completely.'

'You think I might let you down, even after all the time we've been spending together and what you've seen me do?'

'I'm sorry, but yes, especially now I know you were keeping something else from me. I do trust you more than I did, but for me, the biggest issue is that I feel I'll always be second best to Nicole in your eyes. Even when you tell me you love me, I'm still not sure I completely believe you.'

Thierry let out a long sigh. 'Okay, so that's what it is. I knew there was something. I just couldn't work out what. So, where do we go from here? How can we be together if we don't fully trust each other?'

'I don't know. I do love you, Thierry, but love doesn't seem to be enough for either of us.'

It was the first time she'd told him she loved him, but he wished it could have been in better circumstances. He reached out and took her hands in his. 'All I can say is that I love you and I want to be with you. Nicole was my first love and I can't erase that love or that experience – I wouldn't want to – but I have room in my heart to love again, and my heart is already yours, Lottie.' He paused to let his words sink in. 'And I promise to work on my understanding of your need to be independent, if you can also work on your trust issues. You're not second best to me, and you never will be. You've helped me get past my guilt and my fears, and helped me accept that even if I'm not perfect, I am a good man. But I can't make you take that final leap of faith with your heart, Lottie. That's up to you.'

They left the wine bar shortly afterwards and Thierry walked Lottie back to Henri's house. He held her hand the whole way, hoping with all his heart he'd said enough to persuade her of his love for her and Marie.

'I'll think about what we've discussed tonight, Thierry, but I'm not making any promises. There's still a lot for me to work through. Good night.' She kissed him goodbye and it felt very final.

Once she'd closed the door, he turned to make his way along the darkened path back to the vineyard. He'd been honest with Lottie, but it hadn't improved the situation between them. They'd both kept too many fundamental things from each other, which was why they were still wary of trusting one another. On top of that, he didn't know how to prove to her that despite his love for Nicole, he was ready to move on and start over. And even though Yiannis had never been physically there between them, either, he had everything to do with her reluctance to trust again. In a way, they were both fighting ghosts.

Thierry arrived at the house and poured himself a glass of cognac to help calm his frustrations. He took a sip of brandy, enjoying the warmth of the alcohol on his tongue before it slipped down his throat. He glanced at the photograph of Nicole on the mantelpiece, trying to arrange his thoughts, and he remembered the list of things he still needed to do with regard to sorting out Nicole's stuff. He would start with the photo albums, he decided, and choose which photos he wanted to have on hand and the ones he would put away. Maybe he could give some to her parents, and some of her jewellery. He only wanted to keep her wedding and engagement rings, along with his own, and a necklace he'd given her on their first anniversary.

He sat up straighter. This would help him move on and maybe show Lottie that he was serious about committing to her. He also wanted to remind her that he was happy to look after Marie while she went to work, which was surely the best way for her to know that he took her need for independence seriously. He would send her a text about that tomorrow to reassure her.

And he would never keep anything from her again. He had a second chance at love and he was lucky to be in that position. The big question now was whether Lottie was ready to take that chance with him and to build a future together.

Lottie

Lottie had gone round and round everything in her mind after meeting Thierry at the wine bar, but she was still no clearer about the way forward when she woke up the next morning. It felt strange being in Henri's house, and listening to him and Ellie going about their lives together as they made plans for their travels. They had their whole future ahead of them and she envied them their lack of complications. But despite all her difficulties, she had a beautiful, healthy baby and she wouldn't be without her for the world. She looked down at Marie in her Moses basket and realised how lucky she was. Her daughter began to stir and Lottie smiled.

'Come on, little one, time for your breakfast.'

She sat down on the bed and brought Marie to her breast to feed her. She thought about how caring Thierry had shown himself to be towards her baby. He'd been everything she would have wanted Yiannis to be as a father. Just because Thierry wasn't Marie's biological dad didn't mean he couldn't love her. And he really must have changed his view about having children because there was no doubt in her mind that his love for Marie was real. She definitely wanted to have more children in time and she was confident that Thierry would be a good dad to them, too.

But the trust issues remained. She was so afraid of being hurt again, and of being left in the lurch if the relationship broke down. How did other people do it? She groaned at the thought of making herself so vulnerable again. She finished feeding Marie and made her way downstairs to see if she could talk things over with Ellie.

'Morning, you two,' Ellie said, as she appeared in their little kitchen. 'Did you sleep well?' She tickled Marie under the chin, making her giggle.

'We did, thank you. And thanks again for looking after Marie for me last night. How are you both today?' Lottie glanced at Henri as she popped Marie in his lap before making herself some breakfast.

'We've decided that we want to have a celebration before we leave,' Ellie told her.

'Have you set your departure date then?'

Ellie nodded. 'We have set the date, yes. We've got tenants set up for the house, so we've really got to go now. We've told Fran and Didier, and they're okay with it. We want to have a proper send-off so we can see everyone before we go.'

Lottie took Marie back from Henri and sat down at the table, trying not to be disappointed at the news that they'd found tenants. Now there was no chance of her staying here while they were away, and that meant she had no more excuses not to make a decision about her future. She took in a deep breath and pasted on a smile. 'That sounds like a super idea. A celebration is what we all need to cheer us up.'

'Excellent! Will you ask your mum and dad to come, too? It would be great to see them again.'

'Oh God, I'll have to tell Mum about moving out of Thierry's, won't I? She's bound to be cross with me.'

'You might be pleasantly surprised if you reach out to her. How did your date go last night?'

'It was hardly a date,' she said, pulling a face, 'but it was fine. We had a good talk and we both got things off our chest, but I still feel undecided about what to do next.'

'Do you love him, Lottie?' Henri asked.

'I do love him, and he's been so good with Marie, as well.'

'So what's stopping you going back and getting on with the rest of your lives together?' Ellie asked.

'Fear, I suppose, and the unknown.'

'I think we all feel like that when we meet someone new,' said Henri, with a glance at Ellie. 'But if you love him, it's up to you to take that final step. You can't protect yourself from hurt in the future – none of us can – so you have to decide how much you want to be with him.'

After delivering those wise words, Henri stood up and cleared the table before grabbing his bag and kissing Ellie goodbye. He was meeting Fran at the office for a final handover discussion.

'A toute à l'heure, chérie. Bonne chance, Lottie.'

Ellie left shortly afterwards to go and get some shopping, and Lottie decided to give her mum a ring there and then to invite her and her dad to the celebration. She put Marie down for her nap and picked up her phone.

'Oh, are they going so soon? I hadn't realised,' her mum said.

'I know, it's come round quickly. I'm excited for them, but I'm going to miss Ellie so much. We've become so close this year, especially since Marie was born.'

'I'm glad to hear Henri's going with her. It will be the making of him, to get out of Alsace, and maybe even out of France for a bit, so he knows there's another world out there.'

Lottie was surprised to hear her mum say that, but pleased she recognised the benefits of travelling. 'I have some other news, Mum, which isn't quite so good.'

'Oh, darling, what's happened?'

'I've moved out of Thierry's and I'm staying with Ellie and Henri for the moment. Thierry and I had an argument over him not wanting me to get a job.'

'Oh, sweetheart, I'm very sorry to hear that. How are you feeling now?'

Lottie told her mum about the meeting she'd had with Thierry. 'And so it's all coming down to whether I can trust him. I want to, I really do, but I'm so frightened of making the wrong decision.'

'I liked getting to know him better when you came to stay. It was clear to us then how much he loves you and Marie. I know he's had his troubles to overcome, and I think you've helped him with that. If you want my advice, he's worth taking a chance on.'

After Lottie rang off, she noticed she'd had a text from Thierry.

'Just wanted to let you know I'm still fine to look after Marie when you start work next week. Let me know when and where.'

As she stared at the message, her mum's words rang in her ears: 'He's worth taking a chance on'.

Thierry

After meeting Lottie at the wine bar on Friday, Thierry had backed off a little to give her space to think about everything they'd discussed, even though what he wanted to do was keep calling her to try to persuade her to get back together. He was pleased to receive a positive reply to his text about looking after Marie, but other than that, he didn't contact her again.

Now it was Monday and he was meeting Didier for a vineyard

inspection late morning. Thierry finished his own jobs in the winery first thing before making his way through the estate. The sun was shining and it was a glorious June day. He was able to wear just a T-shirt now it was warmer, and the feel of the sun on his skin lifted his spirits with the promise of better weather to come.

'Morning, Thierry. Shall we crack on?' Didier looked miserable and Thierry was surprised by the lack of the usual pleasantries.

They didn't talk much on their inspection except about the state of the vines, so Thierry didn't know what reception his idea of lunch together would get, but he was determined to suggest it anyway.

'Shall we go out for some lunch? It might do you good to get away for a while.'

'I haven't got time, Thierry.'

'You have got time. You've been working yourself to the bone, arriving first thing and leaving late, and you know that isn't the answer to your problems.'

Didier frowned at him, and Thierry wondered if he'd over-stepped the mark.

'Okay, I suppose you're right.' His shoulders drooped, and Thierry was relieved he'd agreed.

They wandered slowly back through the vines and into the village, choosing their favourite bistro as usual. Once they'd sat down and ordered their *prix fixe* menu, Didier leaned back against the corner seat they'd chosen and blew out a long breath.

'I've been working so hard to try to take my mind off all the problems Fran and I have been having,' he admitted.

'How is Fran?'

'She's finding it hard to keep smiling through everything when the news is always bad. And it's driving me mad to see her so depressed. But the doctor has told us to keep trying for at least a year, and we're still a few months off that yet.'

'What do you think you'll do if you're not successful this time?'

Their meals arrived, so they paused while the waiter served them.

'Honestly, I don't know. It could be the final straw for Fran. For me, it will be as far as I want to take it, not just because of what it's doing to her, but also to us. Chlöe must have picked up on the tension between us now, and I don't want that to get any worse, either.'

'God, I wish there was something I could say to make you feel better. It's such a personal thing that only the two of you can sort out. I can see it from both sides, but I don't know what the right thing is to suggest.'

Didier nodded. 'How's things between you and Lottie now, anyway? Any sign of her moving back in with you?'

'I met her last Friday evening and we talked honestly about everything, but now I've left it with her to decide whether she wants to come back to me or whether this is the end. We've both found it difficult to trust one another, but I do want to be with her and I think she loves me. It's just that we're both wary.'

'That sounds quite miserable, too. We're quite a pair, aren't we?'

They both laughed then. Thierry finished his last mouthful of the *coq au vin* they'd chosen for lunch and put his cutlery on his plate.

'What did you think of the Riesling they used for that?' he asked Didier as he was finishing up.

'It didn't seem quite dry enough to me. Perhaps we should see if they'd like to try some of ours?'

Thierry nodded. They both chose a light chocolate dessert with black coffee, and then it was time to get back to work. Thierry had a quick word with the restaurant manager before they made their way back to the vineyard.

'Thanks for pushing me to come out, Thierry. I needed a break.'

'No problem at all. I'm glad we did it, too. And you can always talk to me whenever you need to.'

'We have a lot of changes coming up round here, with Ellie and Henri leaving soon. That's obviously going to have an impact on Fran, so I may need to rely on you more and more.'

'I know I haven't been much good to you over the past couple of years, but things are moving forward now and I'd like to pull my weight more. And Lottie will at least be able to help Fran some of the time.'

'I wish we weren't all so hard on ourselves. We all have stresses to deal with, and we've all been here for each other. We need to keep doing that and everything will work out.'

'How do you feel about Henri going with Ellie?'

'Well, I encouraged him to go, so I can't be upset now he's taken my advice. He's been so good to us, hardly ever taking any time off, so it's the least we owe him. We'll manage between us all, like we've always done before.'

'I think you're right. Fran knows what she's doing now and she can teach Lottie, so between them they can manage the office. And we can both help with the new Visitors' Centre. It won't be easy, but we'll be okay between us all.'

Lottie

Lottie was due to spend the morning working with Henri. He wanted to show her all his systems for handling the estate's admin, and although she was excited, her stomach was also in knots. She'd agreed with Thierry that she'd drop Marie off to him before she started at 9.30, and the thought of seeing him again was only adding to her nerves.

It was shaping up to be another warm day as she strolled along the path towards the vineyard. At least she'd remembered to pack some sun cream and a hat for Marie. Thierry liked to take her with him in the baby carrier, so she would have to tell him to make sure she wasn't exposed to too much sun.

She knocked on his door a few minutes later and he opened up straight away, as if he'd been waiting for them.

'*Salut,*' he said, clearly delighted at seeing them both again.

Lottie relaxed her shoulders. 'Morning. How are you?' She felt shy now after not seeing him for a few days.

'I'm fine,' he said, lifting the pushchair inside and then taking Marie out. 'I've missed you both.' The look he gave Marie filled Lottie's heart with joy.

'Thank you for looking after Marie for me today. I packed a hat for her and some sun cream because it's so warm, and you've got the carrier, haven't you?'

'Yes, I've got it and I'll look after her, I promise. You've still got your key, haven't you?'

'Yes, yes I have. Okay, well, I'd better be off.'

'Good luck this morning. I hope it goes well.' He grinned and she laughed.

She walked back up the hill towards the office, feeling surprised he hadn't asked her whether she'd made any decisions yet. She was grateful to him for giving her space. But she had definitely missed him and the way he made Marie and her laugh.

She knocked on the door of the office a minute later and stepped inside.

'Morning, Lottie.' Fran beamed and Henri stood to give her his chair.

'It feels so weird to be here without Marie and the pushchair,' she told them, and they smiled.

'You're a free agent this morning. So let's make the most of it.'

For the next few hours, Lottie tried to take in all the systems they had in place for dealing with the post, with emails, with deliveries, with orders, big and small, and with all the day-to-day invoicing and enquiries related to vineyard business. She was exhausted by the time midday came round.

'I think we should call it a day there for today,' Fran said at last, after they'd looked at the final item on Henri's list. 'If we tell you any more, you're likely to forget it anyway. Shall we go and get some lunch? Will Thierry be able to look after Marie for a bit longer?'

'I'm sure he will, but I need to check with him first.'

She fired off a quick text, then said goodbye to Henri, and they went outside to wait for Thierry's reply in the sunshine. Fran's dog

Ruby followed them out to work her way round the courtyard, sniffing curiously at all the new smells since she'd done her morning inspection.

Thierry replied to say he could look after Marie for a bit longer, so Lottie and Fran set off for her cottage to get some lunch.

'How do you feel it went this morning? Do you still want the job after the onslaught of new information?'

'It was a lot to take in, but I loved every minute of working with you. I did miss Marie, but it was manageable, and knowing she's with Thierry makes it easier, if that makes sense.'

'Of course it does. He loves her as much as you do and you trust him with her.'

Lottie was amazed. It was so simple for Fran to see their relationship for what it really was. And she was right: she did trust Thierry to look after Marie. All of a sudden, she felt like a missing jigsaw piece had fallen into place.

They reached the cottage and Lottie followed her sister inside.

'How are things going with you and Didier? I don't like to keep asking you, but I'm always thinking of you both.' She sat down on the sofa and Fran took the chair opposite. Ruby sat by her side, faithful as always to her mistress.

'I've definitely had my ups and downs these past few months, but do you know, Lottie, for the first time, I'm starting to feel okay with it all. Whatever happens this time – and I don't hold out much hope – I'm ready to move on from it now.'

'Really? You do look much better than the last time. What's changed?'

'We've decided that if I'm not pregnant this time, we're going to try to forget about it for a while. And to be honest, rather than being upset about it, I feel relieved, like the pressure's off for the two of us. It was pushing us apart and my relationship with Didier means more to me.'

'I know how hard it must have been for you to make that decision, but I think it's the right one, for what it's worth. You look so much better in yourself. I hope it will still happen for you this time, but if not now, maybe if you're less stressed it might happen naturally.'

'Well, that would be ironic after all this time trying, but yes, maybe. I'm not even going to think about it for now – well, I'm going to try not to.' She smiled wistfully, and Lottie's heart ached for her older sister that something she wanted so much was just out of her reach.

'You never know. But I'm glad you feel at peace with the decision you've made.'

CHAPTER SEVENTEEN

Thierry

Thierry spent a lovely morning with Marie. He took her out in her carrier while he did his inspection, and he enjoyed chatting away to her as he checked the vines. Many of the workers wanted to chat to her too, and she lapped up all the attention. He put her hat on and made sure she was covered in sun cream, just as Lottie had asked, but the fresh air definitely tired her out.

As they wended their way slowly down the hill to his house, he was able to take in the full beauty of the estate. The château was shimmering in the distance with the sun behind it, and in the foreground the vineyards had almost all turned green.

When they got home, he fed Marie and then laid her down for a nap. He had to put her on the sofa because the Moses basket was at Henri's place, so he sat on the floor next to her while she was asleep. He used the time to sort through his old photo albums and to pick out the photos he wanted to keep on display of Nicole. There were only a handful of photos in the pile by the time he'd finished. He left those on the coffee table and stacked the albums on the floor, ready to give to Nicole's parents to look through. He would put the rest in the loft when they were finished. He leaned back against the sofa and sighed. Every time he had to do something like this, it was hard on him, but he also felt a small sense of relief when he'd finished. He was finally giving himself permission to move on and allowing himself to remember the good times he and Nicole had spent together.

Marie stirred behind him and he turned to look at her. He reached out for her chubby little hand and brought it to his face, where she delighted in rubbing his scratchy stubble. He had meant to shave this morning, but in the end he hadn't had time, and it didn't matter most of the time whether he was clean-shaven or not. When Marie shifted to put both hands on his chin, he lifted her up and put her on his chest so she could get easy access to his bristles.

He studied her little face as she concentrated on her task. Her eyes had remained blue after the birth and were a beautiful shade of cobalt. Her soft baby hair was thickening into dark curls, and she was beginning to learn how to do lots of different things. Having had no contact with babies before, and never having wanted to, either, he was astonished by how much he was drawn to her, even though he had no biological connection to her at all. He'd never imagined that he would come to like a baby, let alone experience the depth of feeling he was beginning to feel for Marie. Maybe it was because she was Lottie's daughter that he felt so protective of her. She pulled on one of his whiskers then and he laughed, making her laugh, too.

Lottie's key sounded at the door, and he was sad his time with Marie would soon be coming to an end.

'Look at you two,' she said as she came in. 'You look like you're having fun.'

'She's fascinated by my beard. Anyway, how did you get on?' He stood up and passed Marie back to her mum.

'It was good – a bit mind-blowing, but still good. Thanks so much for looking after Marie, Thierry. Did you have a good time together?'

'We had a great time. All the estate workers fell in love with her and she loved all their attention.'

'Oh, I bet she did.'

'When will you be working next? I can help out again, if you like.'

'I didn't check that with Fran. I'll have to ask her. But I wondered if you had time to talk now?'

Thierry nodded, hoping that this meant good news and not bad.

'I've done a lot of thinking in recent days, but it was only this morning that I finally made up my mind about what I want to do next.'

He tried not to jump in and push her to tell him what her decision was, but it took an almost superhuman strength not to. He breathed out and tried to keep calm. 'And what did you decide?'

'I decided Marie and I belong here with you, and that we'd like to move back in, if the offer's still open, please.' She gave him a huge smile and he stepped forward to put his arms around the two of them.

'It most definitely is,' he said. 'I'm so glad, Lottie. You do belong here and it hasn't been the same without you both.' He leaned down and kissed her and felt Marie reach out for his beard again, making him laugh. He stopped to kiss the baby too, and she giggled.

'I still can't quite believe this is real. I feel so lucky. What made you change your mind?'

'It was something Fran said about you loving Marie as much as I do. I trust you completely to look after her for me. I wouldn't do that if I didn't trust you in every other way, too. So that's it.' She shrugged and he understood that it was that simple.

He went to retrieve the photos of Nicole from the table. 'While Marie was asleep, I started sorting through my photo albums and these are the ones I'm going to have on display.' He went through them so she could look at them.

'What are you going to do with all the rest?'

'I'm going to let Nicole's parents have a look through, too. I'm going to put these ones I'm keeping into a collage and frame them. There are so many happy memories here and I want to focus on that now.'

'I've got so many photos of Marie now. I'd like to make a collage of my favourites, too. That sounds like a lovely idea.'

He smiled at her, and he knew in his heart that they were both ready to move forward.

Lottie

Lottie set off to meet Fran and Ellie a little before midday. It was their last chance to say a personal goodbye to her, and so she'd left Marie with Thierry while they went for lunch. Thierry was desperate to catch up for lost time with the baby, and although Lottie had spent a fair bit of time away from her in recent days, she didn't want to deprive him.

She'd been living with Thierry again for a few days, and it felt like she'd never been away. Marie had quickly adapted back into her routine, and for the first time in a while, Lottie was relaxed. She had let the past go, accepting that she and Thierry had both made mistakes, and now she was ready to look to the future they would share together. Thierry had stepped up when she needed him most, respecting her need for independence, and she'd been able to rely on his help so she could go and do her job. That had been the moment when their relationship had moved to the next level.

As she reached the top of the slope, Fran was leaving the cottage. She waited for her to join her on the path.

'Morning, how are you feeling?' Fran kissed her on both cheeks and they carried on to the courtyard.

'Things are pretty much back to normal, and I'm so much happier,' she replied. 'How about you?'

Fran tucked her arm through Lottie's and hugged her close. 'I'm so glad to hear you're feeling happier. You deserve it. I feel much better too, now I've let go of the stress. It's so good to put it behind me and return to how things used to be between us.'

They found Ellie already installed at a table in their favourite wine bar and restaurant, a glass of wine in her hand.

'Ladies, come and join me,' she cried as they approached.

Fran gave Ellie a hug and sat down. 'It's so wonderful to celebrate your exciting travels with you. We'll miss you, of course, but we're already looking forward to you coming back.' She poured a glass of wine for herself and a glass of mineral water for Lottie, at her request.

'I know I should be happy, and I am. It's just I'm going to miss you two so much.' Ellie released a deep breath. Her lip wobbled and Lottie reached out to squeeze her hand.

'You're going to have a brilliant time, the pair of you,' she told her. 'And you'll meet lots of people. It will be fantastic, I promise you. And don't forget, you're going to tell me all the places you go, so I can live vicariously through you.'

They all laughed then, and Ellie relaxed.

'It's going to feel so odd without you around, and without your help,' Fran said, looking disheartened at the thought of Ellie going.

'Don't start getting emotional, Fran. It wouldn't take much for me to change my mind at the moment.'

Lottie changed the subject to distract them. 'Why don't we order some food? I'm starving.'

They studied their menus and placed their orders, before catching up with Ellie's travel arrangements until their starters arrived.

'How are you doing now, Lottie?' Ellie asked as she popped a panko-coated prawn into her mouth.

'I'm great, thanks. Thierry's been looking after both of us, and it's good to be back with him.'

'You needed to find the right balance and I think maybe you've worked it out now, the two of you. I'm so pleased for you,' Ellie told her.

'It's been wonderful to see Thierry come out of himself these past few months,' Fran said. 'I really feel I've got to know him, and he's been so helpful with the Visitors' Centre.'

'Have you set an opening date yet?' asked Ellie.

'Not a specific date, but it will be shortly after you go, I think.'

Fran turned to smile at her sister. 'Now I've got Lottie to help me, it's full steam ahead.'

'I'll miss the grand opening,' Ellie said, 'but I know everything will go well. It will all be so different by the time we come back, but hopefully the centre will be a great help to the vineyard finances in the next six months.'

'The financial situation has already eased up a bit. We're not spending any money on the château now, and most of the work on the centre is done. It shouldn't be too long before more money starts coming in as we receive more visitors and sell more wine.'

'And how's it been for you, Lottie, working with your big sister?' Ellie asked.

Lottie laughed. 'It's been good, actually. We think alike about a lot of things, don't we?'

'We do. It's funny, isn't it? You only notice that when you work together, despite having known each other all our lives.'

'I'm so glad everything's worked out for you. I don't feel so guilty now about going away, and taking Henri with me, too. But I'll look forward to coming back and finishing off the château. It will be amazing when it's finished and you can welcome guests to stay there.'

'It's incredible to think that a year ago none of us was even living here,' Fran said. 'So much has changed for all of us since last August, hasn't it?'

'God, a year ago, I'd just found out I was pregnant, and now I'm a mum.'

'Did you ever hear from Marie's dad?' Ellie asked.

'No, and I don't think I ever will. He wasn't ready for a family and all that stuff.'

'How do you know when you're ready?' Ellie asked next. 'I can't even imagine wanting to settle down right now.'

'Well, sometimes fate lets you know and then you have to get on with it,' said Lottie. 'And often it all works out for the best, anyway.'

'I'm so glad it's all worked out for you and Thierry,' Fran said.

'It will work out for you and Didier in time, too,' Lottie reassured her. She hoped she was right, and that Fran got her wish soon.

Thierry

'I thought we might all go for a walk this afternoon as it's such a lovely day. What do you think?' Thierry asked Lottie while they were eating lunch.

It was a perfect June afternoon, with clear blue skies and a comfortable warmth, so they set off across the neighbouring vineyard estates. Walking beside Lottie, with Marie in the baby carrier in front of her, he felt at peace.

'It was the second anniversary of Nicole's death recently,' he told her as they gazed across the vines.

'I'm sorry, Thierry. I wish I could have given you more support.' Lottie looked pained.

He glanced across at her. 'You've helped me to start coming to terms with it all. Your support gave me the strength to go and visit her grave for the first time.'

She took his hand. 'How did that go?'

'It was cathartic. I felt strange afterwards, but I'm glad I went. Her parents were there too, which could have been awkward, but in the end it was fine.'

'And are you still seeing the counsellor?'

'Not so often now, but she's been helpful. More helpful than I would have imagined. I've been so consumed by guilt for such a long time.'

'And how do you feel now?'

'I'm still hurt by the pointless loss of her life, but now I accept it was an accident. We'll never know if I could have prevented it, but I've accepted it wasn't my fault she died. I still have some way to go in the grieving process, but I've started to let the anger go now, which is a move in the right direction.'

'I'm glad for you, Thierry. It must have been so hard for you dealing with all these emotions over the past couple of years. And it's been difficult watching you going through it. I could see how low you were, but I couldn't do anything to help. I don't think it will ever all completely go away for you. You loved her and she'll always be a part of you, but at least you're dealing with it all now.'

'Yes, grief's a funny thing, and you're right, it will always be with me. I hope you're happy to still be with me while I work it all out, Lottie. I know I'm asking a lot of you.'

'I understand it's going to take time, but I'm in no rush, and I'm always happy to listen to you when you want to talk.'

'There is something else I wanted to talk with you about.' He waited for Lottie to say something but she stayed silent, giving him time. 'Since Marie was born, and I've spent more and more time with her, I've started to think that maybe I could be a good dad. Although I have lots of regrets as far as Nicole is concerned, I would like to have more children with you in the future.'

'I'm glad about that, Thierry. I feel the same. You've already been so good to Marie and you'll make a wonderful dad to your own child, too. We've both changed, haven't we?' She reached for his hand.

'I think we have, and I have you to thank for a lot of that.'

'So this is a move forward for the three of us.'

'I like the sound of that – the three of us.'

He turned to Lottie and kissed her then, snuggling Marie between the two of them. Marie reached towards them and they took her chubby hand in theirs.

Later that evening, when Marie was asleep, Thierry drew Lottie to him on the sofa.

'Let's leave the clearing up until tomorrow and enjoy this bit of time on our own,' he said as he snuggled up closer to her. Her eyes twinkled and Thierry experienced a rush of desire. He'd never stopped wanting her. It was just that everything else had got in the way.

They both stood and he took her hands in his.

'Are you sure this is what you want?' he asked.

'I am sure. Are you?'

He let his kiss be his reply. His lips settled on hers, and it was like coming home to feel her and taste her. She lifted her arms around his neck, and he cupped her face with his hands. After they were both breathless from kissing, he led her to his bedroom where they shed their clothes in record time before embracing each other again on the bed.

'I wasn't sure we would ever do this again,' he admitted, between kisses.

'You haven't forgotten what to do, though,' she replied with a laugh.

He leaned forward and kissed her again, reinforcing her words, and began to caress the soft skin of her back. The feel of her long, silky hair against him only increased his arousal, and when she moaned her pleasure, he was almost undone.

'Thierry...' Her hands gripped his shoulders, instantly conveying her message.

By the time they finally came together as one, each of them had expressed their desires to the other, and it was only a matter of time before their final release came.

As they lay together afterwards, Thierry's heart was the lightest it had been since Nicole's death. He felt guilty to be thinking of her now, in this most intimate of moments, but it was a symbolic letting go. He embraced Lottie again, delighted they'd finally found a way to make their relationship work.

'I love you, Thierry,' were the last words she said before she fell asleep.

Lottie

'Fran! This is a nice surprise. Come on in.' Lottie held the door open for her sister wondering what had brought her out to see her. They'd seen each other only a couple of days earlier.

'I decided to be spontaneous and come and catch up with you both while I was out taking Ruby for a walk. I can't stay too long, but I needed to get out of the office.'

Fran lifted Marie out of her bouncer and hugged her niece to her. Lottie was glad her sister was nearby and able to pop in and see them so easily.

'How are things with you?' she asked. 'How have you been finding work without Ellie and Henri there?'

'It's been pretty hard. There's so much to do, and although it was a great help having you in for those two mornings last week, I still feel like I'm drowning.'

'I wonder if I should have a word with Sylvie. I could ask her if she would look after Marie for one morning a week, as well. That way I'd be in with you a bit more, which might allow you to do all the other things you need to get the centre open.'

'Well, that would be great, as long as you're happy to be apart from this little one, and also if Sylvie's up to it.'

'I'd be okay doing three mornings, for sure. And I have a feeling Sylvie would be delighted to have Marie to dote on.'

'Thank you, Lottie. You've been an absolute godsend. And if, over time, you want to help out in the Visitors' Centre, I'd appreciate that, too. I have a feeling it's going to get very busy over there.'

'Thierry's been telling me about it. I can't wait to see it.'

Fran went back to cooing over Marie for a moment. 'I have some other news as well, both good and bad.' She paused and Lottie could see she was working hard to keep herself together. 'I'm not pregnant again, as we expected.' She swallowed and glanced up briefly, sadness and resignation etched into her face. Lottie didn't say anything, unsure what the right response would be, and Fran ploughed on. 'We've decided to put getting pregnant on hold for the moment. Or at least, to let what will be, be. Instead, we're going to go full speed ahead with our wedding plans.'

'I'm so sorry, Fran.'

Fran shrugged, having accepted the situation. Then Lottie clapped her hands, making little Marie laugh. 'But that's so exciting about the wedding. Can I help?'

'Of course. We plan to have it when Ellie gets back because I've already asked her to be my maid of honour, and also I'll need six months to sort it all out. That means we should be getting married just before Christmas. I need to tell Mum and Dad when they come to Ellie and Henri's leaving party.'

'So we'll have something else to celebrate, then.'

'I'm looking forward to the party, actually. I know we'll miss Ellie but I want it to be a great send-off for them so they go off knowing how much we all wish them well.'

'Yes, they deserve that.'

Fran picked Marie up again and cuddled her close. Lottie sensed her sadness and wished there was something she could say to comfort her. She hoped with time things would work out for her and Didier, like they were starting to work out for her and Thierry.

'Wouldn't it be amazing if we could hold the wedding in the château, and hold the reception there, too? The downstairs is all finished, so it wouldn't be difficult to arrange it.'

'Ooh, that does sound like a good idea. I'm not sure if we could manage to organise all that as well as doing everything else with the business, but we could give it a good go.' Fran laughed and Lottie joined her.

'Would you want to get caterers in or do it yourself?' Lottie asked.

'I think we'd want to pay someone else. It would be too much to do it all ourselves.'

'Yes, you're right. I'd love to get into that sort of work.' Lottie sighed wistfully.

'Really?' Fran stared at her. 'I've never heard you say anything about that before.'

'I've always loved cooking. I've been doing more since Marie was born, and it feels like something I could be good at.'

'Do you know, it's something I've wondered about for the Visitors' Centre. A café. I don't know when we might be able to make it happen but it's definitely worth thinking about for the future. Maybe you could give it some thought as a project you might like to manage for the estate.'

Lottie couldn't believe her ears. 'I would love to take on something like that when Ellie and Henri return. In fact, I'd be interested in working more in the Visitors' Centre down the line. I think there are all kinds of ways you could develop the centre once you've got the fundamentals in place.'

Fran sat up and shifted Marie deeper into her lap. 'We need to have a brainstorm about this when you're next in the office, which might be sooner than we think, once you've spoken to Sylvie.'

'I'll text her when you've gone. I'm sure she'll be happy to start next week. I can talk to her at the party as well, can't I?'

'Yes, we have a busy weekend coming up. I'd better get back to work now, but it's been lovely to see you both. Do come and see me when you're not working, won't you? Otherwise I might start to go mad from being on my own all the time.'

She stood up and popped Marie back in the bouncer before turning to give Lottie a hug. 'I'm so glad to have you here. I don't know what I would have done without you.'

Lottie waved goodbye to her sister and realised how good it felt to be needed.

CHAPTER EIGHTEEN

Thierry

Thierry was looking forward to the dinner this evening to see Ellie and Henri off on their travels. He'd chosen a great selection of the domaine's wines for the occasion, as they were also celebrating the completion of the work on the château's ground floor. Didier had cheerfully approved his list. Lottie had left early with Marie to help Fran and Sylvie with the food preparations, so all he had to do was gather the wines before heading there himself.

He went to the winery before lunch and then set off for the château. On his way, he thought about his discussion with Lottie the weekend before, when they'd talked about having children together. He had to admit he couldn't wait for that to happen, but he would have to give Lottie some time with Marie before they thought about having another child. But now he knew it was in their future, he was happy.

'Hey, Thierry.' He turned to see Henri running down the hill to catch up with him.

'*Salut*, how are you feeling about your travels?'

'I'm a bit nervous, to be honest. I don't have the same sense of adventure as Ellie, and I'm afraid of the unknown. I like being in control of my life, and I enjoy the life I have here in Alsace. But I'm doing this for Ellie and I'm just hoping it works out for us both.'

'We can all see how much you love Ellie, and she loves you. So it will all be okay, I'm sure.'

'I've loved her from the first minute I saw her, and I couldn't bear to lose her, so in the end the decision to help her fulfil her dream was easy.'

'Good for you. Just think of all the tales you'll have to tell us when you come back.' Thierry clapped him on the back, and Henri laughed.

A few minutes later Thierry knocked on the back door of Fran and Didier's cottage. Inside they found Fran, Sylvie, and Lottie assembling all the food for the evening celebrations. Thierry put the white wines in the fridge in the kitchen before joining them all in the living room.

'Here, let me take Marie from you,' he said to Lottie, as he came up to give her a kiss.

Fran and Sylvie both stopped what they were doing to smile, making him blush. He was more comfortable being affectionate with Lottie in public now. It had taken him a long time, but he'd got there.

'Thanks, Thierry. I was going to see if Mum and Dad had arrived yet. They said they'd get here for lunchtime. I guess you haven't seen them.'

'No, Henri and I walked over together, and we didn't see them on our way.'

'I'll go out and have a look for them,' she said, making for the door.

'What can I do to help, Fran?' Henri asked.

'Oh, Henri, could you drain the potatoes for the potato salad and carry on making that, please?'

Henri set to it at once, leaving Thierry to keep Marie occupied. She was sitting in her bouncer watching them all, but she needed someone to keep her entertained, so he happily obliged by showing her a picture book.

'Mum and Dad are here, Fran,' Lottie said, coming back into the kitchen. 'They're just coming through the arch. Shall we go and give them a hand with all the supplies?'

'I can't go right now. Could you and Thierry manage?' Fran looked stressed and no-one wanted her to be feeling like that today.

'Yep, no problem. Come on, Thierry. You bring Marie and we can meet them halfway.'

Lottie's parents had dressed up for the occasion; Joseph was wearing a suit and tie, and Christine was even wearing a hat.

'Mum, Dad! It's lovely to see you both,' Lottie cried, as they met in the middle of the hill. After kisses had been exchanged, they turned to make their way to the cottage.

They spent the rest of the afternoon laying out all the food on the dining table and putting up decorations, everyone chatting and catching up as they worked. Then they all went off one by one to get ready, before returning to wait for Ellie and Henri to arrive. When they appeared together around six o'clock, with Ellie wearing a colourful dress and Henri a stylish dark blue suit, a hush fell over the kitchen. Thierry had never seen them looking so happy. He passed them both a glass of the domaine's *Crémant d'Alsace* and did a final check round to make sure everyone else had a drink.

'Let's all raise our glasses to Ellie and Henri and wish them well,' Fran announced a moment later.

'*Santé!*' Then everyone began talking once again and the room was buzzing in no time.

Thierry looked around to see where Lottie was and found her chatting to her dad, while her mum chatted away to Marie. Lottie looked so relaxed, and that made him happy, too. Fran and Didier also seemed much less stressed, laughing and joking with each other in a way he hadn't seen them do for a while, and Sylvie was talking animatedly to Frédéric while he tried to keep Chlöe occupied with a card game, which she was in danger of winning. Ellie and Henri were whispering quietly together in a corner, heads touching and lips meeting in an occasional kiss. Thierry was struck by how in tune they were with each other, now they'd decided to travel together. His heart lifted as he took in the cheerful faces of his loved ones, his family.

Lottie left her mum and came over to join him. She kissed him as she reached his side.

'What was that for?' he asked, slipping his arm round her waist.

'It doesn't have to be for anything, does it? I want you to know I love you, and I also like kissing you.' She grinned at him and he grinned back.

'I'm happy for the first time in such a long time, Lottie, and that's all due to you and Marie.'

'It's not all due to us. You've worked hard to get past your guilt. That hasn't been easy, but you've done it. But for the record, I'm happy, too. I love going out and working with Fran, and now Sylvie's agreed to help one morning a week as well, it will give me a bit more time to get to know the business. So everything's good, isn't it?'

He chinked his glass against hers. 'It most certainly is.'

Lottie

'I'm dreading saying goodbye to Ellie at the station today. We're both going to miss her so much.' Lottie had gone to meet Fran the next morning so they could see Ellie and Henri off in style together.

Fran unlocked the car and they both climbed in for the short drive to Henri's place. He'd moved into a quaint house in the village not long after Ellie and he had got together. Henri had rigged up a bell for visitors on a rope next to the door. Lottie gave it a yank when they arrived and then studied the mustard yellow front door while they waited. The façade of the house was painted a glorious orange, which she'd always loved.

Henri came to the door and kissed them both hello before

inviting them in. He had a bag in his hand ready to load into Fran's car for the journey to Strasbourg to catch their train to Paris.

'Can I give you a hand?' asked Lottie, as Fran went to find Ellie.

'How are you feeling after the party last night?' Henri asked as they took more of their bags out to the car.

'A bit tired, but I wouldn't miss seeing you both off for the world. Is Ellie okay?'

'Yes, she's just doing a final check that we've got everything. I'll get her bag and see whether she's ready.'

Lottie followed him back into the little house. The wooden floorboards in the corridor rattled as they made their way past the stairs and down to the tiny kitchen at the back. Lottie spotted Ellie's enormous rucksack as they passed the front room. She didn't miss having to carry one of those.

'Ready to go, Ellie?' Lottie asked, as they squashed into the kitchen.

'Pretty much, although we barely got any sleep. Thank goodness we packed our stuff yesterday, otherwise I'm not sure we'd have had the energy to do it this morning.'

'We'd better hurry if we're going to get you to Strasbourg on time to catch that train,' Fran said.

Ellie finished her cup of tea and went upstairs for a final check round the house while Henri carried the rucksack to Fran's car. Fran had just closed the boot when Ellie joined them.

'It's just as well you're going with her, Henri. I wouldn't fancy her chances carrying that rucksack on her own.' Lottie gave him a smile before getting back into the car and taking her seat next to Fran.

'Have you got everything? Passports, train tickets?' Fran asked.

Ellie and Henri nodded, and Fran pulled away from the kerb.

'You must both be so excited,' Lottie said, once they were on their way.

Henri looked worried. 'I'm a bag of nerves, that's all I can say. I'm still waiting for the excitement to kick in.'

'You'll be fine once you get to Paris and you start sightseeing.'

Lottie turned round and smiled at him. 'Just think of it, Henri. I wish I could come with you.'

'It will be so weird to stay in Paris for a few days rather than only passing through,' Ellie said with a grin.

'Where will you go after that?' Fran asked, glancing at her in the mirror.

'We're going to work our way south, stopping at Bordeaux first and then on down to the Spanish border, or maybe across to Italy. I'm not sure. We'll go where the fancy takes us.' She laughed and turned to Henri, but he could only manage a tight smile. Lottie could see he was putting on a brave face.

'You will stay in touch like you promised, won't you?' She wagged her finger at Ellie. 'I want to see those photos.'

'Of course. I'm going to send you every little detail. You'll be sick of me in no time. And I want to hear all about the wedding plans. Don't you dare choose a horrible colour for our gowns.'

Fran gasped. 'You've let the cat out of the bag now. I was keeping that as a surprise.'

'What, you haven't asked Lottie to be your bridesmaid yet? Surely you knew anyway, Lottie. It'll be you and me walking down that aisle, side by side.'

'Oh, Fran, thank you. It will be so amazing and something to look forward to celebrating with you when you come back, Ellie.'

All too soon, they arrived at the station. Fran went to grab a trolley for the huge rucksack and their smaller bags. They made their way slowly inside the building, none of them wanting to say goodbye. Once Ellie and Henri had found out which platform they needed, they all shared a final hug, including Henri, and then it was almost time for them to go.

'Henri, you will take lots of care of Ellie, won't you? And have a fabulous time, too. Otherwise, it won't be worth you taking this time off.' Fran kissed him on both cheeks and gave him another hug.

'I promise I'll look after her, Fran, and I'll do my best to have a good time.'

'Have the best time, Ellie. You deserve to have a wonderful trip. But if you need to talk, just let me know.' Lottie hugged her friend tight and when they pulled apart, they both had tears in their eyes.

It was Fran's turn to hug Ellie. 'If there's any good news, Fran, I want you to let us know straight away. I'll be keeping my fingers crossed for you. Take care of yourself, won't you?'

'You too,' Fran whispered, pulling Ellie to her.

'Good luck with the job, Lottie. And whatever you do, don't mess up my desk!' Henri laughed and Lottie saw the twinkle in his eye. They'd already worked out that Lottie was much tidier than him, and he'd told her he was looking forward to seeing how organised his desk was when he returned.

Henri took Ellie's hand and they pushed the trolley off together, towards their platform and their big adventure.

Thierry

The first month after Ellie and Henri's departure passed quite quickly. Thierry settled into a regular pattern of looking after Marie twice a week so Lottie could get to work, and he was loving being back together with them.

He'd had his final meeting with the counsellor and it had gone well – well enough for them both to agree that he could manage without their sessions. As he considered that, he felt a sense of relief wash over him. He picked Marie up from her bouncer on the floor and swung her in the air. She giggled with pleasure, and even more so when he gently rubbed his beard against her cheek.

Lottie emerged from the hallway wearing a colourful dress he hadn't seen before. 'You're looking gorgeous,' he told her.

'You too,' she said, fingering the lapel of his jacket. It was the only smart one he had, and he didn't wear it very often. Everyone was gathering for dinner at the château that afternoon, and he was looking forward to spending time with his friends.

They popped Marie into her pushchair and set off shortly afterwards.

'I've been thinking about Ellie and Henri and the wonderful time they must be having together. Have you been back to Paris since your childhood, Thierry?'

'Only passing through on my way to Bordeaux and back. Have you been?'

'Yes, I went a few times on my travels and I always tried to stay for a couple of days. I found something new to do every time I went. I'd love to go again one day.' Lottie looked wistful, and Thierry longed to take her there, despite all his bad memories.

'Maybe we could go together for a long weekend some time.' He could hardly believe he was saying these words out loud. He hadn't made plans for a long time, and certainly not ones that included Paris.

'You wouldn't mind travelling then, or going back to Paris?' she asked hesitantly.

'I'd be happy to travel more. And... maybe it's time for me to make some new memories of Paris, with you.'

Her eyes glistened. 'I'd love to go away for a weekend with you, just the two of us.'

'You wouldn't mind leaving Marie with someone?'

'Not when she's older. I think that would be okay.'

He loved the sound of that.

When they arrived at the château, Chlöe rushed out to greet them, and it was clear she'd been keeping watch for them.

'*Salut, ma petite,*' Lottie said as she came out.

'I don't think you can call me that any more now Marie's here. I should be *la grande fille* now.'

Lottie laughed as Chlöe puffed out her chest. 'You're right. I will try to remember.'

They followed her inside, tucking the pushchair away in the hallway. Chlöe was full of energy and always keen to look after Marie, although everyone else kept an eye on the baby, too.

'Hey, Lottie, good to see you, and Thierry, too.' Fran took off her apron before joining them all in the living room. She kissed them both on the cheek and gave them a glass of *crémant* each.

Didier sat down on the floor with Chlöe to make sure the baby was all right.

'It's been a funny first month without Ellie and Henri, hasn't it?' Fran said. 'I hope they're having a good time.'

'It has to be better than how they'd be feeling if they hadn't gone together,' Thierry replied, and they laughed.

'These six months will pass soon enough,' Didier said, 'and they'll be back to tell us about all the lovely places they've visited.' Thierry caught the smile Didier exchanged with Fran, and he was glad they were more at ease with each other.

'And after that, it will be a new year, and we'll have another baby to celebrate with,' Chlöe blurted out, before covering her mouth with her hands, her eyes wide.

Didier gave her a hug to reassure her while Lottie and Thierry caught up with what she'd said.

'Oh my goodness – Fran, Didier, is it true?' Lottie could hardly contain her delight. Fran nodded and Lottie threw her arms round her. Thierry reached out to shake Didier's hand and Chlöe left her dad to take care of Marie so she could jump up and down.

'We could hardly believe that it happened naturally after all the difficulties we went through, but at last, yes, we're having a baby. It's due next spring, so we can get married before the baby comes.'

'Oh, how exciting.' Lottie was as pleased as Chlöe. 'You're going to have a baby brother or sister then, Chlöe. Won't that be wonderful?'

'I know and I'll be the oldest!'

Thierry laughed at her priority. 'Cheers to all of you,' he said. 'No-one deserves it more.'

They chinked glasses with Fran, who was drinking mineral water, and with Didier. Thierry appreciated his closeness with Marie even more. He loved her like his own child and he was so grateful for the opportunity to be part of her life. He glanced over at Lottie to see her looking straight back at him, as if she was able to read his mind. Her smile told him all he needed to know. Finally, his past was being laid to rest and he could look forward to the future.

Lottie

Today, it was Lottie's turn to entertain everyone for lunch. She wanted to take the opportunity to thank Thierry and her family and friends for all they'd done to help her since Marie was born. Her parents were coming with *Papi*, Sylvie was bringing Frédéric, and Fran and Didier were coming with Chlöe. And by her side from the outset would be Thierry.

They made an early start; Thierry took Marie with him into the village to the *boulangerie* to pick up all the fresh bread, while Lottie got started on making her famous onion tart, along with some salads. Her mum was going to bring a quiche, and Didier was making a dessert with Chlöe. Sylvie had offered to make a *tarte flambée* as well, so there would be plenty of food for everyone. Thierry had also been given permission to choose some wines from the domaine's cellars again, so it was shaping up to be a very good celebration.

Soon everyone was arriving, and by the time Thierry returned, the house was almost full.

'Here, let me help with that.' He passed Marie over to Didier and took the onion tart from Lottie to put on the table, which they'd moved into the living room.

The two of them carried on adding dishes and salads, including a delicious-looking potato salad Fran had made. Didier had put their dessert in the fridge for now – an equally tasty-looking *clafoutis* that smelled divine.

'*Salut, tout le monde,*' Sylvie called, arriving next with Frédéric. She deposited her *tarte flambée* on the table as she came in, along with another bowl of salad. Lottie wondered whether they might have far too much food in the end.

Didier passed Marie over to his mum and gestured to Thierry. 'Shall we go and get the wines now?'

The two men disappeared, and Fran and Lottie took over pouring the *crémant* for new arrivals. Finally, her parents arrived with *Papi* and everyone was there. Lottie breathed a sigh of relief when the last plate of food was put on the table. Just as she was wondering where Thierry and Didier had got to, they reappeared through the front door, and at last the party proper could start.

She and Thierry were the only ones who knew about Fran and Didier's good news, so this would be a chance for everyone to celebrate once the announcement was made. Lottie chinked her glass and everyone fell silent.

'Welcome, everyone, and thanks so much to all of you for coming today. I hope you've all got a drink because there's a lot to celebrate.' Didier and Thierry went round filling glasses as she spoke. 'First of all, I wanted to thank you all, mostly for putting up with me while I was pregnant, but also to thank you for your support since I became a mum. I know it's been hard, but your love and patience has got me through. So thank you, and I'm sorry.' They all laughed and raised their glasses. 'Now I'm going to hand over to Fran.'

Everyone looked expectantly at her sister. 'I'd like to echo Lottie's words and thank you all for coming. Didier and I are so pleased to see Thierry and Lottie settled in their home with Marie.' Lottie looked over at Thierry and smiled. 'I'd also like you to raise your glasses to our absent friends, Ellie and Henri. Fingers crossed that they're having a wonderful time!' Everyone cheered that one. Didier came over to join Fran for her final announcement. 'And finally, we'd like to share the good news with you that I'm pregnant!'

The cottage erupted and suddenly everyone was talking and coming over to congratulate them both. When everyone had spoken to them, Didier took his turn at addressing the room.

'Just one small request from me – can I count on you all to help us with the harvest this year?' He received a resounding yes. 'And finally, you're all invited to a wedding around December time, when Ellie and Henri should be back, and our new baby will be almost due.'

Lottie put out plates and cutlery then and encouraged all their guests to tuck in. Thierry was holding Marie and she went to join them.

'It's great to have the whole family here, isn't it?' she said.

'It is, and it's a lovely chance for us all to celebrate with them.'

'Are you okay with Marie for a bit longer? I wanted to have a word with Sylvie.'

Thierry nodded and Lottie went off to find her.

'Hello, darling. How are things with you now?'

'I'm fine. It's great to be working again. Thank you so much for agreeing to babysit one morning a week. I hope you know how grateful I am.'

Sylvie beamed at her. 'Oh, I can't tell you how much I enjoy it. It's going to be the highlight of my week.'

'I wasn't sure whether to ask because I didn't know what your plans were for the future. I didn't know if it might be too much for you.'

'Not at all. I can't sit indoors for the rest of my life, no matter how much everyone might want me to. Anyway, Frédéric loves it when we have Marie and Chlöe to look after. He loves having children round.' And she laughed.

Lottie left Sylvie to go and find her mum.

'Hello, sweetheart. How are you?' They shared a hug.

'I'm good, Mum. I wanted to say I'm sorry, once again, for being such a pain these last few months. I don't know how you put up with me.'

'Lottie, I love you. I know how hard it's all been for you. But I'm so pleased everything's now working out for you. And you and Thierry are so good together.'

Lottie glanced over at Thierry holding Marie and couldn't have agreed more. As he raised his glass to her, she did the same, confident that things would only get better and better for them as they moved forward into the future.

The End

Because reviews are vital in spreading the word, please leave a brief review on **Amazon** if you enjoyed reading *Starting Over at The Vineyard in Alsace*. Thank you!

FREE BOOK: The prequel to my début novel, *From Here to Nashville*, is available **FREE** when you sign up to my newsletter. Find out what happened between Rachel and Sam before Jackson arrived on the scene in *Before You*, at **www.julie-stock.co.uk**.

READ AN EXCERPT FROM THE VINEYARD IN ALSACE

BOOK 1, DOMAINE DES MONTAGNES

Fran

'Here, you can have this back!' I wrenched my engagement ring from my finger and flung it in the general direction of their naked bodies huddled together under the sheet on the bed. *Our* bed. 'I obviously won't be needing it any more.'

'What the hell, Fran?' The thunderous look on Paul's face as the ring pinged against the metal bed frame almost made me doubt myself. I closed my eyes briefly. *Don't let him control you. You are definitely not the guilty party!*

I took one last look at him and then I turned and ran. I kept on running, as far and as fast as my legs would take me, blood pounding in my ears, my long hair whipping around my face. The whole time my mind raced with thoughts of his double betrayal.

Eventually, my body couldn't take any more and I stopped on the pavement near an underground station, doubled over and panting from the effort. Once I'd got my breath back a bit, I gave Ellie a call. She picked up on the first ring.

'Hey, Fran, how are you?'

That question pushed me over the edge into full-blown sobbing and once I'd started, I couldn't stop.

'What's the matter? Where are you? Is Paul there? Talk to me, please!'

'Hold on a minute,' I managed to choke out, wiping my face on the sleeve of my T-shirt. 'I'm at the Tube station and I need a place to stay. Paul... Paul... well, there is no Paul and me any more.'

I heard her sharp intake of breath before she said, 'Of course you must come here. Will you be okay on your own, or do you want me to come and get you?'

'No, I'll be okay. I should be about half an hour. Thanks, Ellie.' I rang off and made my way down into the depths of the Tube, grateful that I would have somewhere to stay so I didn't have to go back home tonight. Afterwards, I couldn't remember finding my way to the platform. I was so distracted by all that had happened, and in such a short space of time, but the next thing I knew, I was squashed into a seat on a crowded rush-hour carriage, trundling north on the Northern line.

No-one spared me a second glance on the train. It was oddly calming to be sitting among complete strangers in my misery and to know I didn't have to explain myself. I wrapped my arms protectively around my body. *Why on earth has Paul done this to me?* I wracked my brain as the train rattled on, but I could make no sense of it.

When I arrived at Ellie's, she scooped me into her arms at once for a hug, which only made me start crying again. She patted my back comfortingly, and eventually the tears subsided.

'Why don't I get us both a drink and then you can tell me everything that's happened?'

I nodded silently. While Ellie was gone, my phone buzzed with yet another text message. It was from Paul, no doubt trying to find me, but I deleted it along with all the others and set the phone down on the table in front of me. Ellie returned shortly afterwards with two cups of tea. I wouldn't have minded something stronger under the circumstances but it probably wasn't a good idea to get drunk just now. I'd need a clear head for whatever was going to come next.

'So, what the hell has happened?'

And I told her.

'I can't even begin to process it, Ellie. Why would he do that to me in the first place, but even worse, why would he do it to me just after we'd got engaged?'

'I don't know what to say, apart from telling you that I never really liked Paul – I'm sorry – and he's proved what a bastard he is by doing this to you. There's no excuse for cheating and you'll never be able to trust him again now.'

I winced at her honesty and at her harsh judgment of Paul.

'In just that one second, my life's been turned upside down. Everything I was planning on – you know, getting married, settling down, starting a family – is now in doubt. I feel like my life is over.' I set down my cup and let the tears roll down my face. My phone buzzed once more with another text. This time, I read it first.

'*Where are you? I just want to know that you're okay. I'm really sorry, I've been incredibly stupid.*'

'Well, at least he realises that much,' said Ellie, her lips tight with anger as I read it out to her.

My fingers hovered over the keypad, but in the end, I deleted the message and turned off the phone.

'I'm going to bed, Ellie. I'm exhausted, and I just can't think straight. Hopefully, things will be clearer in the morning.'

Once I'd climbed into the little single bed in Ellie's spare room, sleep just wouldn't come. I tossed and turned restlessly as images of Paul in bed with this other woman invaded my mind. I thought again about what Ellie had said about never really liking Paul. Had I been taken in by him all this time? I covered my eyes with my hands, embarrassed by my foolishness. I lay there for hours, railing against the injustice of the situation and wondering how I would explain all this to my parents. By the time I finally fell asleep the sun was coming up but I had the beginnings of an idea about what I was going to do next.

ALSO BY JULIE STOCK

From Here to You series

Before You (Free prequel) - From Here to You

From Here to Nashville - Book 1 - From Here to You

Over You - Book 2 - From Here to You

Finding You - Book 3 - From Here to You

From Here to You series

Domaine des Montagnes series

The Vineyard in Alsace - Book 1 - Domaine des Montagnes

Standalone

The Bistro by Watersmeet Bridge

Bittersweet - 12 Short Stories for Modern Life

ABOUT THE AUTHOR

Julie Stock writes contemporary feel-good romance from around the world: novels, novellas and short stories.

She published her début novel, *From Here to Nashville*, in 2015, after starting to write as an escape from the demands of her day job as a teacher. *Starting Over at the Vineyard in Alsace* is her latest book, and the second in the Domaine des Montagnes series set on a vineyard.

Julie is now a full-time author, and loves every minute of her writing life. When not writing, she can be found reading, her favourite past-time, running, a new hobby, or cooking up a storm in the kitchen, glass of wine in hand.

Julie is a member of the Romantic Novelists' Association and The Society of Authors.

Julie is married and lives with her family in Bedfordshire in the UK.

Sign up for Julie's free author newsletter at **www.julie-stock.co.uk.**

facebook.com/JulieStockAuthor

twitter.com/wood_beez48

instagram.com/julie.stockauthor

ACKNOWLEDGMENTS

Thanks to you, my lovely readers, I was able to leave my part-time job in October 2019 and commit myself full-time to my writing career from that point onwards. This is the first book written since I became a full-time author.

I submitted the book to my editor for a first look before Christmas 2019, and as we were going on holiday to San Francisco and Los Angeles in January 2020, I didn't plan to get back to my book until after we returned.

Fortunately, we were able to have a wonderful holiday and to return safely before the coronavirus pandemic took hold. And so I was able to finish this book during the many weeks of lockdown that followed.

Writing can be quite a solitary occupation, especially when you write full-time, but it has been good to have some of my family round me during this difficult time. It has also been a godsend to have something specific to do!

I am fortunate to have a strong group of writing friends around me as well, some of whom helped me by reading an early version of this story. I would like to thank the Beta Buddies in general for their support, and especially, Jennifer, Liz, Sally, and Sara for their early feedback.

I'd also like to thank my writing friends, Kate and Ros, who have been a constant support since I first started writing in 2013.

And finally, I'd like to thank all members, past and present, of my branch of The Society of Authors, known as The Herts Writers Group, for their cheerleading and their advice over the past few years.

Made in the USA
Coppell, TX
24 August 2020